# Meat

ULTAN BANAN

Also by Ultan Banan

*Notes from a Cannibalist*

*A Whore's Song*

Cover art courtesy of Dave Migman © 2020
Editing by Paul @ Seminal Edits

blacktarnpublishing.com

ISBN: 978-1-914147-02-9

'What did I need, I who had rejected
with such disgust the loveliest of mankind!
What I needed I could not say.'

Maldoror

# Meat

# Part One

# Me and Meat

Show me a man's present and I'll tell you his future, isn't that what they say? At least I heard it that way once, I think. I'm a graduate with a half-decent degree, but I work here, in this grill. That's my present. Some might get all Jungian, tell me workin in a grill is the reason for what came later, ya know, the cannibalism n'all that, but truth is I'm lazy — I've little motivation for gettin ahead, so instead of a career I choose to work here, in this dead-end job.

Our reputation is on the slide. Most of the savvy diners have moved on to find the nearest Cuban pulled pork truck or the latest fusion joint. Who goes out to eat steak now anyway? Meat peaked long ago, and has been in steady decline ever since vegetarianism cast off its reputation as a mental illness. But we get em, we do, the diehard meat-eaters — usually men, middle-aged, red in the face and heavy in the gut, and if I'm honest, with unhealthy levels of frustration and rage simmerin just beneath the surface. Your average meat-eater is angry. I mean, not those who have the occasional chicken wrap, but the ones who like to eat meat off the bone with their fingers, or who enjoy the blood that leeches from a rare sirloin as they tear at the flesh. I dunno which came first, the meat or the anger. Why the frustration? Why the rage? It's probably sexual. What I'd like to see is a study on the instances of rape in a meat-eatin society compared to those in an equivalent population of vegetarians. I wasted four years of my life studyin drama when I should've been in the sociology department. Cause I wonder about things.

Joe, who's our head chef, doesn't wonder about these things. Joe has even less motivation than I do, so it's a surprise every day when his wife brings him lunch. Joe is the most single-lookin married man you've ever met. The only explanation is that Joe's wife is even lazier than he is, which I don't buy, since she has the resolve and the persistence to come visit him every day. She's concerned for his health. She likes to see him for a half-hour. She's invested in him. Joe, so far as I can see, is invested in absolutely nothin.

Joe, I say, what do you think about that? I point at a man at a table eatin a mixed grill with his hands.

About what? he says.

Your man over there, eatin like a savage. D'ya not think he looks like he wants to go out n'kill someone?

Joe's pickin at the remains of his wife's tuna pasta. He shrugs.

I mean, look at the face on him, I say.

He could probably do with a few hours on the Stairmaster, Joe says.

But it's more than that, Joe. There's a kinda animal aggression about him. That guy's a bomb waitin to go off.

Joe shrugs. He's not a man for psychology or sociology. Maybe that's why his wife loves him — he brings a welcome simplicity to life, in a world that's just too complex, and, let's say it, sometimes proper fucked up.

I need an all-day breakfast and a steak sub, says Janine.

Janine is one of our waitresses and she's workin three tables out there, which is a busy lunch for us.

I got it, Joe.

Joe's sittin on a stool in a small staff room out beyond the kitchen.

I throw oil and some strip steak on the grill and listen to it sizzle. Smoke rises, the stench of cooked meat fills the air. I like this job, I do. But the smell. The stink of meat is the thing. It goes with me everywhere. Follows me around the city. I leave work and it comes with me down the street, it gets on the bus with me, exciting the nostrils of dirty old men and repulsing the noses of modern urban wives. It makes children in prams squeal. It drives dogs fucken wild. It makes the homeless glare at me with murderous intent. And I'm sure my girlfriend is about to leave me. I have a girlfriend — Jules. We live together: her, me and two others in a shared house. But the stink of meat has taken our relationship to the point of collapse. She won't come near me til after I've come in, stripped and put all my clothes in the wash, had a shower and changed into somethin clean. Even then she swears she can smell it on my fingers and in my hair. What can I do? I could find another job, sure, but that kinda upheaval would require a level of determination that I'm just not equipped with at this point in life. So she puts up with it, until the day comes that she decides she no longer has to. It's either me or the meat, she'll say. And I won't have the answer she wants to hear. And that'll be it.

But back to the meat. There's one point when it intervenes in our relationship in a positive way. She's a good girl, Jules, but about once a month I convince her to take a little ecstasy with the rest of us. We dabble, I more than her; she'll play along just to keep me happy, and on that night... that night she's an animal. And I can't put it down to the pills — it's the meat. On that night I'll come home from work and I won't put my t-shirt in the wash, instead I store it upstairs. So we get to poppin pills and it's all nice and lovey-dovey, and right before we go to bed I'll put on the t-shirt and she gets fucken wild. The animal comes out. She doesn't know it, but it's the smell — the stench of meat turns her into a right hoor. I suggested this once, night after rollin, and she got mad, insisted it was the pills. So I never mentioned it again. But I know, I do, that it was the dirty hamburger smell off me that turned her into an animal.

But what can I do? I can't keep my girl doped up on pills every night o'the month. I just have to prepare myself for the inevitability of our split.

Don't char the steak, Joe shouts.

I'm fiddlin with a tin of beans and perhaps I'm lost too much in thought.

Right-o, Joe.

I plate up the steak and turn over the black puddin. Fucken stinks, the black puddin.

Jules works as personal trainer, which brings me to perhaps the most important thing about my choice of employment: Jules isn't one of these ketogenic types, she's a proponent of raw, of green. She's no vegetarian — she does chicken and even a bit o'minced beef now and again, but I'm sure the smell reminds her of all the good things she's forced to deny herself. Come to think of it, she does have a temper. This might be the ultimate cause of her anger issues.

One breakfast and one steak sub, I shout.

Janine's over to pick up the plates. She hurries away, her fat little bum shakin.

I wander down to the staff room.

Goin for one after work? Joe says.

We're next door to a bar. As if that wasn't close enough, there's a strange back alley linkin the two establishments, so we don't even have to go out in the street to get there. We just go out the back door and we're in. Too easy for a coupla men with zero motivation in life.

I shouldn't. Jules is finishin early so I told her I'd take her to dinner, I say.

Where you takin her?

Dunno.

What about Kibby's?

She's a personal trainer, Joe.

Sarah likes Kibby's.

*You* like Kibby's, Joe, I tell him. Your wife just goes there to keep you happy.

They got the best pork ribs in town.

Yeah well, fuck meat, I say.


Lunchtimes are over before they've started, and then we kill time til dinner. Sometimes we sneak out back for a drink. Today, we don't. I'm sittin in the staff room while Joe does a bit of cleanin. I'm readin Joe's paper, an article about how they're injectin mice with antibodies from convicted murderers and rapists — does somethin to the mice, drives em fucken crazy like. Wonder if I could try that here, at the grill — get my hands on some rapist antibodies, start pumpin it into the meat, see what happens to the customers, what it makes em do? A social experiment, like. Just to pass the time. Where would I get antibodies from a rapist? Or a murderer? How would I go about that?

Please don't think I'm fucken crazy. Afternoons are slow here and my mind wanders. I'm killin time.

How about a hand here? Joe says.

Don't mess with the system, Joe. I did the cleanin yesterday, I tell him.

About three o'clock Jules texts me and cancels dinner. Second time in two weeks.

*Fuck it, then. What else am I gonna do?*

Joe, I say, you still up for a swift one after work?

What about dinner?

Fuck dinner, I say.


So at six we go next door, but we don't go in the front we go in the back, through the alley like, cause we get a kick outta walkin in through the mystery door at the back of the bar, cunts lookin at us like, *Where you comin from?* We gotta special door, lads. Just for us. So there.

Cyril's on the bar. Cyril's a good sort, he knows what we drink so we don't have to ask and we never have to shout him for a refill, so folks at the bar be thinkin, *Who are these cats, come in by their own door and don't even say anything and drinks appear in front of em?* Well, that's how it works when you have your own door.

Soon we're sittin with two Guinness in front of us and Joe's lookin at his watch.

What's eatin you? We just got here, I say.

Sarah said she might drop in, he says.

For fuck sake, Joe, can you not go five minutes without the missus?

Joe gets all defensive like, doesn't like to be ribbed about the missus.

She bring him his packed lunch today? Cyril says, and we snigger, cause poor Joe is the butt of many jokes at the bar, probably cause he's in a stable relationship and the rest of us are on the brink of disaster or simply unfit for companions.

I look round the bar. *Yep. Sad, lonely and single, all of em.*

Where's Lenny? I say to Cyril.

Lenny is the captain of sad, lonely and single, but he's a great man for laughin at himself which is why we like havin him around.

You didn't hear? Cyril says.

I didn't.

Lenny was found dead last night.

*Nah,* I say, and I stretch it out, all long and unbelievin like.

Yeah, Cyril says, and he leans over the bar and we understand we're about to hear somethin juicy.

Found dead in his apartment yesterday mornin. It's not clear how long he was dead, but get this — his dog had started chewin on him by the time they found him. Ear and a couple of fingers missin, and a lip chewed off.

Fuck off, I say.

You fucken believe it? Cyril says.

Expletives are like the milk of magnesia we need to process the news.

Jesus fucken Christ, Joe says.

Yeah, Cyril says.

We sit around shakin our heads for a few moments.

An ear? I say.

Cyril nods.

You'd wonder why it didn't go for the forearm, or maybe a bit o'cheek?

What's wrong with you? Joe says.

No look, I explain, I'm just thinkin out loud. I mean, there's not a whole lotta meat on an ear. If the dog was starvin like, which it musta been, there'd be more eatin in an arm, no?

The two of them are lookin at me like, *What the fuck's wrong with you?*

I'm just thinkin out loud, I say.

Well, maybe you should keep your thoughts to yourself, Cyril says.

A few fellas around us are noddin their heads like, *Yeah, maybe you should.*

And they're probably right. Lenny was well-liked here. They just don't get my predilection for scientific enquiry. It's not a crime to ask questions, is it?

I have to ask Cyril for a fresh pint, an indication of his annoyance.

Have one for yourself, Cyril, I say.

*Gotta stay in the good books.*

And the rest of the lads too, I add.

Nods all round.

Let's drink to Lenny, I say.

Hear hear.

We'll miss him, I say.

Nods of assent.

*Well, the parts of him that are left anyway.* Of course I don't fucken say it.

I'm not home late. In fact, it's only nine when I go through the door but Jules is on the sofa waitin. She's cryin.

You're drunk, she says.

Astute, I say.

Do you care about me at all?

Mel, who's our flatmate and a shit-stirrin little bitch who's always stickin the knife in me with Jules when I'm not around, gets up off the sofa. She goes out to the kitchen with a snide look over her shoulder.

*Little bitch. Stirrin the shit.*

You cancelled dinner Jules, I say.

And you didn't even reply, she shouts.

And I realise I'm in one of those arguments that are circular in nature and there's no winnin, even if you're fucken right. But I start shoutin anyway.

If you hadn't cancelled dinner I wouldn't be drunk.

You don't give a shit about me, she says, and she weeps into two balled fists in a way that makes my heart melt. I sit down beside her on the couch and reach out to put an arm around. She leaps up.

Jesus, you fucking stink, she says.

She flees the room.

Now I'm angry and I get a beer from the fridge. Mel passes me in the kitchen on her way out, says, *Well done*, and those words, those two words... I could bounce her head off the fucken wall.

*Well done*. Are there two more malicious and spiteful words that one can use at a point like this? Mel is the high-cunt of *Well done*.

— You missed her birthday? *Well done.*

— You didn't text her about being late? *Well done.*

— You burnt the chicken? *Well done.*

*Well, Mel, fuck you Mel. One of these days I may take a knife to you, and you know what, maybe we'll pump you full of rapist antibodies and cook you up too, see how you taste.*

— How do you like your Mel, sir?

— Well fucken done.

That little joke cheers me right up, and I sit in front of the TV and drink til I'm done fumin.

At around eleven I go upstairs and Jules is in bed. She's not sleepin, cause I can feel that tension in the air.

But you know what? Tonight I'm not fucken showerin. Fuck you. I'm even keepin my t-shirt on. I climb into bed, all meat and beer.

Silently, she climbs out and goes downstairs.

# Meat Kills My Relationship

Well Joe, I say, I think I went too far last night.

We're standing in the kitchen. I've a twisted head on me and I'm sweatin like a hoor, hangover eatin at the edges of me like some degenerative disorder. The rank smell of bacon fills the air. It feels like my stomach is tryin to leap outta me. I'm holdin on to my motor skills by a ball-hair.

Whaddaya mean? Joe says.

I think I blew it.

What happened?

She got mad when I showed up drunk.

But she cancelled dinner, didn't she? he says.

Yes! I say. That's it, that's it right there. She cancelled, now she's pissed at me.

Doesn't seem right, Joe says.

Thank you, Joe.

I stab holes in the sausages on the grill with more venom than is necessary. Joe understands.

Hey Joe, I say.

Yeah?

Sarah ever complain about the smell?

What smell? Joe's nose twitches in the direction of his chef's jacket.

You know, the smell o'meat?

Off us?

Yeah.

Nah. I think she likes it.

Are you sure, Joe?

I think so.

I turn around, look at him. Ask her for me, will ya? I say.

You want me to ask my wife if she likes the smell of meat?

Yes, Joe.

Nah, he says, all coy like.

What's the matter?

I turn back to the grill and flip the potato bread.

I'd be embarrassed, he says.

She's your wife, Joe.

I know, but ya know…

I *don't* know, Joe.

It's weird.

It's not a bit weird. You work in a grill, I tell him.

Still, he says.

Then I go and tell him about Jules, and about how once a month when we go poppin pills together the smell makes her fucken wild and she does shit she wouldn't do in a million years if she were straight.

Really?

You never tried it, Joe?

Sarah doesn't touch drugs.

Well, maybe you should make her.

Why would I make my wife take drugs?

You don't have to force her. You could slip a little in her tea, like.

And I turn around and wink, and make that little poppin sound with my tongue off the roof of my mouth. *Tcha!*

In her tea?

Or in her veggies, I don't know. Just a little slip of E.

That's not right, man, he says.

*Poor Joe. A good man with a good wife.*

We goin for a pint today, Joe?

I get the text around three. It's Jules, sayin she's had enough and that I don't care about her and I've never cared about her and I only think about myself and I'm not normal. Says she's moved out and taken her stuff and gone back with her ma. Just like that. No warnin.

I hear Mel's voice in my head. *Well done.*

*Fuck you, Mel. And fuck you too, Jules.*

*Not normal.*

I know what it's really about, I do. It's not about not caring, or comin home late and drunk, or not replyin to her texts. It's about the smell. It's the smell of meat that's killed us, and why can't she just come out and say it?

*It's the smell of meat, Jules. Just be fucken honest with me.*

Well, what can you say to a woman like that, anyway, who doesn't know how to say what's on her mind?

*Fuck it.*

I leave the cleanin and go down the staff room where Joe's lookin at the paper.

Hey Joe, I say.

You should read this thing about Salmonella, he says.

Forget about Salmonella, I say. I tell him about the text.

Just like that? No warnin? he says.

Nothin.

What are you gonna do?

What can I do, Joe? Nothin for it.

You know Janine likes you, he says.

Janine? Yeah?

Yeah.

*Janine.* Janine's nice. Cute little bum. Nice smile. Plus she smells o'meat too, so there's problem number one taken care of immediately. We could be meaty lovers, with no fucks to give about the hum of lamb chops or pork sausage.

Are you sure, Joe?

Yeah. Sarah told me, he says.

Maybe I'll ask her for a drink, then.

Bit soon, isn't it?

Whaddaya mean?

After just breakin up with Jules n'all.

Well, she finished it Joe.

S'pose.

Yeah. I'm gonna do it. I'm gonna ask her out.


Right after dinner I ask her. Hey Janine, wanna have a drink next door after work?

She smiles. Yeah. Sure.

Okay.

I need to finish up here, she says. Why don't you go on through and I'll see you there in a bit?

Great.

She smiles and turns, and her meaty little bum trembles.

So I go through and Cyril sets me up and I sit and have a drink.

Lenny was buried today, Cyril says.

God rest him.

Good turnout, he tells me.

Closed casket?

Yeah. Because, you know…

I know, Cyril.

We bow our heads, all remorseful like.

*Poor Lenny.*

Where's Joe? Cyril says.

Joe's not comin. Janine's comin through, we're gonna have a drink.

Janine?

Yeah.

Cyril nods all barman-like, sage and understanding. Doesn't need to know why.

The TV drones low in the background, over it the sound of early evenin bar tittle.

Cyril puts down a second pint.

It's after six when Janine texts, say she can't come, she's got somethin to do.

*Ain't that sweet?*

I put the phone on the bar and I must have a face on me cause Cyril gets it.

Like that, is it?

Yeah, Cyril.

We sigh, two men with the weight of thousands.

What you gonna do? he says.

Guess I'll go home, I tell him. I've the place to myself the night. Maybe it'll do me good.

Sure why not, he says.

I drain the glass.

Be seein you, then.

And I scarper.

*I'm goin home.*

I cross Victoria St into Amelia Street, headin for the bus. But it's eatin me now, it is. Dumped then blown off.

*Fuck it.*

I turn around. I'm about to head to the Crown and kill an hour and a few more brain cells when I look up and see the sign of some joint I wasn't aware existed. Right on the corner. I pause for a second, but only a second, then I'm headin for the door. There's a name up there. Can't hardly read it, but it's there.

*The Screamin Pope.*

# Screamin Pope, Belfast

**Location:**
*Screamin Pope, Belfast*
**Time:**
*18.20, Thursday*
**Present:**
*Hugo: bartender, butcher*
*Ducasse: punter, odd-job man*
*Sweeney: punter, unemployed*

And fuck knows why I do, but I walk down the dirty unlit staircase. It's kinda creepy, disquietin like. I turn a corner at the bottom and I'm in the joint, a basement bar, queer green glow and a strange ambience about the place. Three heads turn to look at me as I walk in. I got that voice in my head, ya know, the one I never learned to listen to, sayin to me, *Turn around and walk.* And I mighta, but I'm three pints in now and the hesitation comes on me… two pints I mighta done it, turned and walked out, but I'm half-cut and I pause. Then I'm committed. So I walk up to the bar, these three cunts lookin at me as I go. *What can I do?*

Two of the boys are sittin, and the barman, hand inside his shirt strokin his belly, gruff head on him, big beefy moustache, he raises an eyebrow as I put a foot on the rail and lean in.

I'll have a pint, buddy, I say.

The barman nods, Good man, he says, still rubbin his belly through his shirt all queer like.

So he lets off pokin himself with his big hairy fingers and pulls me a pint, the other two cunts still watchin me all the while, and he sets it front of me, winks, and he's about to turn away when I see his nose twitch, then he gives the air a proper sniff. Leans right over at me, sniffin. I'm just outta work, still in my work clothes. I know the score.

That's a smell I love, he says. Yes, that's fucken tremendous. Hey Ducasse, he says — come and get a noseful o'this.

And the other one, leather jacket on, kinda rapey air about him, comes over. Now he's sniffin at me too, he starts growlin, a real dirty kinda growl.

*Mm-hmm*, he goes.

And the barman's fingers have drifted back in his sweat-stained shirt and he's fingerin his belly button.

Fuck sake, lads, I say, I'm just outta work. I get this shite everywhere I go. I work in a grill.

I love it, the barman says. There's nothin I appreciate more than the scent of a good chop. *Yes*, he says, and he moans.

And I think, *These cunts are alright*. So I say, You wouldn't believe the day I've had, lads, then I go on to explain about Jules and the smell of meat and how it's broke us up and she's left me.

The two lads are shakin their heads, the third, queer spectacled fella, sittin back eatin a burger, watches me as he licks mayonnaise from his lips.

Girl's got it all wrong, the barman says. Meat's the thing. Meat makes the world go round. That's our speciality here. We got some of the best meat in town.

I look back at the guy eatin the burger, then I look round the bar — greasy, dank, spooky, and I'm thinkin salmonella, I'm thinkin bovine spongiform, I'm thinkin bacterial infections and a dose of the shits... what I'm not thinkin is, *You know what pal, I'd like to try your specialities. In fact, serve it up, cause I just can't wait to try your ribs.* Wouldn't wanna offend the guy though, so I keep schtum.

Never seen you in here before, the barman says.

Never been in, I say. Screamin Pope? What's that about? Doesn't cry out 'fine dining'.

All about the bacon, he says, and the others are laughin but I don't get it.

So you're in the meat business? he says.

I work for a business which sells meat, I tell him.

Fuckin Wordsworth here, the other one says, the rapey one in the leather jacket, and he claps me on the shoulder. And even though there's somethin amiss about this guy, amiss as in, *This guy's an out-and-out wrong'un,* I have to say, I kinda like him. He holds out his hand.

Ducasse, he says.

I shake his hand.

That's Hugo. He points to the barman, who nods.

That strange one's Sweeney, he says, gestures over his shoulder at the paedo-lookin guy with the mayo on his face.

Here, go and throw on a tune, the barman says, and tosses a coin over the bar at Ducasse.

Any requests? he says to me.

I've no idea what kinda joint I've wandered into, but I'm content to see what way the night goes organically, ya know?

Knock yourself out, I tell him.

So he goes over to the jukebox, back of the bar, throws the coin in and I hear it fall into the belly of the machine, then Tammy Wynette comes on, and I think, *Yeah, I fucken knew these guys were wrong'uns.*

Ducasse does this little Christopher Walken shimmy, slides across the floor, singin,

*It aint easy bein a woman,*

*Giving all you can for your man...*

Shot? the barman says.

Before I can reply it appears at my elbow, and it hits me then that I'm not goin back up those stairs anytime soon. I'm four pints in and the word *No* has packed its bags and fucked off to Dingle. We lift two shots and clink glasses as Hugo winks, then we throw back the green fairy. Ducasse is still swingin, and now Hugo starts his own little thing behind the bar, hand in his shirt strokin himself as he watches Ducasse, some kinda unspoken thing goin on between em.

Now, I didn't think I'd stumbled into a queer bar, but fuck, the whole thing was right queer.

I'm struck how feminine Hugo is for such a big, meaty fella. He moves like a woman. Not a bender, but a woman. Then, in a flash, he's out from behind the bar. I hardly saw him move, but he's there and he grabs my arm and pulls me to my feet and holds me tight, and with him right there, holdin me, I'm struck by his magnificent odour; he smells of meat, like me. I hadn't noticed it over my own hum, but now, with him there holdin me, the scent is overpowering, a big fleshy man who smells like me, smells like barbecue and hamburger and ribs.

*If you want him you'll go get him...*

The smell of him, so thick and meaty and commanding. I give way and let myself be danced around the bar.

Here is a fleshy commander, a meaty general. This is a man.
*She needs two arms to hold onto,*
*Somethin hot to come to...*

And then he spins me and I'm back on my stool, and Ducasse is laughin, Sweeney is laughin, Hugo is laughin, and fuck it, I laugh too.

Lads, I say, this isn't the Thursday night I was expectin.

Thursday, Friday, Monday, what's it matter? Hugo says, and he throws up another line of shots.

The voices in my head make their last desperate pleas for reason, for retreat, but the glasses clink and we neck some more of that green fire then it's *Goodnight, Dorothy.*

I'm not worried. I was, but now I'm not, cause you know what? There's somethin strangely familiar about the weirdness, and there's somethin reassuring about finding a man like Hugo, a man of such regal and fleshy countenance.

Another round.

Wanna make a toast? Hugo says.

And I look round at my peculiar companions, my head swimmin, Tammy Wynette playin and the strange green glow of the bar, the smell of meat in the place, off me, off him, and I hold up my glass and I say, To meat.

Hugo smiles, Ducasse smiles, Sweeney grins, and we all drink.

*To meat.* Here I am in company where I'm not judged, where the smell off me after a day's work doesn't mark me out as somethin low, somethin degenerate, somethin dirty. Aye, meat, and here are men who understand.

Ducasse claps a hand on my shoulder, says, You're alright kid.

I take issue with 'kid', but fuck it, I'm feelin pretty good right about now and I just come right out with it.

You know, there's somethin off about you, somethin proper anomalous — *some word from my uni days, outta nowhere, but it has Hugo in fucken wrinkles* — I dunno, somethin weird and rapey, I say. But I like ya.

Now Ducasse is fucken howlin.

He's got the measure of you, Hugo says.

Hugo lines up another round, and just as he's about to pour he stalls, bottle hoverin over the glass.

Sure there's no woman waitin at home for ya? he says.

Nah, I say. I told ya, she's fucked off. And I get to tellin him about her leavin and goin back to her ma, and how she couldn't talk about things and blamed me instead.

That's not right, Hugo says.

Then I tell him about pill night, about how once a month we pop pills and Jules goes fucken wild at the smell o'bacon when she's off her tits, and at the mention of bacon, this weird cat Sweeney, hoverin in the background, starts playin with his balls.

The smell of meat makes her crazy when she's on E? he says. Hugo fucken loves this. His eyes light up. He looks at

Ducasse who's listenin closely, the two of em noddin sagely.

Girl has repressed issues. Don't take it personally, Ducasse says.

Did you ever experiment? Hugo says.

Whaddaya mean like? I say.

I mean, did ya ever try goin home with different scents on ya? Like bacon, pork chop, beef sausage — see how each one fires her up different? he says.

No, I say, but now he's said it my mind's firin off, me with my propensity for scientific enquiry, like, *Why didn't I fucken try it?*

Then he goes and tells me about how he had an ex-wife with a serious coke and pill habit, and how he figured out that the smell of cooked meat turned her into a masochist, but the smell of raw brought out her sadistic side. Then he goes into detail, shit I'm not gonna repeat, but now I can see that this man is some kinda genius, and there's some sorta meaty brilliance to the way his mind works.

What's your favourite cut? he says.

Meat?

Yeah.

I like brisket, I tell him.

He winks. We're gonna get along just fine.

Ducasse has somethin else on the jukebox, I can't put my finger on it but I know the lyrics.

*All of them gonna get used by you...*

Come on. I wanna show ya somethin, Hugo says. He nods towards the back of the bar.

I get up. That queer one Sweeney is watchin me, hasn't said a word since I came in, just sittin there with that creepy grin.

Ducasse comes over, puts an arm around my shoulder. You gonna show him? he says to Hugo.

Aye.

Follow us, Ducasse says.

So we go in behind the bar and through a door, out into the kitchen. There's nobody in there, no chef, just a big side of meat on the counter. A big, glistening, meaty slab.

Five hundred quid a kilo, Hugo says, points at the cut.

Is it dipped in MDMA? I say.

And he laughs. We don't deal in any cut-price shite, he says. We only do the best.

He goes over to a door back of the kitchen, above it one of those safety signs, flickerin. *EXIT*. The sound of the jukebox is comin through the door behind us.

*I travel the world and the seven seas...*

Follow me, he says.

He opens the door.

# 4

# The Past

Sometimes things happen, ya know, that you just can't explain.
Cunts'll be thinkin at this point, like, *How did things turn so
fucken quickly*? Well, I dunno what to tell ya. Things turn. You
might say it was the breakup with Jules that set things movin,
or maybe you're the Freudian type, likes to dig in the past,
like there was somethin lurkin back there just waitin to be
triggered... but who ever really knows? All I know is I was
dumped, then things turned fucken mental. That's just the
way it went. Story o'my life.

I never had much success at relationships anyway, truth be
told; I wasn't really one for compromise. Not that I couldn't
do my bit when it was needed, ya know — I never had any
problem sittin down to watch a romance with the girl, on the
sofa with some popcorn and a couple of cans. And in the early
days I even bought her things — I'd come home with some
flowers or a nice bottle of wine, and that was all good and
wholesome while it lasted. I'd cook her dinner sometimes too,
and I can mix it up in the kitchen with the best of em.

Hey Jules, I'd say — how about a chickpea curry tonight?

Sounds great, she'd say, and then I'd knock her up a killer
dinner, or maybe I'd put together a superfood salad and
some goujons, cause I can do that stuff. I'm a chef, and I have
no problem turnin on my skills outside work if it keeps her

happy. Of course, it wasn't so rosy as all that. We had our ups and downs, we did, all of the eight months we were together — not like we were ever gonna get married anyway.

Then before Jules it was Kelly, which was, how can I put it, not quite the stable thing I had with Jules. Me and Kelly met at an underground rave in Belfast back in the day, and after goin home together that first night it soon turned out we both had a love for pharmaceuticals. Not so much the Es, but both of us were into blues, that cheap Chinese knock-off Valium which flooded the city back then. Lookin back on it now, I wonder why the fuck I was puttin that shite into my system, but around the time we were both eatin em like Skittles. Thirty or forty a night between us at the height of it, we'd go three days and not come up for a breath. Boozin too on top of it, and a host of other stuff, and then there was the fucking. We'd go out drinkin all night, then stumblin home we'd find an alley to fuck in — that was Kelly's thing, she liked to be fucked in dirty alleys, and it'd finish up with her weepin, sayin, I feel like a hoor, but wasn't that the whole kick? Why else am I standin here in piss and broken glass with my trousers round my ankles?

I was raped, Kelly told me once, when we'd both been high for a week straight, and I didn't know whether to believe her cause she was as fucked in the head as I was, but then her sister told me, yeah, it's true, and after that things started to go south. The last night we were together I was stayin at hers, the kid was with her ma, and we got so twisted on every kinda powder that she begged me to beat her with the hurley she kept under the bed. I mean, that thing was substantial. We're talkin GBH, or maybe manslaughter given the quantity of pills we'd taken, and all for a bit of sexy fun. That was it, man — that's no kinda relationship to be in when your greatest responsibility in life is your drug habit. The next day I turned it around… I was off the blues, off the powders, and I got myself back into full-time employment. Changed man.

Then I met Jules. We met in a juice bar — how about that

for new man, turnin over a new page? Truth be told, I'd only nipped in to take a piss, but I'm happy I did, and we hit it off right away, and I was lookin for a new place to stay, new leaf and all that, and Jules says, We're lookin for a new flatmate. So I moved in. Two weeks later we were together. Brand new me...

So there. I tried, I did. I tried to make a go of it. They say self-development's the thing, and Christ I had a go. But if you can rely on yourself, you can't always rely on other people, can ya? I'm not blamin Jules. I'm really not. All I'm sayin is, I don't think she gave us a fair go. I think she bailed at the first sign of trouble. It wasn't her fault entirely, she had that little bitch Mel feedin poison into her ear, too... I mean, that one was a cunt. She had it in for me from the beginning. When the world's against ya, whaddaya do? To me it seems simple — you gotta rely on yourself, go it alone, cut out your own path, plough your own field and shovel your own shite. A man's way, and that's the way I went.

Things turned. That's the way it goes. And luckily, I'm a man of considerable internal resources. So I dug deep. I followed the river, went with it. Lest I haven't made it clear to you yet — things fucken turned. And I turned with it.

# 5

# Inducted

Turned out these guys had a string of joints all across Europe, and whaddaya know, sometime later that's where I ended up. I cast off the yolk of the home city, stepped out into the world, the wanderin philosopher, the rogue mick, the grand touree. Fucken went for it I did, stepped out and found myself goin places.

Things turn.

So we're in the back room of the bar and there's a row of sacks hangin on the wall, maybe half a dozen, one of em shakin. I look at Hugo, who's side-eyin me.

*Big fucken man-sized sacks, three or four of em strung up on the back wall.*

This your cold room? I say.

Hugo nods. Ducasse is at my back. He takes out a cigarette and goes to light it.

Not next to the stock, Hugo says.

Sorry Hugo. Ducasse slips the pack into his jacket pocket.

Yeah, good European produce, he says. He slaps a meaty hand on the sack and gives it a fondle.

The sack shakes.

Still alive? I say.

Yeah, he says. We got our own peculiar type of curing process. Takes time.

But the bar's empty — you got demand for all this? I say.

He nods. We're in the supply business too. We take deliveries twice a week. Some comes in, some goes out. Across the border, across the water, we just keep it movin. Fresh meat, is all.

I find the whole set up off, somethin not right about it all, and maybe Hugo senses I'm uneasy.

We've got other lines too, he explains.

Other lines?

All in good time. Take our new friend here over to Ambroos, he says to Ducasse. I'm gonna get started on one of these.

Man's gotta work, Ducasse says, and takes me by the arm.

He leads me out. Hugo nods, turnin to the sack. I see him run his hands over it the way a man might enjoy the curves of a new wife, his fingers explorin the rolls and expanses.

I'm thinkin, *He really likes his work.*

So we head out into the street, me and Ducasse, and it's cold, and I'm not really dressed for it but I'm lit on absinthe and it's like I can feel my atoms vibrate, all electric like. I'm walkin on air. I could be shirtless and it wouldn't bother me cause I'm lit up like christmas. My breath freezes on the air and I blow clouds at the sky.

Where we headed? I say.

Ducasse lifts his collar and wraps it around his neck. To see Ambroos, he says.

Ambroos?

Ambroos is a cat we do business with only when we absolutely have to.

Don't ask me how I know, but I know we're goin to get drugs. I'm new to the game, so I don't ask.

Dutch cunt, is he?

He's a cunt and he's Dutch, Ducasse says.

I wouldn't have my local dealer any other way, I say.

We leave Keizerstraat and cross Nieuwmarkt, and we turn into one of those dingy little alleyways. We pass a few windows, you know, Amsterdam fuckboxes, and it's early so they're empty, except for the last one where a big black girl stands, a mornin hoor: wide, gross, unfuckable, but Ducasse pauses as we pass the window and I can see he do it, he'd fuck her, cause clearly I was right about him and he's a pure anomaly. She blows me a kiss, I grin, Ducasse follows after me down the alley.

You'd have to be on your last legs, I say.

When you've seen what I've seen, you see beauty in all places, he says, and leaves it at that, and I don't ask cause his statement has a cruel kinda weight to it and, honestly, I just don't wanna know.

Ducasse stops at a door. There's a busted 8-ball sign on it. It even looks like a crack den.

Here we are.

High end, I say.

Come on.

He pushes the door and we step right into a living room. No hall, no foyer, just right onto the carpet. Three junkies are lyin there, two on the sofa, one on a beanbag. Smells like they haven't moved for days. There's a coffee table with every manner of paraphernalia on it. I mean, me and Jules and Mel and Pete lost it now and again, but we never let it go this far. This is another level of dedication.

The guy on the couch looks up at Ducasse, sighs, says, Sit down, just don't fuck with anything, and don't try to fuck my woman.

Ducasse's reputation goes before him.

Relax, Ducasse says, and sits down next to a gas heater on the floor. I sit other side of the beanbag.

The guy looks at me, throws a chin in my direction. Who's this? he says.

Ambroos, this is our boy, the chef, Ducasse says. Winks at me.

The chef? The chef got a name?

You can call him 'Chef'.

Fuck's your story, Chef? Ambroos says.

Just blowin through, I say. I pull off my jacket.

Ambroos gives me the eye, all distrustful. Ducasse was right — he's Dutch, and he's a cunt.

See this? Ambroos says, and he points to the melted girl next to him, See her? That's my girl. Don't fucken touch her.

I hold up my hands, all placatory like, then the girl stirs, she's proper gone, and while Ambroos runs his tongue up the side of a big spliff he's just rolled, the girl leans over to me. Do you love Jesus? she says.

Hey, I love Jesus as much as the next guy. I pray from mornin to night, I tell her.

Her eyes are rollin in her head. I fucken love Jesus, she says.

I'm all for Jesus-love, I say. Ambroos is givin me the evil eye, thinks I wanna fuck Jesus-girl.

I'm Mary-Lou, she says, and holds out her hand and I shake it.

I feel Jesus in me all day long, Mary-Lou says, meltin back into the couch.

This is one freaky show, and I'm lookin at Ducasse like, *What are these cats on?* and Ducasse nods like, *Give me a few minutes and we'll get outta here.* Some next-level wordless communication goin on between me and Ducasse.

Hugo sent us over — need some pills, he says.

At the mention of pills there's movement from the dirty hippy in the beanbag. Ambroos lights the joint and pushes it into Mary-Lou's mouth, and she takes a tug on it and splutters.

You need pills, do you? Well, I've got a guy in Den Haag askin after meat, Ambroos says.

So let's trade, Ducasse says.

Ambroos reaches behind the sofa and pulls out a bag of ecstasy. I mean, like a sack. Tosses it at Ducasse. Take what you need, he says.

Ducasse pulls a cloth bag from his pocket, opens up the sack and starts countin out pills.

Here, pass a couple my way, Ambroos says.

So Ducasse pulls out a handful and passes em to Ambroos then throws one at me. I watch Ambroos push a pill into Mary-Lou's mouth.

Here, get some Jesus in you, he says.

Mary-Lou's slidin down into the sofa. Gone girl, goin places. In the name of the father, the son, and the holy spirit, he says.

I look at the pill, a little Mitsubishi, speckled like the good old days, and I pop it and chew it up. Get it goin like.

Ducasse is countin away: 50, 60…

The comatose guy behind me in the beanbag suddenly kicks, shakes his head. I look at the guy; he looks like he's been on the business end of a needle for several weeks. Sure enough, Ambroos picks up a syringe off the table and passes it to me. Stick that in his leg, he says.

Will I fuck, I say.

Ducasse says, Nah, it's alright — poke him with it.

I'm looking at Ducasse like, this is not what I do mornins, but he's givin me the nod like, *It's fine, just stick it in him.*

So I plunge the needle in his leg and squeeze, and that settles him down some.

What about this one? Ambroos says to Ducasse, pointin at the junkie.

For what?

For meat.

Fuck knows what's runnin through his veins, Ducasse says. He looks away, goes back to the countin.

I know exactly what's runnin through his veins, Ambroos says, cause I been pumpin him with it all week.

What is it? I say, droppin the needle.

Some kind of horse tranquiliser, Ambroos tells me.

Not much eatin on him, Ducasse says.

Then Mary-Lou starts groanin, the pill comin on her, and Ambroos slides his hand between her legs, those fat American thighs, brown thighs, thighs that belong to Jesus and which open like the Bible, only for those who believe.

Do you feel Jesus? Ambroos says.

Mary-Lou's moanin, *Yes*...

Ducasse's eyes are followin Ambroos's hand, and I can see he's thinking about jesus-cunt, bible-cunt, and I'm startin to see just what kinda prayin Ducasse is into.

Where'd you find her? he says.

Ambroos tokes on the spliff. Christian Youth Hostel, round the corner. I came to the aid of one God's lost children, he says.

Aren't you the high priest of mercy, Ducasse says, and the jealousy in his voice is palpable, and I don't blame him, cause those big fat American thighs are the stuff of manna, of plenty. We're talking feed the five thousand. You'd part the sea and cross the desert to climb up there, and what must be waitin there at the top? Deliverance, that's what, and Ducasse knows it. He'd kill to open that Bible and hear God's word.

160, 170...

Ducasse is still countin, fillin up his cloth sack with pink Mitsubishis, not bad either, cause I'm feelin it come on me now too. It's started in my balls, where it always does, and soon it'll move up into my stomach, then *bam*, I'll be chewin the face off myself.

Mary-Lou's comin up, moanin, her own two hands slip between her legs now. I feel him, I feel Jesus, she says.

Yes, but do you *feel* him? Ambroos says. Is he explodin in you?

No...

And he stands up and takes her by the hand and pulls her from the sofa, and I can see Ambroos wants to climb the Temple Mount, he's had it, he needs to bathe in the Word, swim in it, open those thighs and bathe in the Word.

Come, he says, and he's hissin it. *Come on*...

Man's out of control. Put those back where you got em, he says to Ducasse. And he leads Mary-Lou out to go part the ocean.

Let's get the fuck outta here, I say. These are some strange ones.

Two hundred and fifty, Ducasse says, and he pulls the string in his little pouch and slips it into his pocket. Then he dips his hand in the sack and pulls out a handful and hands it to me. Here — for the poor fucken hospitality in this place, he says. And cause he's a cunt.

I pocket the Es, and Ducasse takes another handful for himself.

Let's get the fuck outta here, he says.

We head back down the alley, by now I'm flyin, the pill proper on me, and it's on Ducasse too cause he's all over the alley like a man gone, but I know it's not just the E, it's the pussy too, the man's got cunt on the brain. So when we pass the window with the big black hoor in it Ducasse stops, his jacket's already comin off him, and I say, Nah, Ducasse man, you've gotta be fucken lunatic for that, but he is lunatic, I see that now, and he's high and he'll tackle anything. Big girl has her ass up against the window, winkin at me over her shoulder, but I'm not half the man he is.

Go on down the corner and have a drink, he says. I'll be down in a minute.

What are you gonna do? I say, like an idiot boy.

Fuck do you think I'm gonna do? he says.

Yeah, he's off on one, so I watch him go in the door and I'm thinkin, *Poor fucken girl, doesn't know what's comin at her.* And I head down the corner.

So I find a café down the end of the alley, all black on the outside, and bounce up the stairs. I go in the door, nice place, and I smell the smell of warm breakfast pastry, cinnamon rolls, raisins and chocolate, all these things, there at the back wall I see the bar, couple of staff all dressed in black, but between me and the bar there's no way through. I mean, it's wall-to-wall tables and chairs, a fucken maze, like the Takeshi's Castle of dining experiences.

Sir, she says to me, we're not open for another fifteen minutes.

What? I say, and I try to push my way through, but it's not happenin, it's like a jungle.

Sir—

Just hold on a minute — I'll come to you, I shout, and I back up and take a runnin leap at it.

*Bam!* The first chair I hurdle takes me down, and I'm on the floor writhin and squealin, like a wild pig floored by hyenas.

Sir—

I'm wrapped in chair legs and table legs, sabotaged by the café with too many chairs, and I'm shoutin at the poor woman who's run over, Get me up out of it, will ya!

And two of em lift me, me thrashin and kickin.

Are you okay?

Jesus, I say, what kinda place is this?

Sir, we're not open yet...

I need a drink, I tell em. Jesus, I need a drink. Put me on a sofa.

And they drag me to a sofa and drop me in it, and by now they've caved and they're lettin me stay.

What can I get you? she says, and I see a kinda terror in her eyes, cause now I'm a man who makes women afraid.

Got any absinthe? I say.

They don't.

I'll have a Black Russian please, I tell her, and she nods, and I can see what she's thinkin. *Give him what he wants and maybe he'll leave.*

Okay, sir. Wait here.

*Like I'm goin anywhere. Fucken place makes the Temple of Doom look like a Jungle Jim's.*

So I sink back in the sofa and look up at the ceilin, which is too high, way too high, and this is the strangest café I've ever landed in, and I'm thinkin, *You better throw up a good beverage.*

So she comes back over with the Black Russian and puts it down on the table with a little napkin, the way they do in nice places, and I say, Thank you, and smile, cause I don't wanna be the guy that scares women. She seems more chilled

36

and heads back over to the bar, and I take a sip of the cocktail and *jesus-fucking-christ*, it's the finest thing I've tasted in my life. I mean, it's fucken revelatory. I bliss out there on the sofa and take to starin at the glass, all cold and condensation and muscat-brown, and I sniff it, then I take another sip, and then repeat, each better than the last. Blissed out on Black Russian, I don't care about the ceiling or the chairs or the fucken spill on the floor, I don't even care what Ducasse is doin to the hoor down the street, cause I've found the best thing since pills, which is alcohol, prepared by someone who know what they're doin. I look at the girl behind the bar, and I don't wanna open my mouth and break the spell of the moment, so I just wink and I think she gets it. She knows.

Bliss.

Then the door bursts open, and I look up and see Ducasse come in, all arms and fury, and the girl at the bar is shoutin *Sir!*, but Ducasse doesn't give a fuck he just barrels through, chairs, tables, everything flies, and without a bother he drops down beside me on the sofa.

How'd you get over here?

What are you on about? he says.

Through the chairs, I say.

He shakes his head. You're wrecked, you clown, he says.

And the girl's over to chase him out, but Ducasse takes no notice and orders a beer, and the girl, poor thing, has no fight and retreats to get his drink.

That blood on your shirt? I say.

Ducasse flicks at his shirt, mumblin some shite, then picks up a napkin and rubs at it. Why you drinkin a girl's drink? he says.

Ducasse, you won't fucken believe how good this thing is. It's heaven in a glass.

Get a bit giddy, do ya, when you get high? he says.

So I tell him about the flying leap across the tables and the spill on the floor, and the strangely high ceiling, and how I've been sittin here drinkin purple rain.

You wasted prick, he says.

Doesn't get it, Ducasse. He's a man of crude tastes.

The girl comes back with the drink and Ducasse swallows his beer, gone in one, me here tryin to savour, relish, luxuriate in my sublime cocktail.

Ready for gettin back? he says.

Slow down, will ya? Where ya rushin off to?

Gotta get back, he says. Hugo's waitin on the pills.

Let me finish this, I say, but he pulls it outta my hand, downs it, then he turns to look at me, like, *That thing is a revelation.*

Prick, I say.

We're comin back for one of those, he says, and he gets up and blows through the café — chairs, tables, nothin to him, and I stand up and all I see's a fucken assault course.

Help me through, will ya? I shout.

Fucken imbecile, he says.

# 6

# Screamin Pope, Amsterdam

**Location:**
*Screamin Pope, Amsterdam*
**Time:**
*14.51, Thursday*
**Present:**
*Hugo: meaty swinger, ABBA fanboy*
*Ducasse: sex offender, aggro lunatic*
*Forsythe: manufacturer of high-class pharmaceuticals*
*Group of businessmen: aficionados of Hugo's meat*

We get back to the bar, Hugo's back there doin his thing, and it's pretty thin for the afternoon, but there's a group of suits in the corner goin savage on plates of meat, no messin around with salad, garnish, none of that shite, these guys are just goin at the flesh, big slabs of it, thick and bloody, rare, like lions at the kill. A pride of bankers, an ambush of accountants, a streak of suits. Fucken savages. There's the acrid, metallic scent of bloody meat in the air and it gets me strangely excited. The pills, see? Like used to happen with Jules, I figure, but I never got that kick outta the scent before, but now my balls are tinglin.

We head over to the bar, Hugo's leanin over talkin to some guy I don't know, he turns as me and Ducasse come up behind him. I get that pill thing, seein two faces on the one guy — the one everyone sees, and the other face, the one MDMA brings out, a mask face, which is actually their real nature, hoverin just over the physical one. A shimmer face. Smacked on E you really see people. This one looks like a bit of an evil prick, like a wiry Lavrentii Beria. Or like James Joyce in the final stages of HIV. Thin, haggard, eyes hard and cold.

The conversation stops as me and Ducasse rock up. Aids Joyce is watchin me, me a newcomer n'all that. I'm off my head and probably starin him down too.

You two look twisted, Hugo says. What the fuck you been at?

This one here's a pillhead, Ducasse says, and I start gigglin.

This one was throwin little pink Mitsubishis at me. What the fuck can I say? I tell Hugo.

Degenerates.

I'd like a Black Russian, big fella, I say.

Fucken yuppie, Hugo says.

And none of that bottom rung stuff, limme have the Grey Goose.

So, Hugo says to Aids Joyce, as he unscrews the top of the Goose, we need you back on your game quickly, cause I had to send the boys over to Ambroos for some sassy and you know well as I do there's no guarantee what that Dutch prick is gettin in his pills. We're gonna fuck up the meat.

Does he need to be here? Aids Joyce says. He's lookin at me.

He's in, Hugo says. Ducasse nods. Matter of fact, Hugo says, he's gonna help you get your shit back.

How's that? Aids Joyce says.

He's gonna rob back your PMK, Hugo says.

I'm gonna do what now? I say.

*I may be off my tits and not completely at the wheel, but who likes havin shit planned for em?*

Don't worry, you and me partner, Ducasse says.

Hugo puts the Black Russian down in front of me.

This is your last, by the way. We need you straight tonight.

What kinda fuckery are you gettin me into? I say.

Kinda like stealin, but not really, Hugo says. More like takin somethin back that's already ours. You and Ducasse are gonna go and retrieve it for us.

Paid work, I presume, I say. *I'm an honest guy.*

Five grand for the job, Aids Joyce says.

Ten, Ducasse says.

Aids Joyce isn't swingin with it. It's two hours' work, he says.

Nah, Ducasse says. Get with the fucken payscale.

Hugo nods and Aids Joyce caves. He looks at me. You on? he says.

I shrug. *Why the fuck not? Gotta make your way in this world, don't ya?* Yeah, I say.

Hugo puts the Black Russian down and I tear into it, one of those unquenchable pill thirsts on me. But it's not like the other one, not like the one in the café which blew my fucken mind.

Then Hugo introduces me, after I've gone and agreed to rob somethin for the cunt.

This is Forsythe, Hugo says.

Forsythe nods, all cool and evil. I nod. *Aids Joyce is your name, and I'm stickin with it.*

I take a stool and lean back against the bar and scan the room. The suits are finishin up their meat feast, all grease and fingers.

Who are these cunts? I say.

Customers. Connoisseurs. Men who are ruled by their appetites, Hugo says. Here — go and put my song on.

He throws a coin at Ducasse, who heads over to the jukebox and throws it in, and then I hear *Winner Takes It All*. Now, I'm not an ABBA man, nor is ABBA pill music, but in this oddball place nothin is too strange.

Hugo heads out across the floor, gone with the music, dances over in that feminine manner, big sweaty meaty Hugo, his movements hypnotic. He's like a well-practised drag queen without all the get up. Perhaps that's what he does on weekends, I dunno. But there's somethin womanish about the brute. I look at the table of suits, who watch as Hugo slides over to the table to collect the plates; they eye up Hugo as he swings to ABBA, lookin on with a voracious hunger, swollen with meat and desire.

*Right queer place, the Screamin Pope.* But I'm pilled up and it's all mad compelling, for a man like me who's fascinated by weird shit.

Then the four suits start turnin into some kind of obscene caricature of Hugo himself, hands slidin between the buttons of their shirts and fingers in bellies, strokin beneath the tailored cotton, another with his balls cupped in his hands, the last still suckin the traces of meat juice from his fingers, lickin one after the other in a lecherous and ecstatic agony.

*Right queer business altogether.*

Aids Joyce breaks the filthy spell. I got ten million euros tied up in those goods, he says. I hope you're up to the job.

I'll get it done, I say.

Just do it right, he says.

I could get into it with him, but I don't. Prick's eyein me like he's got the measure of me, but I see his face, his real face, his shimmer face, hoverin there over his skull, and it tells me all I need to know. Aids Joyce is a cunt.

Hugo's still out there, meaty hips swingin, some of the suits gropin at him. I look at Ducasse who now has violence in his eyes, and I don't know if it's a queer thing or a lunatic thing, like he's already fucked someone and now he has to fight, cause there's strong waves of lunatic off Ducasse. Aids Joyce senses it, cause he's squirmin in his chair.

Perhaps Hugo senses it too cause he pulls away, plates in hand, but still movin, the big thick meaty meister is still shakin, ABBA playin,

*Someplace deep within, I know you missed me…*

And I can see his gyrations are inflaming the suits, the

gyrations and his meaty scent casting a strange fleshy spell over us all. I have to admire his élan. He's a barman, a showman, a sex fiend. I see it in the eyes of the four bankers or whatever they are, they're thinkin, *Yes yes yes, move you big fucken bear, move for us...* Hugo plays up to it, puts on the show, then disappears out back.

I am surrounded by maniacs and perverts.

*Thinkin I should be here*
*Thinkin I may fall*
*Building me a wall...*

The suits get up off their stools, headin off out to the savannah. They move like animals move. They are gettin to somethin like a frenzy, driven wild by meat and the sight of a thick man moving like a woman. Hugo's barbecue spell has set them off on one. I can see where they're headed. Now they're gonna wander into the Red Light to make some hoors very uncomfortable.

Hugo comes back out through the door. See ya. Behave yerselves, he shouts.

The men wave and go ape-like up the stairs. I see Ducasse relax and turn around in his stool. I gotta say, I wanna see him in a scuffle, but I'm not really in the mood for blood.

Then he pulls the bag o'pills from his pocket and tosses it over the bar at Hugo. Hugo opens the pouch and pours them onto the bar. Two hundred pills look like nothin. Two hundred shining pink Mitsubishis.

Hugo shakes his head. Gonna fuck up the meat, he says.

We'll be back in business in a few days, Ducasse says.

I'm blissin out across the bar and Ducasse gets up and claps a hand on my shoulder. Time for you to get some rest, he says.

Oh yeah?

Yeah.

Go n'lie down for a bit, get yourself straight, he says.

Sure, I say.

Never had much willpower when I was flyin off my tits.

I get up. Be seein ya later fellas.

Aye, Hugo says. Aids Joyce says fuck all. Hugo's pickin up the pills, droppin them back in the pouch.

So I head upstairs. I got my own room. Top of the stairs I take a right turn, fumble with the key, stumble inside. Home. I peek through the curtains. The street outside is empty save for the odd pervert.

I pull off my jacket and fall on the bed.

I have a room where the hoors go. A fuckbox. Never used though. It was never rented out, so I got a nice clean bed, a shower, lots of mirrors. It's clean, and it's free. Livin cheaply. But when the money starts comin in, I'll splash on a nice place.

*And if my new life of crime doesn't work out, I can always sell my ass. I'm surrounded by perverts anyway — may as well make some money while I'm at it.*

# 7

# PMK

This way, Ducasse tells me.

We head up Keizerstraat and cross the canal. I don't know the time, but it's gone dark. Amsterdam has that cold winter sheen. It's crisp, jaunty. It's like walkin around in a postcard, or the magical land found only on the lids of Danish biscuit tins. It feels like that, but it could be my blood levels are still way too high in MDMA.

Ducasse takes a set of keys from his pocket and he's janglin em maniacally, stridin high, all over the street like the high priest of *I'm-walkin-here-get-the-fuck-outta-my-road* and I'm just tryin to keep up. He stops at a white van, self-employed plumber kinda shtick, I dunno if it's the perfect van for whatever the fuck we're doin or whether it's so inconspicuous as to be conspicuous.

We're goin in this fucken thing? I say. We'll be lucky to get outta the city in it.

She's rock solid, Ducasse says, and he opens the door with that clunk you get on twenty-year-old motors.

He slides in and opens the passenger door, and I bounce in after. I shut the door — *clunk* — and blow into my hands and rub em, not cause I'm cold, but growin up in a cold country you develop habits, don't ya?

Ducasse starts the engine then turns to look at me all solemn like, hands in his lap like he's about to take my confession, degenerate minister that he is.

We can't fuck this up, which is why we gotta be *tight*. I mean, you gotta be shootin straight tonight, he says, lookin me in the eye, dead serious like.

He then pulls out a wrap of coke, pulls the streetfinder from between the seats, and empties out the contents of the wrap. Some higher-level logic right there.

He pulls out a metro card and gets to cuttin up lines. We'll get our heads clear then we'll fuck off, he says.

Aye. Clear heads, I say.

This isn't some dirty ye-ya from some Dutch pillhead, he says. This is the cleanest coke that can be found this side of Machu Picchu. A line of this stuff and you feel like Sai Baba, he tells me.

Then he rolls up a fifty-euro note, snorts a massive line, and passes me the streetfinder.

I hit it, and he's right. My brain lights up like a switchboard, synapses *ping-a-lingin* all over the show.

*Jesus-fucken-christ*. White christmas this year.

Ducasse winks. Sai Baba, he says, and he starts up the motor, snatches up the handbrake and pulls into the street.

Where we headed?

Tilburg.

Where the fuck's that?

About an hour away.

Got more coke?

Enough for the trip.

Ducasse turns down the canal. I sit back.

I been to Machu Picchu, I tell him.

Course you have, you filthy backpacker, Ducasse says.

Six years ago I was in Peru, hiked up to Machu Picchu with three Argentinians. We got arrested cause two of em decided to take a shit in the main temple. Spent three days in a Peruvian jail cause three Latinos ate some bad tamales, I tell him.

You've poor taste in company, he says.

Yes I do.

He pulls a cassette outta the glove box — twenty-year-old van, course it has a cassette deck — and he jams in a tape. *Clunk.*

Then I hear this wailin, or howlin, or chantin — some Indian jiggery, *sixty-times-anticlockwise-round-the-temple* kinda racket, and I look at Ducasse and this is no joke, he's settlin in for the ride.

You fucken kiddin me? I say.

I reach out for the tape deck but his hairy hand claps on my wrist.

Trust me, he says.

Ducasse knows. Ten minutes later I'm wired on the sound of *Om Sai Baba*, off my tits on coke and with the lights of Amsterdam zippin by. I'm havin a religious experience.

*Om sai namo namaha, jai jai sai...*

Coked out on Sai Baba, we sail outta the city.

Coked up and zoned out we are, and an hour later the thing is still playin. By now I'm frayed at the fucken edges, Ducasse is too, cause he pulls over and we bang another couple of lines.

Enough's enough, Ducasse — wanna put somethin else on? I say.

It's nearly over.

How long's it go on for?

There's a hundred and eight repetitions.

Bit fucken excessive, innit?

Hindus like to pray, he says.

You Hindu?

Ducasse is peerin through the glass at the bottom of the windscreen cause our fan's given out.

Nah, he says. But I studied theology. I was in the seminary.

I can't help it, I laugh. Christ, I fucken laugh.

You takin the piss?

We've pulled into an industrial estate and Ducasse hushes

47

me. We're here, he says.

And just as he says it, Sri Sai Baba gives over, all prayed out, and I'm impressed, like, *this guy knows time*, knew the song would take us A to B and not a second lost. He fucken knows.

Down there, he says.

He slows the van and kills the lights, and we crawl down the road. No vehicles about. I peer out the window, Ducasse is pointin at a warehouse two hundred yards up ahead. It's fenced off, one police out front.

That it? I say.

That's it.

Ducasse takes out another wrap.

Maybe we give it a rest with the coke, I say.

This isn't coke.

He pulls latex gloves from his pocket, slips them on, then carefully opens the wrap and empties in onto the streetfinder. He slides it onto the dash.

Don't touch that, he says. Don't fucken breathe either.

We roll down the street towards the warehouse. The cop's turned, watchin us draw up. We reach the gate and Ducasse turns the van like he's gonna drive right in and the cop starts waving his arms. Ducasse rolls down the window.

Officer — we're lost. Need your help.

The cop comes over, looks at Ducasse, peers over at me.

Give me directions? Ducasse says.

He nods, even smiles. Dutch police — good cunts.

Ducasse lifts the streetfinder from the dash, holds it out the window and the cop leans in, and he blows the powder in the cop's face. The cop flinches, takes a step back, reaches for the 9mm, but then comes over all disoriented like.

There's no problem, Ducasse says. There's no need for your gun.

The cop looks at Ducasse and his hand drops.

We need in. Open the gate for us and close it up after, Ducasse says.

48

You need in, the cop says, then walks over and slides the gate open.

Ducasse salutes, drives inside. I look out the back window. Sure enough, the cop is closin the gate after us.

What the fuck was that? I say.

Ducasse smiles. Kissed by the devil, he says.

What'd you do?

Scopolamine, he says.

Fuck's that?

Some Colombian craziness. Grows in the forest, makes you do whatever you're told, he explains.

Scopolamine? And this shit is on the streets? I say.

In very tight circles. Only if you know the right people.

Jesus fucken wept.

He drives the van round back to a large loading door.

Is that it? Just one cop? I say.

One more inside.

You gonna spike him with that shit too?

Nah. We'll just crack this one over the skull.

You keepin any that Colombian shit for yourself? I say. Cause I don't wanna wake up some night in a fuckin spin with you lickin my ear and fondlin my balls.

You've trust issues, Ducasse says.

I don't wanna see that stuff again, I tell him.

You won't, he says.

I don't believe him.

Let's get this done, he says.

We get out.

Stay down a minute and don't move, Ducasse says.

So I slide down behind the passenger side and Ducasse walks up to the door and raps it with a giant flashlight he's lifted from the van. He hugs the wall and waits. Nothin. He raps it again. Then I hear a lock rattle. The door opens and the capped head of a Dutch police pokes out. Ducasse cracks him on the back of the skull with the torch and he goes down.

I stand up.

We're in, Ducasse says.

*That fucken easy.*

We drag him inside and drop him between two pallets, bind the hands and feet and pull a bag over his head.

That it? I say. There's gotta be more.

Just two, Ducasse says.

How do you know?

We know some people. We got the heads up. There are only chemicals here, no drugs. It's a low-priority seizure, he tells me.

The warehouse is long, low and low-lit. We head down the central aisle. Rows of barrels line each side, every few feet a stack of boxes. About halfway down he stops at a pallet. It's stacked to chest height with white plastic bags. He checks the tags.

This is it, Ducasse says.

What is it?

PMK-glycidate. Precursor for MDMA — there's about ten million worth of pills here, he says.

*Jesus fuck.*


We pack the last of it away in the van, white bags stacked to the roof, and Ducasse goes back to close the door.

What about the cunt inside? I say.

We leave him, Ducasse says. Shift change'll get him in the mornin.

We done here?

He nods. I shake my head.

*Easiest five grand I ever made.*

I think we need a celebratory line of Charlie, he says.

He pulls out the coke and divvies it up, and we take a line. Then we're drivin out the gate. Ducasse stops to talk to the law.

That'll be all for tonight officer, says Ducasse. We're all done.

You're all done, he says. He tips his cap.

One more thing, officer, Ducasse says. Show us your cock.

Fuck sake, I say, but he's doin it, the cop's pulled out his cock and is showin it through the window.

Nice cock, isn't it? Ducasse says to me.

Tell him to put it away, I say.

Leave it out for a bit officer — give it a bit of an air, Ducasse tells him.

A bit of air, says the officer and nods, like he's well-pleased with the suggestion.

Goodnight captain, Ducasse says, and drives off.

I turn to look, the police is pullin the gate closed behind us, prick swingin in the wind.

Ducasse pops the tape out and turns it over.

Sai Baba? he says.

# 8

# Meat Lovers United

*Location:*
Screamin Pope, Amsterdam
*Time:*
03.20, Friday
*Present:*
Hugo: witchy barman, retro saviour
Ducasse: chemical connoisseur, lunatic swinger
Sweeney: weird lurker
Lots of party boys and girls

Back in the city we pull into a lock-up in Czaar Peterbuurt around three in the mornin. Ducasse kills the engine and pockets the keys and we get out and close up. Twenty minutes later we're back in the Pope.

It's a shitshow. Somethin's kicked off while we've been gone and the place is heavin, wall-to-wall freaks and perverts, music kickin, the joint alive, a joint that only hours before was a seedy, lonely dive bar.

A hen party's in and are goin ballistic on the floor to 'Voulez-Vous'. Hugo's at it again, with his queer, ABBA-induced carnality. On the floor the women are whipped up, while around them the predators circle. It smells like meat, sex and violence. This is no kind of scene to do straight. I shout over the music at Ducasse.

What happened in here?

Sometimes it just kicks off, he says.

Giz a coupla pills, I shout.

He pulls a fistful outta his pocket and drops em into my hand. I chew a couple and we head to the bar. It's freaks end-to-end, and in back, Hugo, doing whatever the fuck it is he does, holdin everyone in thrall. He sees us, winks, not breakin his stride, and soon he's passin two glasses of Jameson over the heads of the cattle.

Job done? he says.

Ducasse nods.

Hugo winks. He's clappin his hands to the tune.

*Ah-ha! Ah-ha!*

Ducasse necks a couple o'pills, pulls off his jacket and tosses it over the bar at Hugo. He turns to the floor. He's goin off on one. I take my Jameson to a table by the wall where two women sit. I make eye contact, puttin my glass on the table, just so there's understandin what I'm doin there — I'm not there to hit on anyone. I just want a place to watch the madness. Crazy fucken scene.

That weird cretin Sweeney's sittin down the far end of the bar. He waves.

The heads along the bar are in every state of inebriation and undress: bare chests and tits are the responses to Hugo's greasy charms. A couple of male model types are competin with a few slutty hangers-on from the hen party for his attention. There's a couple of beat-lookin trannies tryin to climb onto the bar in eight-inch heels. There's another group of suits in, not the ones from earlier but others, but same animal ways about em. There's one bent-over crackhead runnin up and down, eyes on the floor; why no one's thrown him out I dunno. Then there's a weird clique of Japanese who look utterly fucken enthralled and terrified at once. Young fellas, hard-ons for the crazy scene, look like they'd fuck a hole in the wall. It might even be possible in here — likely there's a gloryhole somewhere in this slippery joint.

*Here we are again, we know the first, we know the last,*
*Masters of the place...*

Hugo flings his arms out, Christ-like, to the music.

They all go fucken wild. He's swingin, they're swingin, everybody's swingin.

I inhale it all.

Ducasse is dry-humpin one of the hen party on the floor, I think it's the bride, her friends gettin right into it. The little Japanese kids are buckin the air wildly, I don't even know what they're at, dry-ridin, air-fuckin, they just wanna stick their pricks in somethin, gone Asian kids lettin it all out in a room full of perverts.

I'm up in some craziness. I'm comin up on Ambroos's pharmaceuticals, the sweaty green swell of the Screamin Pope fillin us all with some meaty mania. The room is pulsin, I'm pulsin... it's in me: the desire, the heat, the madness.

Crazy in here, isn't it?

It's the girl across the table, leanin over.

I grin, nod. Don't really feelin like tryin to talk — this scene is too good. It's like Passolini on his best day.

You know him? she shouts. She's talkin about Hugo, of course.

I shrug.

Is this a new place? Just we've never heard of it before.

She's not lettin up.

Anything about this place look new? I tell her, and she smiles.

Well, it's crazy, she shouts.

I nod.

Got any gear? she asks, and then I get it. *It's fine, we're all loved up here — I'm loved up, and I don't mind spreadin it about, either. It's all about the love here.*

So I pull out a coupla pills and hand em over. She grins and eats one straight up. The other, her friend, hesitates. Never done it before, I can tell. Her friend puts a hand on her arm, whispers in her ear, then she slips it in her mouth and holds it there. *Mistake. Just swallow it.* She'll be spittin it out. Her friend pushes a drink into her hand and lifts it to her mouth. *Bam*, it's down. Give her forty minutes, the virgin, she'll be doin lines of coke off a stranger's cock, or lickin it outta some sweaty navel.

It's all happenin tonight.

I lean back against the wall all buzzed up, watchin the scene.

*We've seen it before and now we've come for more…*

I see Ducasse slip a pill into the mouth of the bride-to-be with his tongue. Dirty fiend. She's right into it, he's leadin her right down the road, down the Ducassian *rapey-theologian-cokefiend* road, and she's in it all the way.

*Ah-ha! Ah-ha!*

The gone Japanese kids have lost it and are at the two trannies. Big tranny hands playin with little Japanese cocks, *ooh mama…* one o'those kids is cummin in his pants. This shit's probably normal in Tokyo.

The little explosions have begun.

Wanna dance with us? the girl across the table shouts at me.

I'll follow you up, I shout back.

Then somethin happens. A big platter of meat comes through the kitchen door, held aloft by a now shirtless Hugo, a great silver tray, somethin you might see in a history book, you know, like, *This votive tray was dedicated by Pytheas to the goddess Athena in the year 290 as a gift from the people of Massalia.* It's massive, a great mountain of meat on it. A cheer goes up from the bar.

The hyenas attack.

Hugo's out on the floor, tray out in front of him and they're at it. Teeth bared, meat is stripped from the bone in seconds. It's feedin time at the waterin hole.

Hugo holds the tray out to me. Try the ribs, he shouts.

I grab a fistful. The two girls at my table are all over it too.

It's merciless. Frenzied.

Mouths smeared with meat-grease, bones clenched in closed fists, meaty snarls... we are reverted to our primeval state, bloody and gorged. We are one: freaks, trannies, suit and Asian, all animal to the core. Meat.

I look at the girl next to me. She's eatin steak with her fist. No longer a good girl, civilised, well-heeled — she's a hunter by a fire in a cave in sub-Saharan Africa. We're all hunger and instinct, pre-civilised.

I tear at the meat in my own hand, the grease drips down my arm. I suck it up off my hand. The synapses in my head spit.

Juicy.

Greasy.

*Gorgeous*.

Something happens in my brain, my mind on fire. This is what Hugo does, then. He's a meaty wizard, a magus of the flesh, the conjurer of delectable cuts.

I'm rippin the meat from the bone, gone savage like the rest of em.

Gorging on gorgeous gristle and grease.

A glutton.

*Filthy fucken Gs.*

I'm feastin at the table of the ancients in some secret and now-lost ritual that has been revived here in the shithole basement of the Screamin Pope. We're all in on it, all united by it. We are the lost tribe, the first of earth. We're at the epicentre.

*We've seen it before and now we've come for more...*

The place is ballistic.

We're all in it now. We're ridin it out, all together at sea, a big meaty ride on the good ship Ecstasy. And this ship is fast sinkin.

The four suits, Amsterdam's business elite, are on the floor on their hands and knees, lickin at the empty tray, suckin up the last of the juices. Animals on the floor, cleanin up the remains of the kill, eyes wild, furious.

I'm suckin on a rib bone watchin all this go down, the last of the flesh now in a downward descent towards my bowels, but its flavours have already disseminated in my brain and body. My limbs are comin alive, I feel like I could take a beatin off eight men and stay on my feet. I feel fucken invincible.

The shy girl from across the table has come over. She grips my head in her hands and proceeds to suck on my chin. She's sucking up the meat juices. She bites my upper lip, drawing blood. Her eyes are mad. I grin. The blood tastes good in my mouth, and if I wasn't into it before I'm into it now, and I'm feelin that howl come on me like a wolf. I gettin this buzz off the girl, some kinda savage connection now she's drawn my blood, vampiric like. She's mine, and I'm hers. Or perhaps we all belong to each other, joined in thirst and savagery.

She turns around and pushes herself into me, and I claw at her. The more viciously I push my fingers into her flesh the more she loses it. She pushes her face into my neck and I smell the meat juices on her. I grip her and she thrusts her body into mine. We're joined now.

There's mayhem on the floor. They're all clawin and bitin at each other, hungry for flesh. Flesh is king now. Cooked or raw, they gotta have it. Ducasse has the bride held up above him, his head is between her thighs and he's eatin her out. Feasting.

Everyone here's ready to fuck or kill.

I take the girl by the hand and lead her through the debauch. We go up the stairs and into my box, clothes ripped off before she throws me to the bed. She climbs up on top of me, and I've never seen such hunger. She wants to rip me apart. She cracks me across the face with the back of her hand.

Eat me, I say.

Then we get to eatin.

# 9

# A Man's Needs

I wake up naked, bloody and thirsty in my Amsterdam fuckbox, and the girl's gone and the curtain's open. I climb outta bed, sheets stuck to my back, and crawl over to pull the curtain. Place is a fucken mess, like a murder scene: blood, semen... *skin?* I pick it up, and it is, a bit of flesh... human flesh on my bedroom floor. And then I feel it, the pain kicks in, and I find a lump missin from my shoulder and a bite chewed right outta my thigh, and piece gone outta my arm... girl clean ate me. That doe-eyed, good little Dutch girl ate fucken lumps outta me. I mean, I've pieces missin.

*Jesus fuck. What am I into?*

She's gone, and it hits me then — what's *she* like? Is she tore up like me, and will I be gettin a knock on the door?

*Christ.*

I climb up off the floor and go over to the shower and turn on the water, but there's no gettin under it hot cause my skin is screamin, so I go freezin cold and the blood runs off me in rivers, spirals down the plughole into the sewers of the city, Amsterdam's rivers, rivers of coke, semen and now my blood mixed in. The river of life.

I stand under the freezin water for ten minutes. I shake, exhilarated, flashes from last night leapin into my head: the meat, the frenzy, men on the ground like dogs fightin over scraps, little Asian kids climbin up on six-foot trannies, girls eaten out right on the floor, strangers goin vampire on each other after a taste of meat; Ducasse, madman, all up in the middle of it takin his pleasure here, there and everywhere, and Hugo, the marvel, the meaty maître d', our savage charge d'affaires, whippin us up into some kinda ritualistic miasma; and then me, all teeth and prick, all over her, and her goin at me, teeth, nails, tearin pieces off me...

I turn off the water. I feel kinda human again. Almost. Torn and shredded, but alive.

I get out. I look in the mirror and see a man who's been caught in the middle of a dogfight. I dry off and put on some clothes, and head out the door into the cold empty street, hoofing it up to Oudezijds Achterburgwal.

There are a few derelicts around, scouting the mornin scene, beat guys, more beat than me, cunts who've been too long in the city and have no way out. That's not me and that'll never be me, cause I got ideas and I'm movin up, and now I'm back in steady employment. I made five grand last night, fuck sake, and that reminds me I gotta get my money of that cunt Aids Joyce. I got a way out, I got my eye on the door, but first I'm gonna make somethin o'myself.

I cross the bridge and cut round the back of the Oude Kerk towards the Damrak, up to the Grasshopper where I know I'll score a fried breakfast and a cold pint. I'm ragged as hell and need things, like food — a man can't live on pills and booze, can he, pills and booze and vampire women and strange, hallucinatory meat? No. A man needs other unavoidable necessities. Like salad.

So I head inside and up to the bar next to a few Americans and hang there for a second, and the waitress comes over all smiles like, cute little thing, Scottish, asks me what I want.

I'll have a Duvel, I tell her. And make it a Red Eye.

Sure, she says, and starts pullin. I take off my jacket and she sees my neck, and she nearly drops the glass. I don't get what she's lookin at at first, then I get a stab of pain down the side of my head and I understand.

Sweet loving fuck, she says — shouldn't you be seein a doctor about that thing?

And the Yanks have turned around and they're lookin at me too, and they're sayin, Yeah, fuck bro — who the fuck did that to you?

So I slide the jacket back on, Nah lads, I say, nothin to worry about. I got with this mad savage lass last night and she tore lumps outta me, I tell em.

Savage? says the Scottish lass. She was a pure vampire by the looks of it. That's nasty.

Yeah bro, the one dude says, that is *nasty*.

And the bargirl puts down my glass.

I've had worse, I tell em, and I don't think I have but that's what you say, innit?

So's not to get caught up in all this banter, I take my pint. I'm gonna take that table over there — send over a menu, will ya? I tell her.

Sure. Want a first aid kit too?

The Yanks are laughin. Scottish girl's a joker.

So I take the table and a camp little Filipino guy brings me a menu, and Ducasse was right, ain't no Dutch left in Amsterdam.

What's your best burger? I say.

The Wagyu is popular, he tells me.

Better give me one of those, medium, I say. And I'll need a salad. You do a Caesar?

Of course, he says.

That'll do it then. Cheers buddy.

Caesar salad, the obese prick of salads… I mean, if a superfood salad is your gym meathead, then the Caesar is the fat bastard who lives in the flat below ya and hasn't left his sofa in four years. But fuck it, it's got greens in it and a bit of parmesan, and some days that's what a man needs.

I'm sittin lookin out the window up the Damrak, thinkin, maybe I just eat my lunch and head out into the street, and walk up to the station and get on a train down to Arnhem, or better, keep goin on to Antwerp, or fuck it, Bruges — that looks like a city where you can get away from things, where you don't risk gettin eaten by little Dutch vampires inflamed on strange hallucinatory meat, where you wouldn't think of keepin company with rapey types and drug dealers, or where you'd go robbin drug precursor from the law, and who's to know you weren't picked up on a camera outside the warehouse and are now bein hunted by the Dutch police, those nice Dutch police with their friendly smiles and their cocks swingin free, just swingin in the wind... who's to say?

But I know I'm not goin anywhere, cause even though I'm up in some strange business, I feel like I'm finally doin somethin with my life, no matter how strange and weird it all is, I feel like I'm into somethin worthwhile, somethin wild and free and kickin.

*Fucken hoo-ha.*

My burger and salad make their way over, and I re-acquaint myself with somethin called food, and all of the good stuff that comes with it, like proteins and minerals and vitamins. Oh, yes. I love poppin pills as much as the next guy, and I've gone three days before on liquid lunches, but I gotta tell ya, when ya need it ya need it. My body says, 'Yes, oh yes, it's about fucken time'.

I wave for another beer and the Scottish lass brings it over.

You look better, she says.

Do I?

So long as you keep that neck covered up.

That bad, is it?

You haven't seen it?

I looked at it once. I can't do it again.

Gonna be weeks before that thing clears up, she says.

Aye, I say.

I dab it with the napkin.

She puts a tube of antiseptic cream on the table. From the first-aid kit, she says. But I'd get to a doctor if I was you.

I'll be fine.

Your shout, she says.

She smiles.

She wanders off, fat little bum on her shakin, and I think about Janine and wonder where I'd be now if she'd shown up for that drink.

So I disappear into the jacks and put some cream on it, fucken rare sore-lookin it is, and there's no doubt someone's taken a bite outta me. A good mouthful. I put my jacket back on and pocket the cream, and head back out to the bar.

Can I pay ya? I say.

She says aye, totes up the bill.

I go into my pocket for some cash, but out comes the hand with a handful of pills, and I didn't know they were there but now I do, and I know just what's gonna happen when I walk out that door.

I pay the girl and give her a nice tip, and she winks. Stay away from the vampires, she says.

I'm tryin, I say, and, So long, I tell her, and I hoof it out the door and pop a pill.

I'm just too fucken predictable.

I cross the road and go buy myself a scarf, terrifyin the sales girl — who's Moldovan, by the way — cause she's never seen a man with a bite outta him before.

So I wrap myself up, determined not to disturb anyone else, and not only that, but to not draw attention to myself, me, a cunt who broke into a drug warehouse only the night before.

I cross the road again headed for the Red Light and I cut down an alley where there's a tranny slappin her cock off the window, and another big black girl pullin on her nipples, and I feel the pill come on me, balls tinglin, and I hurry out of the alley before I do somethin I might come to regret.

Now I'm buzzin, and God bless Amsterdam, it's fucken beautiful, even here, and God bless pills and booze and Caesar salad for givin me the eyes and the health to see it. Life really is somethin else.

Then I have a glorious idea... Yes, I'm thinkin, I'll go and find that café with the Black Russians, that'll do it, that'll push me right over the edge, for even if I'm tore up and sore I feel pretty fucken good right about now, and a Black Russian will top it right off.

So I hoof it over the bridge and down the main strip and up the alley, past Ambroos's place and up to the end of the street, but it's not there, not there or nowhere... no café with the too many chairs and tables and Black Russians to kill for. *Nah, can't be*, I'm thinkin, *it was right here*, so I walk round the block this way, and I walk round it that way, endin up on the same corner, but nothin. It's not there.

What do you think about that?

Fucken crazy it is, but it's true. So I wander down the canal lookin for another place, and I pass this little bookstore tucked away in the basement of a house, so I nip in, just to get outta the street, and who knows, maybe I'll pick up somethin, even if my drug habit's such that I don't have much time for readin.

I nod to the guy on the desk, give him the old *how-are-ya*, no words just a flick of the head, and I wander up the back. It's like I've been here before, cause my radar leads me right to the English books. I hoke through the shelves, and it's got all the usual second-hand stuff, *Thus Spake Zarathustra* and Montaigne and Bram Stoker and *what-have-ya*. All too heavy, and I'm thinkin maybe some Manley-Hopkins, somethin to trigger the brain, get it hoppin around, all those melodies just trippin off the page. But there's no Manley-Hopkins so I pick up another, a book with no title on the spine and a bland cityscape for a cover. I flick through it. It's just fucking, cover to cover. A jerk book. Guys suckin off guys in the park, guys blowin guys on beaches, motel rooms, alleys... just fucking all the way. It's sweaty and meaty, and I think of Hugo. The main character of this fuck-book could be Hugo. Hairy, sweaty, smellin like meat. Hugo, meatmeister and star of queer fuck-books. I'm gettin strangely into it when the clerk appears at my shoulder, me deep into this strange queer fuck extravaganza.

Help you? he says.

I jump. Jesus Christ, ya scared me.

Interesting choice, he says.

I look at the book in my hand and jam it back onto the shelf.

Perhaps a man like yourself is looking for something in particular? he says.

I think I know what he's gettin at, then he waves a hand towards the back, the store room out back.

I'm just browsin, I say. But he insists.

Something more to your *tastes*, he says, and he really fucken enunciates it. *Tastes*, all long and drawn out and confidential.

So I follow him up the back and he opens the door, and he flicks on a light to show me the rack for the man of *particulars*. 'Special Interest' it says, so I take a peek at it.

You're from the Pope, yes? he says.

The Screamin Pope?

He nods. I can smell it off you, he tells me.

Smell what exactly?

The meat, he says.

You can smell meat off me? I say, and I'm gettin flashes back to the grill, to Belfast, to Jules. Maybe this guy needs a crack in the jaw.

*Mm-hmm*, he says. I'm a patron myself.

You drink at the Pope?

He nods. I'm a long-time customer, he tells me. When you've been going as long as I have, you get to see the signs. Hugo shops here regularly. Look, he says, and points at the shelves.

I look.

There are medical journals. Travel journals. Books on recreational drug use, books on animal testing. Books on bovine genealogy, books on surgery and books on pairing wines with meat. Books on forensic science and psychopathology next to whole tomes on the endocrine system. And a fuckload of other 'peculiarities'.

What's all this?

I'll leave you to browse. I'm sure you'll find something to your liking, he says. And with a queer little grin he disappears out the door.

Yeah, I'm into somethin peculiar alright.

I pull a large colour glossy from the bottom shelf. It's not a book, more of a magazine, and dated. Must be thirty years old. It's called *Ecce Homo*. It's on cannibalism. It falls open at the centrefold, which is a double page spread of a naked woman with every edible part of her outlined in red marker. Front and back. It even delineates the type of cut to use. The *doctor-slash-butcher* stands next to her pointin at her thigh with his red marker. Ass, tits and thigh, all edible. Shoulder. Shin. Ribs. There's a dotted red line around her cunt too, obscured by a thick curly bush. Labia, edible. Neck and lips, delicacies. Over the page, there's a step-by-step account of how to cut, hang and prepare the meat. Recipes too. A cannibal's bible. I can't fathom the kind of maniac that comes up with this stuff.

I put it back on the shelf and pick up a scientific journal: Growth Hormone and Steroids in the Meat Industry.

I pick up one on Ecstasy synthesis. I like the subject matter but it's far too scientific.

There's a novel wedged in among all the academic stuff and I pull it out: *Notes from a Cannibalist*.

Might be worth a peek.

I turn off the light and go out and head down to the desk.

You can have that, he says. If you have anything on you.

He's talkin about pills. This cardigan is the most discreet pillhead I've ever encountered, but it takes all sorts, right? I give him the last of my *ye-ya*, whatever was left in my pocket.

Enjoy your reading, he says, and I watch him pop a pill right there in the bookshop.

Yeah, I say. See you down the Pope.

Some days are just strange.

66

I slip the book into my jacket and bounce out into the street. I'm feelin good but I'm on the comedown now and I start to figure that Ambroos's pills are probably fifty per cent speed. Cunt.

I still want that Black Russian so I have another look for the café, but it's still not there and now I'm gettin antsy.

I think about walkin up to Ambroos's but the thought o'that filthy room puts me right off. I need some real pills. I'm keen to see what Aids Joyce cooks up with that pallet of PMK we plundered for him. He must be good.

A bitter wind blows down the canal so I head briskly down the road. Then I remember that I'm owed five grand. That'll pick me up. Maybe I'll treat myself to some coke.

I head back to the bar to find the prick with my money.

# 10

# Time and Money

**Location:**
*Screamin Pope, Amsterdam*
**Time:**
*12.20, Sunday*
**Present:**
*Hugo: meaty sex wizard*
*Ducasse: aficionado of fine gentleman's establishments*
*Sweeney: self-abuser, cat lover*
*Starlet: transsexual hooker, part-time beautician*

Back in the bar, it's business as usual: Hugo back there doin his thing, skeleton clientele, a few cunts around with a whiff of loneliness and desperation about em... there's a faint metallic tang in the air, ya know, like a crime scene the mornin after. Place has had some cleanin.

I don't see Ducasse. Sweeney's down the end of the bar and he's got a cat in his lap. One of the trannies from last night is in. The jukebox is on low, Elvis playin. Up at the bar, Hugo steps outta the kitchen wiping his hands on a bloody rag.

Ducasse is lookin for you, he says.

Where is he?

He nods out back. You wantin somethin to drink?

Absinthe, I say. I pull off my jacket. The trannie takes a look at my neck, I hear her suckin air in through her teeth.

How's *she* looking this morning? she says.

Dunno. She ran before I woke, I tell her.

Probably best, she says.

Hugo puts a shot glass in front of me. I sup of the fairy and she's good. Hugo's two hands are on the bar.

Ducasse needs your help again, he says.

I'm still not paid for last night's job.

He's got your money.

*Fucken A.*

Hugo eyes my neck and arms. You look torn up, he says.

She fucken ate me.

Yeah? And what'd you do to her? He howls.

Things got fucken mental in here last night, I say. You puttin somethin in the meat?

He grins. Things kick off from time to time, he says.

I drain my glass and pass it over the bar.

Wanna buy me one o'those? The tranny next to me leans over and winks.

Go on, Hugo, I say, and Hugo lines up a shot for the three of us and says, To health. And not gettin eaten in your sleep.

And we all have a chuckle and drink. Outta nowhere — two beers, two shots and one little pink Mitsubishi in — poetry wells up in me, Manley Hopkins swims through my head, some verse from down deep, just flits through,

*That, like this sleek and seeing ball*
*But a prick will make no eye at all,*
*Where we, even where we mean*
*To mend her we end her,*
*When we hew or delve...*

Such alliteration. Absolute wrong'un, that fella. Maybe he was eatin horse meat adulterated with hormones and formaldehyde. Who knows?

A moment of poetry, then it swims away.

You okay? Tranny's lookin at me funny.

What's your name?

Starlet, she says.

Never have normal girl names, do they? They're all Starlets and Angels and Diamantes... or maybe Mercedes, cause she's the ride of your fucken life, *wink wink*. Starlet is no Mercedes, but maybe an Alfa Romeo after its third MOT. She's hangin in there.

Where's your little plaything from last night? I say.

The little Asian boys have no staying power, she tells me. They're good for a quick fuck, that's all.

He'll be back, I say. You had him eatin out of your hand.

She laughs. The poor boy woulda stuck his prick in a wet ciabatta, she says.

I was thinking the same thing last night. She's straight up, Starlet.

Fuck's with the music? I say.

This is the home of the classics, Hugo says.

Fuck that, I tell him.

I wander over to the jukebox. I'm wired on pills and it's always ABBA or Elvis or some shit. A fucken change is what's needed. What we need is some *Manley-Hopkins-absinthe-horse-tranquiliser* music.

To be fair, the jukebox has a solid selection of tunes. *The Cure? Not quite what we're lookin for. Beach Boys? Maybe. Maybe a touch too chipper for this crowd.* Gettin warmer. *Aphex Twin. That's it. That's what we need. The very thing for a bar full of windowlickers.* I slip in fifty cents.

Fuck are you playin? Hugo says, as I slide back onto my stool.

Some proper fucken music for a change.

Hugo mutters, shakes his head, wanders off down the bar.

I like it, Starlet says. She slides one stool over towards me.

Gerard Manley Hopkins would like it too, I say.

Who?

Never mind.

You got any pills? she says.

I ate my last one an hour ago babe, I tell her. But if ya hang

71

around I've a feelin there'll be more on the go. I've been livin on pills and booze since I found this place. I promise I'll sort you out when I get my hands on some.

Don't forget me, she says.

Excuse me a minute, will ya?

I head out to the toilets for a piss. The Pope toilets smell like a hole in the ground in a Delhi railway station. I'm in the cubicle and I hear the door open behind me, so I'm thinkin, *She's followed me in, Starlet, for a bit of afternoon delight.* I shake off and turn around and Sweeney's standin there, kitten in arm, standin there starin at me.

Fuck do you want? I say.

I'm goin for a piss, he says.

Yeah? Use the other one you fucken clown. What are hoverin over my shoulder for?

Waitin, he says. Strokin his fucken cat.

Get the fuck outta my way.

I push past him. Guy smells like dog and semen. Creepy clown.

I go back out to the bar, slide onto my stool.

Why don't you go n'see Ducasse? Hugo says.

Yeah, I say. Alright Hugo.

So I go out through the kitchen out to the back, and Ducasse is out there in the cold room on his phone, perched on a table next to a stack of trays. He hangs up as I walk in, pulls an envelope from his pocket and tosses it at me.

Your money.

Sweet, I say.

I open it up, flick through it — can't say I've ever looked at five grand in one go before, and it doesn't look like much but it's all in hundreds. Still, five grand is five fucken grand.

You busy? Ducasse says.

Nah.

Wanna make another hundred? Half hour's work.

Sure, I say, but I'm kinda distracted. I'm lookin at the instruments of sexual torture on the walls around the room.

Right then. Stop starin at the fucken walls and help me get these into the van.

We load up the van and set out. The mornin's dry, winter-bleak.

Where we headed?

Just across town. Forty minutes there and back.

Right, but no fucken Sai Baba.

Ducasse lights a cigarette. We tear across town. Traffic is a bitch, slow, but he's right, twenty minutes and we're there. Wherever there is. Fucken tourist — take me out of the Red Light and I'm lost.

Where are we?

Near Vondelpark, he says.

The banal Amsterdam street is lined with abandoned bicycles. We're outside a discreet little two storey red-bricked place.

That it?

Yep. Ducasse flicks a cigarette out of the window and gets out.

We grab a tray each of meat from the van. The sign by the door says 'Park Lane'.

Gentleman's club, Ducasse says.

A hoorhouse, I say.

A big meathead opens the door and leads us through reception, across the dance floor and out back past a sauna to the kitchen. The kitchen is smart, all pristine stainless steel, and we drop the trays on a counter. The big fella, maybe a bouncer for the place, lifts the paper and takes a sniff at the meat.

Some of our best cuts, Ducasse says.

The meathead nods. He approves. I had some of your steak the other night, he says. Fucked for forty-eight hours straight. Yeah, I fucked, he says, then he goes on to explain how he banged three strippers from the club for two days, two Ukrainians and one Moldovan, no breaks no Viagra, just pills and meat, fucking here, fucking there, fucking up down left right, wore them right out he says, they had to beg him to stop, couldn't take any more.

Yeah, that's some fucken meat, he says.

Ducasse is noddin along, yeah yeah yeah, then he goes off on his own story, about how he fucked four players of the English national football squad and one of their wives after a UEFA cup play-off a few years back, three days in the InterContinental livin off coke and room service and cunt and cock, non-stop. Yeah, he says, that meat does somethin to ya.

And then the meathead goes, Boys, yeah? Wait til I tell ya about the World's Strongest Man three years ago, we were in Reykjavik, and yadda yadda yadda, and I'm stuck in the middle of this cock one-upmanship, Ducasse and this meathead swingin their cocks at each other, so I wander out to the van and keep unloadin the trays.

They're still at it when I unload the last of em into the kitchen, swappin cock stories, and I say, Ducasse man, let's be gettin on.

Yeah we should be movin, he says.

The boss extends an invitation to you any night of the week, the big meathead says. Come see us.

Ducasse grins, nudges me in the ribs.

Come on down and I'll hook you up with a couple of Ukrainians, or we got this one Nigerian who can fuck like Cleopatra, cunt like a vise, he says, and he has his two hands cupped in a hole as he mock rides this Nigerian fuck-princess.

Christ, this guy's had only a whiff of meat and he's off on one. Like I said, innit, big angry guys and meat and fucking. Somethin goin on there.

Come on the fuck, Ducasse.

Right, we'll be seein ya, Ducasse says. We'll be down, fucken-A we will.

And the big meathead salutes and closes the door.

You into hoors? Ducasse says after we've climbed into the van.

I nod noncommittally, cause I never had much cause to pay for it, truth be told. From time to time, I say.

Wanna head over to a little place I know, kill an hour? he says.

Why not, I say, because I have an hour to kill. In fact, I got nothin but fucken time. My day is open.

# 11

# Baptised at Madame Zhu's

We head back over our side of town. Ducasse stops on Oude Waal at an innocent little black and white place tucked away between two tall buildings. Now, I know the story of how the Dutch buildings are so skinny, but I get claustrophobic just lookin at em. They spook me. I'd have said, fuck your taxes and your skinny houses, we're gonna live like normal human beings. The fucken Dutch, they sucked it up, and now every house in the Dam is like a standing shoe box. I dunno about The Hague or any other Dutch city, but the Dam is claustrophobic.

We park up, get out, and Ducasse raps on the door.

You know all the hoorhouses in the city?

All the good ones, he says.

The door opens. I can tell right away it's a classy establishment, cause this woman that just opened the door, she's got poise. And she's beautiful. A cut above. She knows Ducasse cause she nods, and Ducasse, who's a cunt through and through, changes. The violent edge softens, and the man who beats hookers and fucks brides and footballers and any other fucken thing, is suddenly a gentleman. Who knew.

The woman looks at me and nods. Come in, she says.

Inside, I relax. The place is gentle, all burgundy and violin. The incense must be some kinda soporific, cause I inhale and feel fucken fine. I mean, *fine*.

She steps in behind a small desk and opens a book. Will it be the usual?

Naturally, Ducasse says.

*Naturally.* Lord of the fucken manor.

He pulls out a roll of bills and throws down about a grand. I put my hand in my pocket but Ducasse grabs my arm. It's my shout, he says. I'm now curious to see what kind of perversion this man pays half a grand for that he can't get for fifty from a backstreet hoor.

Follow me, gentlemen.

She leads us into a sauna where a black girl sets two towels on a low wooden bench next to a large circular bath. She's robed, but she turns to us, smiles, and drops the robe to the floor, and I look at her, Christ, she's flawless, woven from the dying dreams of some Ethiopian prince, cut from the mind's diamond, the God mind, the mind eternal, the super, the meta, the original... she's the undying idea of woman.

Take off your clothes, she says.

*Yes, oh yes. Let's all be naked together.*

The madam smiles and nods. I leave you in good hands, she says, and she swishes out of the door, the folds of her black gown trailin after her.

So I get outta my clothes. I'm not in bad shape; I drink too much and don't play sport, but I'm young and my metabolism is still kickin pretty hard. Once outta my clothes though, standing in front of this black girl and the impossible perfection of her, I'm confronted with the pathetic reality of my cut. I'm inadequate. Thin and flabby at once. White. Insubstantial. Not a man, but a boy. The reality of it is like the crack of a hand on my flushed cheek.

But she smiles, she's seen it all, she's seen worse, and hey, I'm not all that fucken bad.

Then, *fucken-shoot-me*, another one comes out. Identical in every way, twins, two sisters perfect in their dark bareness. I slip quickly into the water, cause ya know what, one I can handle, but two, I'm outta my depth now. Ducasse takes off his jeans and turns around, and his hairy thickness makes me glad I'm in the water. That's a man. He's also hung, a thick cock like a third arm between his thighs. He knows it too, cause he's stood there with his cock swingin.

Get in, the second girl says, and he doesn't fuck around, he gets in, cause these two are commanding.

We're sittin in the tub, me and Ducasse, him in front of me, and I don't really wanna be lookin in his eyes right now, cause there are some things ya just don't do, ya know, certain levels of intimacy that are unacceptable, but I can't help but look at him and he's grinnin like a little boy, and I'm not sure, but there could be the hint of a blush on his cheek too. Fucken Ducasse, blushin.

One of the black girls comes around behind Ducasse, and kneels, her hips spreadin out, wide and incredible, and she places two hands on his shoulders then straddles him. She slides in behind him as I feel two hands on my own shoulders, and those hands push me forward gently, two legs wrap around me, and the thick warm body slides in behind me, pulling me in. Her tits are on my back and I'm locked between her thighs, and she leans back and holds me. I close my eyes. Were I alone I'd fucken weep with joy, but that cunt Ducasse is there in front of me, male and hairy and imposing.

She takes a sponge and runs it over me, belly, balls, thighs, and while she's doing this she's raising me slowly up and down with the hard grip of her thighs so that I'm being slowly massaged by her tits. She caresses me all over with the sponge, then she abandons it to the water and goes at me with her hands. Her fingers glide over my chest, my belly, thighs, balls… then one hand slips between my ass and a finger plays with my asshole… I wanna scream or weep or fucken kill myself, or all three, cause I'm already fucken gone, two minutes in I've already reached the peak, seen the light, prayed with the ancients, and I swear, by Christ, after this I'm finding God.

Fingernails on the insides of my thighs and scratching my belly, and my eyes are closed and I'm thinkin, *Don't look at that fucker Ducasse, don't look at him or the spell is broken.*

Fingers gently scratching my neck. She's found it, it took all of two minutes and she's found my spot. I'm fucken putty, gelatin melting in the warm waters of the tub.

Fingers in my hair, massaging in some kind of lotion, cause I feel the cool tingle of eucalyptus or honey or I don't know what, but it's fucken gorgeous, and I hate the word gorgeous, but it's resanctified under her hands... *gorgeeouuus.*

She pushes me down under the water.

I am baptised. Made whole in the waters of the Nile, wrapped in the Eucharist of her body, held in the prayer of her hands and swallowed by the depths of her tenderness.

I am raised up, God's anointed.

Fucken blessed.

I open my eyes and Ducasse is there lookin at me, and he looks like he's about to weep n'all. Two of us, destroyed.

Then the bullet: she kisses my neck, and that kiss, I know, will mark me for the rest of my life.

Then she slides out of the bath, the touch of her body sendin waves through me as she rises.

Don't go, I say, like a boy, a child, and she laughs softly.

Ducasse laughs too, the cunt. He prods me with his big toe. Eh? he says.

Fuck you, I say. Just fuck you.

But the girl comes back with a tray, sets it by my arm, and slides back in, her sister too. On the tray is a pipe and a small brazier, and she wraps her legs round me, holds me tight, and I melt in the warm chocolate of her body. *Fucken hold me forever til I melt and become part of you, and I swim around inside you like a symbiotic parasite...*

She lifts the pipe, jams in a lump of thick oily tar, and drops in a coal from the brazier and puffs on it til it sparks. She takes a hit then passes it to me, and I take the jade-silver pipe and toke on the thing, her hand on my chest and fire in my lungs, and I set sail, my veins the river and my breath the breeze, the golden breeze, and I sail on it downriver, nothin to see or hear but the golden breeze and the warm whisper of the water, that's it... I sail on down the river carried by the breeze and the warm kisses of Nubian princesses, princesses who were servant girls but became royalty with a power to make men weep oceans, oceans that carried their funerary pyres on their final night, the pyres lit by the spark of a pipe or the collapse of stars, fierce lucent stars blinded by beauty; those girls that became princesses that became whores, who dictated how men die and leave this earth, and who administered the last rites as bodies burned on golden oceans... whores who sat by Christ and whispered in his ear and found his everlasting love because they bore him too, that same Christ who married a whore and fathered a whore and who loved them more than all other women, even his own mother.

I saw all this as I was carried out on the golden ocean, even as I heard her whisper in my ear, golden whispers too, for I felt them drip into my ear and into my veins, whispers like honey that took sail through my veins, blown by their own crystal music, she whispered song-like,

*Follow me and I'll show you what became of Helen, and Hephaestus and Apollo, and Manjushri and Avalokitesvara, and Alexander, for he saw it too, Alexander, when he went East and died at thirty-three, but only after he saw Meru and the glass ocean of Mansarovar, and that's why he had to die...*

She whispered this as my boat sailed out onto the crass ocean filled with the tears of men who were not worthy and who burned on those waters, but I sailed right over it, golden whispers carried me over, and I hadn't the fear of drowning men for I saw my time was not near.

Somewhere out on the ocean I chanced upon an island, an island like an eye where there existed only lepers who lived on a diet of salt water and unripe dates, so I got off the boat and, filled with whispers of golden honey, kissed each of them one after the other, and those missing limbs I healed;

those without arms I licked their stumps and their arms grew back, and those without ears or lips I kissed the holes where their appendages had been and soon they were whole again, and like this I cured all those wretches so that they became men and women again. The women gave themselves to me and the men became my acolytes, so that I was revered here and they named the island after me, and it was called Isa. Isa was my home for a century, until even the last died and I was the only one, so I buried my last wife and acolyte and dug out my boat, buried in the sands for a hundred years now, and after a decade's prayer I put it back on the water.

I left Isa and sailed to the hyperboreal north on the breath of whispers, and this time she said,

*This is where you come after it all, this is what's beyond the glass ocean, dive in and you come up here where all things are remembered and not remembered, and all things are recast in the diamond wind;* this is what poured through me in the golden-honeyed breeze of her whispers.

She held me, and I knew she would always hold me, for I was her sacred son, even if I caressed her brown nipples and lapped at the anointed rivers of her cunt, and buried my cock between the earth of her thighs and the oceans of her womb, I was her son and she would hold me for eternity and more. And I knew it and was blessed.

A last whisper blew through me like a soft wind, *Come back to me*, she said, and so I climbed off the ice and back into my boat, and sailed years back across the ocean of tears until I felt it, I felt the coffee caress of her body, I felt a hard brown nipple in my mouth, sucking on it like the pipe of the dying I was, and I felt those lips on my neck once more, destroyin me with gentle devastation, and I felt the lips of her cunt ride me slowly, each thrust drawing my boat closer to the shore, pulling me home, and she sucked on my ear and licked at my neck and buried me deep inside her, until the boat hit the shore in a frantic thrust, the waters breaking on the hard land, my boat capsized, me flung onto the earth with a scream...

82

broken, consumed, annihilated.

My prick slipped from the shores of her cunt and I fell into the golden sleep of the immortals.

# 12

# In It

I wake, naked, on a warm bed in the dark, alone, the ghosts of golden whispers runnin through me. I rise like Lazarus, find a basin and clean myself, and I look in the mirror, seein no one, which doesn't worry me because I know I'm alive. Extinguished as I am I've never felt so fucken real in all my life. I mean, I've been down the river and have come back and know that I'm here, whole and alive.

There's a gentle knock on the door so I get dressed, open it, and the madam's there.

Your friend is waiting for you, she says, smiling, cause she sees me, knows how I came in and how I'm goin out a different man, sees me devastated and is proud of her girls who know how to destroy men.

Can I see the girl? I say.

I'm sorry, she's not available.

Alright.

*Down the river and out to sea.*

So I got out and Ducasse is there waitin, all blissed out like me, all *man-who's-been-across-the-ocean-and-knows-the-other-side.*

He just looks at me, grinnin, doesn't have to say anything, and I don't really want to. Once we're out the door and talkin, the spell ends.

But he gets up and opens the door, and we step outside.

Good day, gentlemen, she says, standing in the doorway, and I get a last hit of the heady perfume as she closes it behind us.

I look at Ducasse, he looks at me, and I just shake my head.

That was the greatest hour of my life.

We were in there for three hours, Ducasse says.

Nah, Ducasse man, I say.

He nods. Three hours.

I look up at the door, the house, placin it in a mental map in my head.

I'm comin back here tonight, tomorrow, and the day after, I say.

You can't overdo it with Madame Zhu's, he says. Gotta be like a rare treat, like lamb, or duck, somethin you only go to once in a while when the time is right. A man can't be destroyed like that every day. It takes fortitude. Give it a couple of months.

Madame Zhu's? Chinese place is it?

Nah. They say she's from London, but nobody knows. 'Zhu' is just for the whole oriental vibe.

Madame Zhu's. I'm not sure I can wait a couple of months.

Hold yourself, he says.

Fuck knows, maybe he's right, but I know nothin's gonna be the same again.

He looks at his watch. Will we get back? he says.


We head back to the Pope, me and Ducasse walkin on air, our souls cleansed, when this girl comes flyin down the alley towards us outta nowhere. She gets right up in my face, panicked, afraid, angry, then I recognise her, the girl from last night, not the one that chewed me up but her mate. She starts yellin.

Where is she? she says. Where's Cristina?

I don't know, I tell her.

She left with you, now she's disappeared, she says.

I can't help ya, I say, but she's gettin aggressive, lashin out, needs someone to have a go at.

I swear, if you've hurt her…

Now I get angry. Look, I tell her, pulling off my scarf and showin my half-eaten neck. Your friend did this. Then I pull up my sweater to show where a lump of flesh is missin from my ribcage. And this, I say. Your fucken friend ate me alive then pissed off. I woke up in the mornin, bleedin, she was gone.

Ducasse steps in. Ducasse the peacemaker.

I can vouch for what he's sayin, he says. Mornin, she was gone. We haven't seen her.

A tear is forming in the corner of the girl's eye. She moves from anger to desperation.

Where the fuck is she? she shouts.

I don't fucken know, I say.

She shakes her head, turns and runs off.

I look at Ducasse.

Forget it, he says. Not your problem.

We go downstairs.

*

*Location:*
*Screamin Pope, Amsterdam*
*Time:*
*17.45, Sunday*
*Present:*
*Hugo: meatmonger, all-round greasy wonder*
*Ducasse: MDMA authority*
*Aids Joyce, AKA, Forsythe: amateur surgeon, arrogant prick*
*A few random weekend cunts*

Aids Joyce is at the bar, and he spins round in his stool as me and Ducasse come in, leans back against the bar. His hands are bloody, bloody like he's been rootin around in the entrails of a sheep he's just gutted, or he's just had an accident with a filleting knife.

You been doin some carvin? Ducasse says.

Helpin our man here with a little surgery, he says.

Bring anything for us?

Hugo drops a bag of pills on the counter, we all crowd round it like we've just been handed the original Dead Sea Scrolls. Little green fuckers. Sea green, speckled, like the good old days of doves and superdoves.

What are ya callin em? Ducasse says.

Kaiser Sozes, Aids Joyce says.

I can't help myself, I grin. We all do.

Nothing else for it, Ducasse says, and scoops a handful out, passin some to me and Hugo. We all pop one. What else to do? The merch must be quality controlled.

So let's not fuck about: those pills were on us like shit on a dirt bike. I mean, they caught us like a tram side-endin a stalled Yugo at the lights. *Bam*. Out of nowhere we're all liquid-honey-love, smiles and heartbeats. And high as I am, I can see Aids Joyce just sittin back and basking in the effects of his handiwork. Prick. But fuck it, I let myself go, I cut my ropes and sail away. We're all nutted, nachoed... I lose all linguistic control, spawnin new words left, right and centre.

I know exactly what this needs and I go to the jukebox, and whaddaya know, they've even got the tune: 'Crispy Bacon'. I throw it on, and the three or four of us at the bar who are high go fucken nuts. Then some other random cunts join us. About eight people at the bar and a proper rave kicks off and we don't give a fuck. We're lovin it. Hugo throws up a line of absinthe and we scream with delirium and bounce off the walls.

But where to go from there? I've started out with the most bouncin track there is and where does it go then? So I sit back, I'll just chill, let someone else play DJ, cause that's a big fucken responsibility and a thankless one too. The track peters out and a random cunt at the back tries to fill the hole, throwing on some rockabilly psychedelica. *Thought ya'd be a smart cunt, didn't ya?* Probably a student. We all crash down and sink into a kinda dark pensive mood.

What we need in here is a full-time professional DJ, I say.

That's me, Hugo says.

Nah nah, fuck that with your ABBA, your Monday-to-Sunday, mornin-to-night ABBA and Elvis and *what-have-ya.* Nah, we need variety. Sometimes a strawberry milkshake is good, I tell him, but you can't have em for breakfast, lunch and dinner.

Ducasse laughs.

I disagree, Hugo says.

Yeah well, you're entitled to, I say, but we gotta live here too. I pull out my wad from my pocket and I peel off a couple hundred. What night's it? I say.

Sunday, Hugo says.

Saturday night comin, we're gonna have a real DJ in for the night. On me. No patchwork quilt of tracks from every random prick who comes through the door played on a tired jukebox — we're gonna have a real night, I say.

I throw the money on the bar.

And who's gonna find him? Hugo says.

I know a guy, Ducasse says.

Fuck that — we're not havin some wispy guru in here playin mantras or hymns, or Sai Baba or *om-sai-namo-namaha…* not fucken havin it. I mean a real DJ.

Now Hugo laughs.

I'll get you a guy, Aids Joyce says. You'll need five hundred, though. This guy is fucken pro.

Fine, I say. I throw another three hundred on the bar.

Aids Joyce pushes the money towards Hugo. I'll talk to him, he says, see if he's free.

We'll need pills, I say, and they all laugh at me.

Fucken comedian, Aids Joyce says. He stands up to go.

Back here on Wednesday, Hugo says.

He nods and disappears into the toilets.

Ducasse leans his arm on my shoulder. Cunt knows how to make pills, he says.

*We're all chewin our faces off, so yeah, cunt knows how to make pills. He's still a cunt. But a professional cunt.*

Why's he all bloody? I say.

He helps me with the meat, Hugo says.

I'm not sure I'd want him touchin my lunch.

He's more the technical side of things, Ducasse says.

Yeah? What's technical about cuttin meat?

We got a particular kinda process here, Hugo says. You know. It's how our product's so refined.

I know, I tried it. It's intense.

Well, it takes preparation, Hugo says. A little tweakin that only Forsythe can help us with.

His hand is on his belly, scratchin.

Like Kobe beef?

Just like Kobe beef, yes. Ducasse pats on me on the shoulder.

How about changin the fucken music here? I say. I head back over to the jukebox.

Throw on some ABBA, Hugo shouts.


I don't remember crashin out but I wake up in the middle of the night, thirsty. A little light comes in through the curtain and I swing my feet onto the tiles. One of these days I'll get my shit together and stock the room. I look out the window, feelin the cold come at me through the glass.

*Nah. Not goin out. Not happenin.*

I pull a robe around me. Complimentary with the room, like. It's cheap white Chinese tack, and along with the slippers I look like the permanent resident of a seedy sauna. Which I am.

I head downstairs. The place is empty, and under the green neon lights I head for the sink behind the bar. Amsterdam tap water, I don't even know if it's drinkable, but I'm dyin. So I fill a pint glass and chug it, and my body drinks it right up.

I stand behind the bar. The Pope. The Screamin Pope,

bastion of lost souls and degenerates of earth, here for us all, welcoming us to her seedy bosom. I sit and sniff her now, the smells comin out of her walls, up from her floorboards, the way smells do in empty bars. Booze, smoke, piss, and, king of all scents, meat.

The jukebox sits by the back wall, an island of light, and I like the quiet. Long time since I had any quiet.

A noise out back disturbs the silence.

I hear it again, the clatter of steel on steel.

I head out back into the kitchen, no one is there, so I push open the door to the back room. Ducasse is there standing over a table, a lone bulb on above his head. On the table is a body hooked up to a drip and some kind of ventilation.

Ducasse hears the door swing and looks around. Then he goes back to whatever he's doin.

Wanna make us a coffee? he says.

*Nah. Nah, just a fucken minute…*

I step up beside him and look at the body on the table. It's her. The girl I took upstairs. The one that ate me. The vampire chick. The top of her skull's been removed but it's her. She's still in the same dress.

What's this?

Her name's Cristina, but you didn't know that, did ya? he says. He looks at me through a pair of clear goggles.

Cristina? Why's she here? Is she dead?

She's not dead. Would she be hooked up to oxygen if she was dead?

Why's the top of her head off?

Look, he says, we found her outside. She was passed out in the street and if we took her to hospital we'd have the police sniffin around. So we took her in.

And her friend? You think she's not gonna go to the police?

We have friends too, he says.

Jesus Christ. I can't look at her and turn away. Then I see em, along the back wall, three more tables, a body on each, head cut open and hooked up to a drip. Three men. Never laid eyes on em before, but they're lyin there, still dressed, probably still alive but not too fucken active, ya know?

I look at Ducasse. He's lookin at me like, *You just gettin this*?

*And I finally get it*. We're in a butcher's. A human butcher's. I mean, fucken *human meat*.

Who're they? I say, pointing at the tables.

Come I'll get you a drink, he says.


We sit at the bar with a couple of Talisker and Ducasse tells me the story. The whole story.

So the Screamin Pope is a front for a market in human meat. *Daa-daa*.

Sustained by a market created by themselves, Hugo and company have spread the craving for their product right across Europe, with new branches openin in a different city every six months.

Hugo, a butcher by trade, got the idea after reading an article about mice who were injected with the hormones of criminals, you know, murderers and rapists and *what-not*. The mice went fucken boogaloo. So Hugo gets this idea to try foolin around with human meat. He gets his first body, Ducasse doesn't go into details, but he starts playin with ways to manipulate the properties and content of the meat. He thinks he can turn it into a drug. Over two years he goes through a series of experiments, settlin on a method of increasin hormones in the body and simultaneously floodin it with chemicals. Nice chemicals, namely MDMA. Then he discovers if you extract the pituitary gland the body becomes flooded with stress hormone. You let this amp up for thirty-six to forty-eight hours then you overdose your 'patient' with a megadose of MDMA. What this does, see, is 'derange' the body, plus you've just pumped up the serotonin and dopamine in your meat to insane levels. You eat this stuff, you not only wanna fuck or fight — your hormones are tellin you to — but you're overcome with all those lovey-dovey feel-great and next-level ecstasy highs. You have the meat with a side of pills, the hit quadruples. It's lethal. It appeals to all the human instincts all at once. Which is fucken dangerous.

Ducasse takes a breath, I sip on the whiskey.

What about her? I say. She's only young.

Ducasse shrugs. Killin two birds with one stone, he says. The meat won't be top scratch, but they won't know.

Pretty sick, I say.

All in all though, I'm more comfortable with this information than I care to admit. I'm not really too upset that there's a girl in the back room on a slab with her head opened and her pituitary gland extracted, who's pumped full of E and is gonna be carved up into prime cuts. And that's not somethin you see every day.

Want another? Ducasse nods at my glass.

*Nah*. I shake my head.

Fuck off to bed then. Get some sleep.

Sleep is right. Maybe I'll wake up, realise it was a dream. Or some kind of absinthe-fuelled nightmare.

I take a pint glass of water and head out.

Sweet dreams, Ducasse says.

If I get any sleep, I say.

Try countin sheep, Ducasse says, as I head out. Little pill-shaped sheep. He laughs.

*Little pill-shaped sheep*.

I head upstairs, wondering what the fuck I'm into.

*I'm in it now. I'm right up in some shit now.*

# Part Two

# 13

# Deeper In It

Now they got me pickin up bodies. Carcasses, like. Meat.

I like the work. I drive up and down Holland in my white van all day, stoned. My particular fucken gripe is I've no cassettes for the tape deck, but then the Dam has some solid radio stations. If I'm just smokin I'll put on RAZO which is usually wall-to-wall reggae and dub. They know at the bar when I've been listening to RAZO cause when I get back I'm talkin pure Rasta, and they laugh me out of it. If I've a pill or two in me I'll go with RAM, which is eighties all the way:

Let's go where we want to, to a home they can never find
And bounce like cats from out of this world
Leave the real world way behind...

Eighties tunes on pills are mental. Ever heard T'Pau or The Bangles on MDMA?

I make do. There's always a way to put the day in, even when you're doin the dullest work, so I get into my routine and it gets me through.

We got two main sources of meat in the city. One is the prisons. Now, since Holland has one of the lowest per capita incarceration rates in the world, this is not our best provider. But we have people workin on the inside. We get a few from the Dam, some from The Hague, but mostly from Rotterdam. An hour down the road. I leave at six and I'm back for breakfast. Still, these are not high hitters — we're talkin two a week at most, four on an exceptional week. Dutch prisons are just too thin.

There's occasionally talk of 'breaking America'. It's Hugo's dream. With the highest prison population in the world, America's like Mecca to aficionados of human meat. Over two million prisoners country-wide, those cunts shivin each other all day long and slicin each other's throats… it's a non-stop production line of highest-quality product. And those fuckers out there, pumped full of testosterone and estrogen and every other meat-altering chemical on the market… well, let's just say the work is half done for ya. Americans are the Humvee of the Meat market: big, destructive and unapologetic. We had one MMA guy a few months ago, some prick from Texas who picked a fight in a bar in Rotterdam and had his ass handed to him on a plate by a bouncer from Serbia. One punch had this guy in a coma. We got a call. I went down in the van and took him up to the Pope and we put him through our process and into the mincer. We got three to five hundred a kilo for this guy at our best restaurants in the city dependin on the cut. I mean, his was some of the best *viande* we ever had come through the shop. I was down in Park Lane one night while this guy's finest steak cuts were being served up to the patrons and it was fucken chaos. The girls had to be escorted off the premises. Instances of sexual assault in the city went up by forty-three per cent that night. I heard this from a policeman — a customer of ours, incidentally.

American Meat. So tainted it's fucken dangerous. A meathead, for instance, who's spent twenty straight years in the gym, pumped full of all kinds of creatine and *what-the-fuck-else*, is good, but of course, you take a guy who doesn't look after himself, eats the richest foods and does fuck all to keep himself in shape, then the meat is of a more supple quality. The athletes tend be on the tough side, so the meat requires a little more cunning in preparation. Hugo can sidestep some of these issues by lettin the meat mature for a few more days, but it still takes a first-class chef. Which most of our establishments have, by the way. A fat fucker is easier to cook, is all I'm sayin.

But I digress. Back to supply. Without a doubt, our best suppliers of meat in the cities are our affiliated drug houses. Such as Ambroos's, for instance. His is just one in the city. We have five in the Dam, eight in Rotterdam, three in The Hague, a couple in Utrecht, Tilburg and Eindhoven, and a handful of others scattered here and there. We even got one up in Den Helder, all the way north. I do a lot of drivin.

We got houses dotted all over the country, and those runnin em are on the lookout for the right sort of candidate. 'Sociopathic loner' is our general type, but we're flexible. Let's take Ambroos as an example. He waits for a type to come in, he sets him up with whatever his poison is and gets him comfortable. Over the course of a few weeks he'll start askin questions: *Where you from? Been here long? Got a wife, boyfriend, a parole officer? Family back home? What's your job, what do ya do for money? Where ya stayin? Landlady's a nosey old cunt, is she?*

Basically, he's findin out who's gonna come askin if you go missin. We're not too fussed on sex. Mostly men come through these places, but we get the women too. The general age range we stick to is eighteen to forty. Over forty and the meat is past its best, and under eighteen, well, it's a moral grey area, isn't it?

We do well. All our houses average one a week. It takes time to suck them in and build up trust, but now that the machine is oiled and the cogs turnin, our operation is runnin tip-top. It amounts to about twenty bodies on a weekly basis, the average weight of those comin through our doors around ninety or a hundred kilos. That's two thousand kilos of meat. Now, the average percentage of prime retail cuts that can be stripped from a human body is about forty per cent. With some creative butchery, Hugo has raised this to about sixty. The head is over five kilos and we don't even bother with it. Feet and hands too. There's ten per cent gone right there. Brain is a delicacy and we get a few orders for brain. The cunts who like it often ask for 'boutique' cuts — they'll ask us to go out and source this or that person, a doctor, or an academic, but we don't do that. Not yet. So the head is out, and that leaves about twenty-five to thirty per cent leftovers. Nothing goes to waste, though. We got a use for everything. But countin the prime cuts alone, and I'm includin minced meat here, with 1200 kilos at three to four hundred a kilo, that's between €350,000 and €500,000 a week. We got a lotta outgoings, but even at that we're makin solid coin. We're mintin it. And now, I'm right up in the thick of it.

I've just pulled up in Spangen, at one of our houses in Rotterdam. Spangen is bland and soulless, a typical example of the Dutch urban nightmare. I feel sorry for the kids growin up there but it can't be bad for business. If I was growin up in Spangen I'd be lookin a way out, if not geographically then in the form of mind-bendin pharmaceuticals.

Our place is out back of a tattoo shop. The owner of the property, Timo, is a sound prick. He knows about the drugs bein sold out back but he doesn't know about the meat, so typically I get down there before ten when he opens the shop. I back down the little alley and stop in front of the door. Pirri, who's been waitin for me, opens up. A shifty Albanian junkie, he darts back into the house and I follow him in. His girlfriend, Roza, lies slumped in front of the TV. Roza doesn't look at me as I come in. Sly little Roza. She's layin there in skimpy pink shorts, one finger in her belly button.

I eye her as I follow Pirri through.

There's a guy in a coma sitting at the kitchen table. What disturbs me is the bowl of cornflakes on the table opposite him. Pirri's been sittin at the table eatin his breakfast with coma guy. Maybe he was chattin to him. The guy's eyes are half-open and he has a confused gaze on him, like he realised a second before he passed out that somethin was comin on him. I'm guessin, anyway — I've no idea what a hit of crack laced with phenobarbital does to a man.

Pirri sits down and picks up his cornflakes. I wonder what else he does with the carcasses when he's alone. Strange little Albanian pervert.

What are you lookin at? I ask him.

Pirri spoons his cereal mechanically into his gob.

Makes you think, he says.

It does. It makes me wonder. Makes me really fucken wonder what makes people tick, gettin kicks outta the comatose. I'm fond myself of a bit of philosophical speculation, and much as I don't begrudge Pirri his mornin contemplations, I got things to do. I pull up a chair next to coma guy and pull out my notebook.

What do you know? I say.

German, twenty-nine. Livin here for fourteen months, he says.

Any family?

Nah. Divorced. His wife's in Germany. They don't speak.

Job?

Doing temp work for one of the agencies in the city. One day here, next day there. Nothin steady.

What was he takin?

Took a likin to meth about a month or two ago. Been comin here four times a week since.

I look at the guy. He's still hefty... I mean, a heavy cunt. Must have swapped an eatin disorder for powder just recently. Possibly, he started out on speed as a way to cut his weight, and Pirri here slowly cooked up his dose til he was on the good stuff. At that weight, uppers'll kill you faster than a hammer to the back of the head. He's a big bastard, and we're gonna break a sweat gettin him in the van.

He got ID? I say.

Pirri pulls it outta his pocket and flicks it across the table.

Bad idea as far as I'm concerned, but Hugo, bein a particular sort, likes to keep em. He scans the ID and then burns em, but he's got the documents of almost everyone who's come through our doors on an encrypted file on a computer at the Pope. Those that carried ID, anyway. Some kind of twisted collector thing. He says it's safe. I'm not sure.

I put the ID in my pocket and put away the notebook.

*Provenance*, Hugo calls it. Some of the sick fucks who like our produce like to know where it came from. They get some kind of added kick out of it. Some of them only eat men, some only women. We need to know these things when we send out the meat.

Right, get up off your hole, I say to Pirri.

I pull out a body bag and lay it on the floor. Pirri spoons up the last of his cornflakes and gets up. He goes on one side of the German, me on the other, and we push over the chair and drop him to the floor. We roll him into the body bag, which is not as easy as it sounds, by the way. I have a technique: I get the body on its side first, then place the bag over the head all the way down to the feet. Then, swift and quick like, you roll him on his belly one-eighty to the other flank. If this has worked, you can then slide the rest of the body into the bag and zip it up. Often it doesn't. If I had capable cunts workin with me it wouldn't be a problem, but when you're stuck with uncoordinated junkies like Pirri all manner of problems arise. This time, we nail it. The big German is zipped up. All that remains is to get him to the van. Push and pull. I take the front end and start draggin, and Pirri lifts from the back. We drag him through the living room. Roza's still on the sofa and pays us no mind. She looks past me at the TV. Her legs are wide open and I see her tight little pussy through the crack in her pink shorts, and I feel my cock harden against the inside of my leg. She's a touch too skinny on it, but she's tiny so she carries it off. I try to meet her gaze but she's not havin it. Sly little Roza. Such a prick tease.

I open the front door and pause for a breath. Pirri's broken out in a cold sweat. This is all the exercise he gets.

Heave-ho, I say.

We pull the German down the two steps to the back of the

van. I open the doors. Gettin the meat in the back of the van also requires some technique. I do it like this: there's a plastic sheet on the floor of the van. You kneel the body right by the open door, then tilt his upper body forward. Two of us then take a grip round the thighs, then on the count of three you thrust upwards. Done right, he'll slide right in.

If he's dead — sometimes they die on us — and rigor mortis has set in, best thing to do is just stand the body and let him fall in. Easy-peasy. Plastic on plastic, he'll slip right in. Of course, we don't like to get there after rigor mortis has set in. Makes things difficult for Hugo.

I get the body back up to the bar. Ducasse helps me drag it down to the basement where Aids Joyce is waitin. We got four lined up, collected last night and this mornin. As business has grown we've knocked through the basement and installed a cold room. We can accommodate twelve at a time. We got four hospital beds for those on the drip, and we got room for about eight in the cold room when they've been chopped and hung. The process is roughly this: I bring in the carcass and we lay em down, and we've usually got it set up so we got four on the tables at any one time. We keep em under, and Aids Joyce comes in and extracts the pituitary gland of each (he's a part-time surgeon, or at least that's how he puts it). We sew em up and keep em sleepin for about thirty-six hours, which is just about enough time for the body to flood itself with stress hormone. During this time they're on a MDMA drip and about 3600mg will be pumped into em in twelve different doses, once every three hours. Then we kill em with a super-massive dose — we give em the equivalent of twenty of Joyce's pills, about 5000mg, which given the purity is like the Tsar Bomba of ecstasy.

This floods the body with inhuman levels of dopamine and seratonin and Hugo goes to work preppin em, and we hang the meat for three to seven days dependin on the fat-to-muscle ratio. Then they're ready. They're sent out to our affiliate establishments up and down the country. I'm distribution. Roundin em up, delivery — that stuff. All told, I'm doin fifty hours a week up and down the country, but for the money I can't sniff at it. It's a livin.

Wanna help me here? Ducasse says.

He zips open the bag and I grab the legs, and we hustle the big German up onto the table. There are three other bodies laid out behind us. I hear Aids Joyce test the bone saw. One of those circular ones with the terrifyin buzz sound. I've watched him work once outta curiosity. He's got his own 'self-taught' style of craniotomy, which to my eye is something more akin to butchery, but hey, whatever the fuck works. He just grinds a big hole out of the head from the forehead to the top of the skull, then goes rootin around for the gland. Takes him about twenty minutes all told. Fuck knows how they survive it at all.

You got any details on him? Ducasse says.

Yeah.

Hugo's out back, he says.

Through a door out of the surgery we've built a makeshift office. Hugo is sat at the desk on the computer. He's laid back in the chair, finger strokin his belly through his shirt. I hand him the ID and pull out my notebook.

German, I say. Divorced, livin alone in Rotterdam. Agency work, no kin.

Hugo is punchin all this into the computer in front of him. I picked up the machine off a dealer in the city. Off the grid, air-gapped, cold. No internet. The thing is for information storage only, and it contains the details of our deliveries across the country and beyond, transaction histories, affiliated houses, contacts and sources of information, payments to our associates, not to mention the record of the upwards of six hundred carcasses that have passed through our doors. All encrypted. I set it up. I'm no wizard but I know enough. It's enough to keep any base-level local police out. Interpol, if we ever cross their radars, could probably crack it. This is a possibility we've considered, of course. Six hundred people in Holland and another 4000 across half a dozen other European countries, it's only a matter of time before they beat down on our door. By then we'll have retired and fucked off to Uruguay.

Wanna open up for us? Hugo says. I've a bit to do here.

Sure.

I get a kick outta doin the bar. Makes a change from sittin in the van, so I hop out through the kitchen into the bar and turn on the lights. I head up the stairs and unlock the door. I step outside.

It's spring and the mornin is openin up like a tulip. Tourists are pourin back into the city and we're seein new faces nightly. The ones that find us are the ones that are lookin for us. A weekender from, say, Munich, knows about us from Munich and knows where to find our place in Amsterdam. He's a meat-eater through and through. Or she. We do have our female clients, though they're outnumbered by the men ten-to-one. The women who frequent our establishments fucken terrify me. Silent types, with a look of utter diabolical hatred about them. I don't get that. The men are controlled solely by their appetites; whatever acumen they have left has dropped into their stomach. The women, on the other hand, retain some kind of higher faculties. In fact, their Meat addiction serves as some kind of evolutionary stimulant. Their senses are intact, rigid and merciless. If one of these women were to tell you to lift a knife and slice off your own arm, I have no doubt you'd do it. They are *commanding*. I fear we're unwittingly producing some kind of advanced being and we've yet to realise it. No-one else seems to notice. I've mentioned it to Ducasse and he shrugs it off, but he's afraid of nothin.

Starlet comes round the corner with a young fellow on her arm. She has a spring in her step. She puts on a good show, does Starlet. She's tootin an Arab boy, maybe eighteen or twenty. She likes em dark. Don't think I've ever seen her with a white boy though I'm by no means familiar with her history. This little Arab boy has a shy grin, looks like the cat with the cream. Got his hand on her ass too. Starlet strokes the sparse hair on his face.

Mornin, I say.

Open for breakfast? she says.

So long as it's liquid, step inside.

Ever known me to need anything else? she says.

She's flirtin with me. Makin her boy jealous. Those little Arab boys are so pliable.

You look like you've already had everything you need, I tell her.

She blows me a kiss and heads downstairs.

I pick up an old plastic shopping bag outside my fuckbox window. This where I live, after all. *Little bit of pride please, people.*

# 14

# Communion

**Location:**
*Screamin Pope, Amsterdam*
**Time:**
*12.00, Wednesday*
**Present:**
*Starlet: lover, seducer of naive boys*
*Mahmoud: Muslim, apprentice carpet-maker*
*Hugo: busy butcher*
*Danglin' Jimmy: Yank, hotel crooner*

Starlet goes to the jukebox and throws on Scissor Sisters. This means she got laid, if it wasn't already obvious from the boy on her arm. Starlet wears her desires on the tunes she plays. She hasn't told me this, I've worked it out from observin her. Scissors Sisters if she's been fucked, and if she wants to get laid she'll put on Iggy Pop. 'Nightclubbin' is a fucken filthy tune and it works for her too. The way she moves when it's on gets every pervert in the bar worked up. If she's had a bad night, maybe got knocked about a bit, usually she'll put on somethin furious, like the Prodigy. She looks fierce those days. Some mornins she'll throw a boomerang our way and stick on 'Heartattack and Vine', and I've no idea if she wants to fuck or fight. I stay out of her way those mornins.

This mornin she's smilin, so I fix her up a breakfast caipirinha. Her drinks also change accordin to her sexual whims.

Somethin for you? I say to the Arab boy.

Coffee, he says.

Strange. Doesn't mind playin with willies but won't touch alcohol. Peculiar worldview, these Arab boys.

I fix myself a coffee while I'm at it. I don't drink much of the stuff but the smell gets me — once I smell it the urge comes on. We got good stuff at the bar on account of one or two of the patrons who really got a hard-on for the bean. Those that Hugo likes, he'll try n'keep happy. So I make a Turkish coffee for Mahmoud and fix myself a cup of Guatemalan. I can't stomach the Turkish muck. Like drinkin camel shite. Gimme some Guatemalan brew, or maybe Ethiopian. Same as it goes for anything — if you're gonna do it, do it right.

Starlet is dancin for her boytoy, caipirinha in hand.

*So I dance along when I hear that funky song...*

Mahmoud's lovin it in a shy, *can't-express-it* kinda way. Tryin to look tough as Starlet rubs her ass against his prick. She looks over at me and winks.

Nothin wrong with this gig at all. Beats workin in a grill.

Hugo pokes his head through the kitchen door. You okay here? he says.

Swingin, I tell him.

He disappears again.

His disappearance is immediately followed by the appearance of Danglin' Jimmy through the bathroom door. He takes us all by surprise. Jimmy comes out tuckin his shirt into his trousers, fedora askew on his head. We're all lookin at him, drinks in hand.

You sleep in there, Jimmy?

I guess so, he says.

He slips onto a bar stool lookin dazed but steady. I dunno how mangled you need to get to spend a night in the Pope toilets, but I've never got there. I don't know anyone else has either. But then Jimmy is known for mixin up some lethal cocktails of powder, pills and booze. He's got a cast iron constitution. Titanium, like.

Whiskey, Jimmy?

Sure, man, he says in that crooner verve of his.

Danglin' Jimmy is a Yank. Plays piano at some of the better hotels around the city. He's good too. We heard him play one night, me and Ducasse, when he played one of the private clubs we supply in south Amsterdam. The man is a wizard. Even bent outta shape like he is most nights he still can stun a room.

Here you go, Jimmy.

I put a glass of water next to the whiskey, but I know he won't touch it.

Yeah man, he says.

Danglin' Jimmy is black. Not tall but slim. Nah, not slim — *wiry*. Taut as a piano string. He's got some peculiar strength too. He likes to rip books apart at the spine to demonstrate this for us. Must be a lifetime of exercisin the fingers.

*Baby*, Starlet croons in my direction. She's holdin up her glass.

*You think that I could hustle up a little quick step dancin way...*

I leave Jimmy to get acquainted with his Macallan and head over to Starlet. I whip her up another.

Day off? I say.

Starlet works a window at the top of the Oudezijds Achterburgwal.

Today is a Saturday, honey — you know I don't work Saturdays. I'm gonna spend the night with my baby, she says, and she pulls Mahmoud's head into her tits.

If today is Saturday then tonight is Feast, which is a pain in my balls.

Feast is a night that grew out of my original idea to have a DJ in at weekends. It turned into a thing. We get a DJ in, throw up lots of ribs, and it turns into a raging cornucopia of meat and fucking that would put Caligula to shame. It's a ticket-only affair, so we usually see the same faces most weeks with a handful of tourists here and there to pepper the evenin. Mostly Germans, but more and more Italians are comin in now. French too. We've got branches in Frankfurt, Hamburg, Paris and Milan. New one openin in Cannes. We get them here, tourists who are addicted to human meat and the hormonal rush it gives em. Human meat and sexual violence. That's what we do here. It sells.

Because I started Feast it's known as my thing, so I'm left to organise the show. Which means I can't quite enjoy it like I should. I gotta keep an eye on things. I can't let go, get crazy. My weekend is Friday and Sunday. Saturday can go fuck itself.

*But I don't wanna kick it when the old hosanna plays...*

Jimmy's dry and I fix him another.

Cheers, man.

How many of those do you need before you get that big snake out? Starlet shouts at Jimmy.

Danglin' Jimmy is named thus cause he's got a prick that swings down between his knees. We know this cause he likes to take it out and show us when he's oiled. After six whiskies and a few lines of coke he'll stand in the middle of the floor and swing that big beast in circles. It's his party piece. It gets folks talkin. With some pills in him, he'll start whippin people with it. Some of our punters, men and women alike, just like to be slapped with that big black appendage. They get off on it. Danglin' Jimmy is happy to oblige. He's a lover, not a hater. He'll beat anyone with his big meaty prick.

Ways off yet, Jimmy says to Starlet.

You just let me know when you're ready, darlin, Starlet says.

Jimmy raises his glass. A gentleman.

I sip my coffee.

A word of advice Jimmy, I say, leanin in. I know you're made of tough stuff n'all, but another night in those toilets might just kill ya.

Jimmy laughs.

I've seen you party with the best of em, I tell him. Nobody's built like you, and nobody can handle what you handle, but there's bacteria in them toilets that make SARS look like probiotic. Just sayin.

I hear ya, Jimmy says. I wasn't plannin on it, but things jus got outta hand, man. There was some pills goin round here yesterday that jus blew ma fuckin mind…

I grin. Aids Joyce, the cute prick, has been playin with the MDMA. I have to hand it to the guy. Seven or eight straight hours on a single pill. He knows what he's at.

I ate three o'the fuckin things, Jimmy says.

Jesus Christ, Jimmy.

I got so high I drank a whole bottle jus to climb down.

Jesus fucking Christ, I tell him. Maybe you need a night off.

Ain't no night off in my game, son.

Whatever you say, Jimmy.

…*Then why can't I find ya when you're the one I lose?*

Built like titanium, is Jimmy.

Danglin' Jimmy holds his whiskey to his face, touchin his cheek or right under his nose, sniffin it. What he's doin is engaging with it using every sense. He's a sensual cat, Jimmy.

Starlet is draggin Mahmoud towards the toilets.

You see, Jimmy, I say. You see what happens in those toilets?

Jimmy sniffs at his whiskey. Uh-huh.

She leads him by the hand, looks over her shoulder and winks at us.

Insatiable, I say.

Uh-huh.

Ducasse comes through the kitchen door and claps a hand on my shoulder. Got a minute? he says.

Sure. You okay there Jimmy? I say.

Uh-huh.

I follow Ducasse out back into the office. Hugo's waitin. We sit down. Hugo's sittin strokin his belly, lookin at me.

We got a mission for you, he says.

More of a *promotion*, Ducasse says.

We're lookin at openin a new branch down in Athens, Hugo says.

I let this information sink in. Athens. Been once. Shithole.

We want you to set it up, help run it. You'll be in charge, Ducasse says.

Run my own bar in Athens?

You'll be full partner, Hugo says.

I'm not sure how I feel about this. I'm kinda likin it here in Amsterdam.

As a partner, thirty per cent of takins goes straight into your pocket, Hugo tells me. No more runnin around pickin up bodies all day. You'll have some grunt to do that for ya.

This can't be sniffed at. Thirty per cent? At what's comin through this place on a daily basis that's a minimum hundred grand a month. That's no sniffin matter.

Gimme a day or two to think it over?

Hugo nods. Ducasse claps a hand on my back. Think it over, he says.

I'll think on it, I tell em.


Hittin midnight the place is startin to howl. All the fiends are out. The smell of meat seeps from the kitchen and fills the room. We got the DJ in the corner playin his filthy tunes. These nights turn dark pretty quickly. There's no pop, house or disco in here, this is straight up dark dub and psychedelica, the filthier the better. It's difficult to see what grows from what — does the music turn dark cause of the atmosphere, or does the energy in the room drive the music into dark places? Chicken and egg kinda situation. Whatever, the music is a cornerstone of the night. That, and the Meat, of course. And pills.

I'm in the corner buzzin with Ducasse and Aids Joyce. Joyce is off his tits on his own pills and shoutin about the Filipino he's had chained up in his house for the past seven weeks.

Like he's tellin us about his new toaster. Ducasse gets a kick outta this but I'm not really in the mood for it.

Boy or girl? Ducasse shouts.

What?

Boy or girl?

It's a woman you sick fuck, Joyce shouts.

What do ya do with her?

Ducasse wants all the details. Joyce explains he has her read to him.

Read? Read what, ya freak? Ducasse shouts.

Joyce has her read Henry Miller to him evenins.

Who?

Sometimes he likes to hear Bukowski.

What kinda strange fuck are you? Ducasse shouts. Why not just fuck her?

Not what occurred to me, but Ducasse has his own *weltanschauung*.

Aids Joyce is shoutin somethin at Ducasse. I think he's quotin Bukowski, at least it sounds like one of old Charlie's poems. Eyes like two upturned espresso cups, Joyce is squealin poetry at Ducasse:

*… with a young boy to write my stuff now,*
*I keep him in a ten-foot cage with a typewriter,*
*Feed him whiskey and raw whores and belt him pretty*
*good…*

Boys? Ducasse shouts.

The smell of meat is thick on the air, and Aids Joyce is amped up on pills and poetry. I am too, I think. I'm wired on pills, that's for sure, but I feel there's a little poetry in my heart also. Or it could be it's just the first ticklings of a bloodthirsty savagery comin on. What's the difference? Look at some of the best poetry, it's fucken bestial. Who knows, maybe the best way to devour poetry is to have it read to ya by a poor wretch tied up in your basement. Probably the only way to stomach some stuff is to swallow it like this. Aids Joyce, surgeon and pharmacist. Sufferer, poet. Who fucken knew?

Things are pilin up at the bar. Hugo's stretched.

What do you feed her? I shout.

Joyce throws me the evil eye, like we've already established she's sustained on poetry and high art.

Rice and beans — what else would I feed her? he says.

*Like all Filipinos live on beans and rice.*

Where does she piss? I ask him.

She's got a bucket, he tells me.

I no longer know what's real and what's fantasy.

The meaty wafts thicken on the air and people are starting to dribble. Joyce is licking his lips. I look out on the floor where a group of some five or six suits are closing in on three young girls. The men are gyratin, swingin and fingerin their bellies in direct imitation of Hugo, for Hugo is still master of ceremonies, king dick — it's his energy that fuels the night, his meaty waves drivin the mad chaos of the place. He's behind the bar now, arms and face raised to the air as the DJ brings up the room in crescendo, like some greasy Christ of the new world, progenitor of a degenerate renaissance, his disciples ready to crawl on their knees over glass for a taste of the enunciatory barbecue. The ribs of enlightenment. The brisket of bliss. The steaks of nirvana. *Feed us,* they are saying. *Feed us… fill us.*

*Fill us up.*

Hugo will fill them with the meaty word.

Ducasse is lookin round him, I know he's scopin for somethin to fuck. Male, female, doesn't matter. Come the Meat, everyone'll be up for anything. Won't matter soon, man woman, black white, rich or poor… the Meat is the great equaliser. I drain my bottle and another appears in front of me. Hugo winks. Greatest bartender alive, hands down. I clasp the ice-cold glass and take a glug.

*Crisssssp.*

I can no longer sit on the seat and I get up. I'm not quite dancin. I'm in more of an adversarial stance on the side of the floor, rockin aggressively, scopin the scene. I probably look

like I'm gonna glass someone, but actually I feel quite lovey...
lovey with a hard glassy edge.

*Far overrr...*

Hard black dub thumps. The walls are throbbin, pumpin. The room is one long, ecstatic heartbeat. Everyone here, we are flesh and blood and we know it. We know who we are. We know why we're here. We live, we beat, we eat. And where is our meat?

*Far ovvverrrrr...*

*Bam bam...* the dub kicks.

We are caught somewhere in the limbo of a desire to fight or fuck. A bloody sexual kick is about to get goin, and we are all alive with the knowledge.

*Feed us.*

The vampires are out.

Then she comes in, comin down the stairs like she owns the place. Head vampire, like. In a long green dress, gracing the room with silent fury. I look over at Hugo and he's seen her, and I can see he knows her. His demeanour changes. No longer king dick, like.

This *emerald-city* lady all in green is down among the vampires, she cuts across the floor where a table kinda mysteriously empties for her and she takes a stool. She's got two minders with her, at least I think that's what they are. Ducasse has come over all shifty. She's changed the mood of the room. I see Hugo take over a bottle, ice bucket n'all — never seen one before, not in here. He's uncorked it and poured her a glass.

The vampires rage on, oblivious, but somethin's happenin. I smell meat.

*Fill us.*

I'm lickin my lips and rockin, demented like.

It comes. We all smell it, wafts hit us as it comes out through the kitchen door, a big steamin tray of meaty ecstasy and we're all about to get fucken high. Higher. Cause we're all high anyhow, off our tits and ready to scream.

*Fill us…*

The tray cuts through the crowd, hands snatchin at it. Hugo goes straight to the head vampire. He lays down a plate in front of her and fills it with the best cuts. I'm watchin. Ducasse is watchin. Rest of the savages are all movin towards it.

*Bam, Bam…*

The music kicks and the frenzy come on.

I watch the woman in green claw at the meat, pulling off strips and feedin it to herself. The two big meatheads either side of her are tryin not to watch her savage the plate.

The tray comes our way. Hugo, sweaty, greasy, lets us pull off what we want — me, Ducasse, Aids Joyce, we all grab fistfuls. Then Hugo's in among the savages and they're attackin the bounty like raw beasts.

I don't care, I'm eatin that sweet steak right off the bone. And is it fucken sweet. The juices are settin off fireworks in my head, that ole fire startin, we're all lightin up, lightin up like christmas. I can see it now: there's a great web of golden light linkin us all, everyone in the room, and with every bite lights sparkle like golden fireflies wakin up around us. The Meat is firin up our psyche, the collective psyche, the golden thread that runs through all of us, and the Meat is the catalyst. We're all connected, one. One, together in feast. And the golden light is centred round that green vampire in the corner — she's at the epicentre, even Hugo's light which is fucken blindin is directed at her. She's directin it, it all flows towards her…

*So who the fuck is she?*

I'm settin to ask Ducasse when I see him jump up. He's let loose now. He's off on it. He grabs a girl and spins her, presses her ass into his crotch. His hands run up the inside of her thigh and I see a greasy trail on her skin, greasy meat juice glistenin on the green glow of her thigh. That gets me goin. I chew my lip til I taste the blood in my mouth.

I catch the green vampire lookin at me and her gaze is frightful. I look for Hugo. He's out on the floor, so I head in behind the bar. The punters are gettin their meat on and no one gives a fuck about drinks. Their only concern is lickin, suckin, chewin, bitin and tearin at each other. They're all high on Meat and ecstasy and chemically-inflamed libidos. Booze has taken a back seat. One cunt is still drinkin — Sweeney's down at his corner of the bar and is holdin up his bottle for me. I place a beer in front of him and he snatches it up. He's just drinkin and watchin. Probably masturbated so much today there's no blood left in him. He's still high though, and he's grippin that cat of his a little too tightly. The thing looks skittish. Sweeney strokes his cat while out there Ducasse slides his greasy fingers into some bigger pussy. Hugo's bein mauled by the punters, his meaty stench too much for em. Their senses inflamed, they are now clawin at him, tearin at his clothes, scratchin his chest and his hairy belly. Hugo the meaty meister, a sweaty, odorous Karajan, playin them like a symphony. The DJ's in on it too, the dub now filthier and meaner. Emanations seep into us from the speakers, the *Uvvv-uvvv-uvvv* of the tunes throbbin in our bellies, shakin our bowels and intestines. Our bowels itch and our assholes quiver… we shudder, we vibrate, our essence disintegrates. We're comin apart at the seams, and that's okay with us. It's our false selves dyin: the id, the ego. The shadows falls away and we become true once more. Flesh, and flesh alone. No soul, no morality… we are only flesh, and therefore we are free. Consumer and consumed, we are one. Indivisible.

Meaty, fleshy Hugo. The fat conductor, the porky controller. Our fleshy, sweaty king. Hugo has been stripped and is being ravished by man and woman alike, right there in front of me. Such power. The woman in green watches. Some kind of interplay is going on between the two, some ritualistic Dionysian thing is goin on but I can't fathom it. My heart is racin. Drugs and adrenalin. Thrills. Blood courses my veins. The apostles are worshippin at the altar of Hugo, and I'm about to see the sacrifice of the high priest of Meat. Bestow us with your graces…

The tongues, the teeth, the hands and fingers all release themselves from Hugo's sweaty delights, and the crowd somehow intuits the approach of the green woman. She has slid off her chair, the silk tresses of her dress clingin to her snaky curves. She cuts through the crowd like a knife through buttery steak, coming up in front of Hugo. His disciples surround him.

*Uvvv-Uvvv...*

Sweaty and unadorned, Hugo falls to his knees. He looks up at the jade woman, she down at him like an obedient child. The emerald lights of the Screamin Pope illuminate the scene. The music kicks and we imbibe of the holy night.

One of her escort takes out a knife and hands it to her. It's a long silver thing, elegant, lethal.

I watch.

She spins the blade in the palm of her hand and holds it out for Hugo. He takes the handle, all ecstatic like. The woman nods. He grips his waist, takes a fat pinch, then proceeds to cut a long strip of flesh from his side. Blood pours from his wound.

He holds it up for the woman in green. I see it move in his hand. It has come alive and wraps itself around his arm. A small head forms at one end, a tail at the other, and it slides up his arm. An asp. The jade lady holds out her hand. The asp, riding Hugo's arm, peers up at her. A tongue darts from its head as it gazes in her eyes. The long fingers of the green woman beckon. The asp slithers off Hugo's arm, its head rising out above her hand. Gently, it passes over. Hugo sags. The asp clings to the vampire's arm. She raises it to eye-level and they gaze at each other. She opens her mouth and it slides down her throat.

Communion.

Hugo falls to the floor.

# 15

# Notes from a Cannibalist

I wake up the next mornin, though I'm not sure how. My body had every right somewhere middle of the night to say, *Nah, you know what, you've done it this time, you've gone and fucken done it this time — heart's not takin it anymore, we've had enough of your shite. Sayonara son, good night sweetheart, be gone into the dark night of eternal rest…*

But I wake. My heart is racin and some kind of freakish chemical reaction is happenin in my body. It feels like individual cells are explodin, or just fizzin out and dyin. It's proper Armageddon. I even say it out loud:

I'm dyin.

I'm not, though. I'm very much fucken alive and the torment is indescribable. I raise my head an inch from the pillow and throw my arm over the edge of the bed. Luckily I've had the wherewithal to put water in the room and I swiftly sink a bottle.

Then I check to see if I'm alone, and I am. Thank Christ. Thank fucken Christ.

I look at the ceiling. The thin light of the city sneaks in through the curtains. I roll up in the foetal position and try to flee into unconsciousness once more, but sleep is gone from me. My body says *No*. My body says, *You've almost destroyed me, and it's imperative you do somethin to keep me alive.*

But I don't know what. I lie there, tremblin, for hours.

At one point I drift into some black nightmare where I scour the canals of Amsterdam followed by some dark force at my back. It starts off as a casual evenin walk around the Dam, through the Botanical Gardens out into the Weesperbuurt and over the Amstel by the Skinny Bridge, but by dark night I'm being chased round the museum quarter by this evil fucken fiend who I cannot see or name… he catches up to me outside the Rijksmuseum in the black night under a great portrait of Christ and pulls me to the ground, and I smell the evil emanations off him as his thin hands close over my mouth. I rip the hood from his face as he chokes me, and he has the face of Aids Joyce…

I snap out of it in a burnin sweat and drink more water.

This is gonna be me all day.


I come to out of a long, anguished and restless stupor. It's gone dark outside and I'm guessin around eight, maybe nine. My body demands food but I don't have the strength to get out of bed. I roll on my side and stare at the wall.

*Battle through it.*

The night before comes back to me. I mind the jade lady and the thought of her gives me the terrors. I recall Hugo, scarrin himself, cuttin his own flesh. *Did I really see that?*

I mind the flesh comin alive and the woman in green takin his live flesh and her swallowin a snake. *Is that what I fucken saw?*

After that, the night is a blank. I lost it after that. I dunno how many pills I ate or how many absinthe I swallowed. I coulda swallowed a snake too, for all I know. Feels like it. Snakes, knives and MDMA… how many have had nights like that and lived to tell the tale?

Not many. I consider myself one of the chosen.

I hear a knockin at my window. Some cunt actin the prick.

I badly need to piss. The toilet is too far and I can't summon the strength. No matter how I try, I can't summon the will

120

needed to propel myself outta bed. So I roll over and piss into an empty bottle by the bed.

*This is how a human turns into an animal. When you cease usin a toilet. This is the first step.*

I reach out blindly for another water and my hand falls on the book on the dresser. I focus on the cover.

*Notes from a Cannibalist.*

I'd forgotten about it. Plain black cover. Just a title. So that I don't have to get up, I open the book. If I'm engagin my mind then I won't be forced to engage my body. On the inside is the name of the author: J.J. Carmichael. Scottish? A Scottish cunt who eats people. Topical, at least. Not hangover readin but I'm not goin anywhere soon. I open at a random page.

*The first was my brother. That was many years ago, but I'll tell the story of it, for it's back there that it started, before I'd ever tasted the meat of man, it was my own kin that I ate.*

*There was three of us left in the house: me, the brother and the auld ma. The two sisters were long gone and the da, well, he was the first to go, way back, maybe a year before but we'd stopped counting. The passage of time's no longer relevant when everyone's starving to death. Hours, minutes and days are simply intervals between meals, their duration meaningless but their passing no less painful. So the da, he was gone, and the two sisters, children only, they went one after the other. They were sickly from birth, so they'd little chance to start. The da got a proper burial, that was way at the beginning, but the girls, they were buried in a hole in the ground at the side of the road in the dark of night. We came home, me and the brother from the digging, to the auld ma. She was housebound already, could barely make it to the corner to piss. We made up a story about the lovely service the priest gave, and the lovely wee words that were spoke over the graves, about the lilies of the field and the fowls of the air, and how the heavenly father feedeth them… and the auld ma smiled sleepily, gaunt and wretched and soothed by the words of the good Lord, but me and the brother knew that nobody was feeding us, not the auld ma nor the good Lord, and balls to his raiment and his lilies for we were starving, and if he was feeding the fowls of the air then it was clear we were lower than the fowl, for no one was feeding us. We looked at the black walls of our hovel and knew it to be true. 'Is not life more than meat?' the old priest might have asked, and we would have answered 'No', absolutely and neverever NO, life was not more than meat, because for us it was meat or death. Our logic was solid as rock. But the auld ma drifted off into her coma-sleep, reassured that the priest had said a few good words, and I swear I never hated priests more than I did at that very moment. Even imaginary ones.*

*In and out she was, one minute awake then asleep for the whole day. The brother, he mustered up the strength to crawl from the hole we lived in once a day to collect firewood. Our home was a mud hut built against the gable wall of an old cottage. We built it around the fireplace — it was a fireplace with walls. Our sole possession, snatched from the hearth of our family home before we were evicted, was the cast iron pot that hung uselessly above the fire, since it rarely heated more than water with maybe a bit of grass in it. If we could stomach it. Usually we went without. We were sustained by despair, hatred, and the dead prayers of the auld ma. Those bitter, useless prayers. When she was still conscious I used to hear her whisper them in the dark and they tasted like ash in my mouth. I would spit into the fire as she would invoke the Lord.*

*One day the brother crawled back empty-handed. I'd come back with a handful of berries and some wild garlic, he'd nothing to show for six hours crawling around in the muck.*

*'What've ya got?' I asked him.*

*'I've nothin,' he told me.*

*And I hated him, the useless beggar. I hated the sight of him by then, sick and dyin, and though I probably looked just like him I didn't need reminding of it. He was a poor, half-dead animal, lower than a fowl. Pitiful creature through.*

*But one of us might still make it out. And I made the decision that it would be me — I'd crawl out of that hole one way or another and get on a boat out of this country to someplace where it wasn't a death sentence to not have some eating in your pot. So I ate what I had in my hand and went out, and I found sticks and got home and lit a good auld fire, the biggest we'd had in a while, and the auld ma she slept through it and the brother passed out in its warmth too.*

*I smothered him with my coat. My coat that stank of grass and soot and shit, I put it over his face and smothered him til the life went outta him, and the life went with a few kicks, more than you'd expect from a man on death's door. Nights in that hut we'd dreamed and prayed for death and it didn't come, and yet when I delivered it he went fighting while the auld ma slept on.*

*That was the hard part, and I did it with no small weight on my conscience. It troubled me, it did.*

*Then I got to work. What happened next was mechanical, for the only impulse in my body was to that of sustenance, and survival will prevail over conscience at almost any deed.*

*I stripped him and washed him off. I took the hot water from the pot and washed down his body, cleaned him good, for we were living in our own filth for over a year at the time. Then I dragged him outside, and by the light of the moon I cut him up. I took off the hands and the feet and the head, and his sorry prick too, wrapped them in his jacket and put them in a hole in the ground right next to where we slept, but it didn't matter cause I'd be away in a day or two. Then I split him and took out his innards, wrapped them in his shirt and put them into the same hole. I took the legs and arms from the torso, carried them down the river and washed them again, then took them home and got to slicing it up into edible cuts. The poor wretch must've weighed sixty kilos when I killed him. I got about twelve kilos of edible meat off him.*

*Then I made a soup.*

*Bones and all went in and the fattier cuts of meat, and I boiled it up for about three hours, and the auld ma came round with the smell of meat in the hovel.*

*'You haven't killed the sow, have ya?' she said.*

*The auld sow was killed a year before.*

*'I have ma,' I told her. 'It was her or us.'*

*And I fed my brother to the auld ma, and I fed myself, and it was a long time since we'd had any eating like it.*

*God bless her.*

*She fell into a warm, sated sleep that night. Then I smothered her. 'Take no thought for the morrow, ma...'*

*I wrapped her in her blankets and sewed her up, and she went into a hole next to my brother. And while I was putting her pillow on the fire, didn't I feel something inside, and I put my hand in and found her purse. She'd five pounds in it, and I sat staring at it in the light of the fire, me, who'd been starving with the rest of the family for over a year, and here the auld ma had five pounds in a purse under her head. I didn't understand it, maybe she'd forgotten it, I didn't know, but I laughed all the same cause I had a full belly and warm fire, and now I had passage out of the country.*

*I filled up the graves of my mother and my brother, and the imaginary priest said a prayer over them.*

*For three days I built up my strength with eating from the brother, and when I was ready the bones went into another hole and it was filled in, and I cleaned out the old hovel. I sat that last night over my soup and my fire, no longer praying for death and glad that I was the one who was going to make it out. And I would make it.*

*On the fourth day I packed up my things, took the rest of the meat that I'd cooked up for the trip, wrapped it up and said goodbye to the family, or what was left of it. We were scattered in holes all across the West.*

*I walked six days to Belfast on the remains of my brother, got myself a ticket and got on a boat to New York. It was on the boat that I met Father James Carmichael, the man that I would become, the man that I am today, the man who has eaten five men and is alive today because of it. I, Father James, once a worthless fowl in a hole in the West of Ireland, am an avowed cannibalist, and it is my notes that you now hold in your hand.*

Not Scottish, Irish. An Irish cannibal. I put down the book.

I've a pain in my stomach, perhaps from hunger and perhaps from somethin else. I lay in the bed and tremble, and pray for sleep. And does sleep come to me? Does it fuck. Instead I tumble into some sweaty, disturbed hallucination, a man on the run, fleeing, maybe from the law, maybe from head-hunters, hell, maybe from myself... I am chased in the dead of night, hunted across Amsterdam like a dog, so I flee the city on foot headin south to Rotterdam where I hole up for three days. Pockets empty, I beg for scraps and steal what I can, until the third night I get in a scuffle with another homeless man, a bum like me, and we are fightin over the remains of a chicken carcass in the bin out back of a takeaway... the guy takes a swing at me but he's past his best, so I rap him on the side of the head with a brick, catch him in the temple and he drops, lights out. I'm out back of the takeaway with this stiff, it's midwinter and I'm cold, so I light a fire, and off come the bum's clothes, onto the fire they go, his shoes too, soon all his belongings are burnin, but now I've this corpse laid out and I think, *Well, I'm hungry and here we are, some good meat laid right there in front of me, shame to waste it*, and that's that, I make the decision then and there to cook him up, so I break into the takeaway and pilfer a cleaver and a filleting knife, and I go to work on him, get to choppin like, and soon I've him carved up nice, so I cook up a bit of thigh, bit tough could use a few days' hangin, but it's warm meat in my stomach and cheer in my heart, for I'm fed again.

I spend the night stokin the fire and cookin him up, and soon I've him nicely parcelled. The remains of him go in the bins, street burial, and I absorb the last warmth of the fire, and as the fire dies around five in the mornin I hit the road, headin south through queer-soundin towns, Stampersgat, Roosendaal, on through Antwerp and Brussels and soon I'm in France, and I run outta meat around Charleroi, the man eaten whole, digested, and now I have the strength of two.

But I've no meat now, so I get to stalkin, and I find a nice plump cyclist along a bicycle path in Charleroi, beat the life outta him and drag him into the woods. I carve him and cook him up, a better quality meat this fellow, richer, cleaner, grass fed and organic no doubt, those fine-livin Belgians. Stocked up again, I head south across the Ardennes, killin again in Reims, the eatin of a plump housewife takin me to Dijon, and the further south I go the finer the weather becomes, warmin up, and the warmer it becomes the less eatin I need, for with each new soul I devour the lighter I become, a golden breeze blowin south for spring.

I cross the Alps on the meat of a young vagrant in Geneva, a runaway, his body communion to my now ethereal husk, across Switzerland and Italy and down into Croatia he carries me, where in Dubrovnik I kill for the last time, not for need of meat but because the eatin of souls is what now sustains me, for each new soul I consume my own flesh becomes lighter, freer, so that by the time I reach Greece my form blows like a warm Sirocco over the land, fuelled by souls, innumerable souls, and when I drift into Athens I see it, the incontrovertible truth of it, that there is only one salvation: to devour, to savour, to consume.

*And ye shall consume, and consumption shall make ye free.*

# 16

# The White City

I hate this fucken city. The sun blisters everything — it's relentless, unforgiving. And the place stinks.

I'm in a café, tryin to enjoy my coffee, when a guy comes up beatin two fingers against his lips, lookin for a cigarette.

Fuck off, I tell him.

I lift my cup and sip it. Coffee's not even good.

I'm readin a story in the paper, the English papers, about the disappearances that've suddenly been noticed in London. That's down to us, of course — most of em, not all of em. London's two restaurants have a high turnover, though. Our one bar in London and its affiliate establishments have the same output as the entire country of Holland. Those rich pricks in the City are the greediest, bloodthirstiest cunts in the world. They take some feedin. We're shippin meat over from France just to keep em sated. They can't get enough. We still haven't broken America, that meaty Mecca, so London is our highest-grossing outlet. And if you only knew who came through its doors...

I finish my coffee and call the waiter over for a glass of raki. I haven't had a pill in two months since it doesn't quite agree with the heat here, but I need the spirits. Afternoons are unbearable without it. Even in the shade the heat is grim.

Sometimes I ask myself what I'm doin here.

Makin money, I tell myself.

And the money's good.

I'm takin minimum eighty grand a month. I work like a dog, but for that kinda sweetener I can live with it. There are other perks. I eat and drink for free, and I've unlimited credit at two of the city's finest hoorhouses. You could say I have the life. Yeah, I'm livin it. I'm fucken livin it.

I make swift work of the raki and call for another. One more before I head back into the street. Back to the bar to take care of the mornin's business. My phone goes and I answer it. It's Hugo.

Ducasse with you? he says.

Nah, I tell him.

He's been gone two nights.

Can't help ya. Ain't seen him.

How's business? Hugo says.

Couldn't be better. We're not hittin record numbers but we're growin. Growin steady.

Fucken A, Hugo says.

Ya comin down sometime?

It's on my list.

Just let me know, I say.

He hangs up. Not much of a talker on the phone, Hugo. He's got more weight in person. He feels talkin on the phone robs him of his selfhood or somethin. Makes him uncomfortable. Makes sense to me — his meaty scent is his secret weapon. Without it he's half the man.

The sun is inchin round the umbrella above my head, and rather that move I decide to go. I drop a few euros on the table and step into the street, and wander down Areos into the square. Monastiraki. I recall passin through here in my backpacker days. Just down the alley in the fleamarket I bought a *tavli*, and of course I ate those *souvlaki* on the square. Middle of summer though, July heat and sticky, there's nothin to be hangin about for. I nip into Psiri.

We scoped out several locations for our shop. First, we

looked at Exarchia. It didn't suit. Too many headbangers, and besides, when any shit kicks off in the city it usually starts in Exarchia, being close to the Polytechnic. Then we looked at Moschato. We all agreed it wasn't seedy enough. We've toyed with goin upmarket but it doesn't quite sit with our aesthetic. We found our home in Psiri. Central, cheap. Raggedy as shit. We liked it immediately.

We found a little place off Sokratous. Underneath what I gather was once a leather shop, we revamped a shithole basement to suit our needs. We bought the whole building just to get access to the yard (we're shiftin bodies day and night), and got ourselves an underground car park into the bargain, which is handy in all sorts of ways.

The bar ended up lookin just like every other Screamin Pope joint: green, seedy, beat, demented. And of course we're smack bang in the middle of the 'red light' district. The city doesn't have an official corner for peddlin ass, but what it does have we're right in it. Psiri is ripe with hoors and tricksters of every stripe. And most of them find us.

I make my way up Miouli to Platia Iroon, which is where I usually take my coffee, but today I had to see one of our dealers up in Plaka. Platia Iroon is one of the more respectable corners of Psiri, though that's relative. I cut up Eschilou, cross Evripidou and I'm there. Outside our steak shebeen, our meaty mansion in Athens, Greece.

The city is destroyed with poverty, but we do well. Athens has its old-money *riche*; all those shipping cunts held on to their wealth when everyone else was losin their house and old men were hangin themselves in the streets from shame. Plus there's a new class of moneyed German about. They're buyin up islands and they've got a base here in Athens, and they go mental for human flesh. Then there's the Chinese. They're buyin up shit left, right and centre and they're into it too, the Meat. Fuck have they gone wild for it. Those Chinese are natural-born cannibals. They want it raw. They'll ask us for prime rib, uncooked and eat it right off the bone. I mean, of all the savages we get through our door, the Chinese have the least scruples. They'll also eat all the other shite no one else will eat: eyeballs, muscle and kidneys, gall bladder — they fucken love it. I suppose when you're used to eatin dog or rat you'll eat fucken anything. Toes. We had one billionaire in from Shenzhen, and all he wanted was a big plate of toes. I mean, for fuck sake — *toes?* But who am I to question? He's payin me. You wanna eat a plate of toes, we can do it. Six hundred euros, pal. Come back soon. And he does. Every fucken week.

Starlet is standing outside the bar. Over her head is a weather-beaten and deliberately illegible sign, sayin 'Screamin Pope'. I look at her, all shemale and shifty. We're in the shade, but beads of sweat sit on a layer of carelessly-applied make up. She stands with her feet crossed, bitin a fingernail.

Thought we talked about you doin business outside the bar? I say.

I'm waitin on Asif, she says.

Who's Asif?

Boyfriend.

What about Mahmoud? I say.

Fuck, try to keep up, she says.

*How can I?* She goes through brown boys faster than she goes through oestrogen.

Asif got money? I ask.

She shrugs.

I know she's got sugar daddies but the boys she falls for are all penniless apprentices for some reason. I'll bet Asif is a trainee coppersmith or cabinet-maker.

Right, I say, can't wait to meet him.

I head down the stairs.

*

*Location:*
*Screamin Pope, Athens*
*Time:*
*13.20, Wednesday*
*Present:*
*Lorelei: nymphet, bargirl, girlfriend*
*Sweeney: creepy continental spook*
*Lenny Sack: deliveryman*
*Kostas: police, Meat addict*
*Starlet: sweaty shemale, ardent romantic*
*Asif: poor Pakistani*
*Culhannan: resident butcher, fugitive, Sex Dentist*

Finally out of that fucken heat. One thing I'm grateful for, is it'll never be warm in this hole. Lenny Sack's waitin for me at the bar. Lenny's my pick-up guy. Carcasses, I mean. He does the drivin, what I used to do before I got promoted. Lenny Sack drives around all day with bodies in his van. Hence the name. I don't really care what they call him, so long as he gets the job done. Lenny is Canadian. Bit of a lumbering dumb fuck, but he's well-liked round the bar. He works. And cause he's Canadian he gets zero hassle from the police — they take one look at his drivin license and he gets waved on. Handy, when you carryin bodies in the back.

He's sittin with Sweeney in the corner. Sweeney waylays me when I step in behind the bar.

Any chance of a beer?

You not me give a moment's peace? I say. Always over my shoulder you are, you creepy clown, fiddlin with your fucken cats.

I smack a beer down on the bar. Heat and perverts are a diabolical combo.

I go over to Kostas. We're in Greece — of course there's a fucken Kostas. In Greece, every bar, *kafenion* and souvlaki joint has a Kostas. Or a Nikos, or a Pavlos, or a Yiannis. But mostly a Kostas.

*Ela re* Kosta, I say.

*Yiasiu filo*, he says.

Kostas does jobs for us. The Greek police salary doesn't quite cut it.

Another coffee?

Yeah man, he says.

Where's Lorelei?

Just as I say it, Lorelei comes out from the kitchen.

Lorelei. Not one of my more solid life choices. We started fucking not long after she took a job at the bar. She's Greek, but goes under an assumed name after she fled some kind of unstable home environment. She won't talk about it, but I'm sure she was abused. Evenins, she likes me to beat her with the buckle end of a belt until she bleeds, then we make love for hours. It's kinda sweet, but fucken messy too. My sheets are all bloody and my walls are a mess, but she won't let me clean. Maybe she sees it as a testament to my love for her. I've never said anything, and she doesn't push. Pain is what she really needs, not words.

Lorelei. Evenings are a torture — all the fucken perverts in the shop are hittin on this sweet, demented little sixteen-year-old, and I have to stand and watch. But I know she's got eyes only for me.

*Oh Lorelei*. She squeezes me as she passes.

Where you been? Kostas is sittin here with no coffee, I say.

*Siga re*, Kostas says.

Even Kostas has a soft spot for her.

I was cleaning, says Lorelei. *Sweet, defiant Lorelei.*

All these drunks, drinking drinking, she says, in that sassy, broken English with her Greek verve.

That's what happens in a bar. That's what I'm payin you for, I say.

*Siga*, Kostas says.

I'm fixin him a coffee. I take the little copper pot and fire up the gas camp stove. We're not so classy that we have coal fire in this place. I put in the water then the coffee then the sugar, far too much sugar. I set it on the fire. And I watch. You can't leave the Greek coffee. I say Greek — the Greeks call it Greek. I call it Turkish. But you can't say that to a fucken Greek. Let them fight over the name, I'll just make the stuff.

You can't turn your back on the Greek coffee. You gotta eye it, cause the minute you turn your back it'll be all over the counter. Then you gotta start over. How many times have I let the coffee spill? I never learn.

How're the kids, Kostas? I say over my shoulder. I don't take my eyes off the coffee.

Good, man.

What they doin for the summer?

With their aunt in Saloniki, he says.

He's a good skin, Kostas. Not perverted like the rest of em. He's a family man. Just got a bit of a taste for human flesh, like us all.

Just you and the missus, eh?

Just me. She's in Saloniki too.

Eh, Kostas… just you and the city, I say. Just you and the city.

I hear Starlet come down the stairs. High heels on the wooden stairs. She likes an entrance.

Take care of Starlet, I say to Lorelei.

I'm not takin my eyes off the fucken coffee.

Hey *yoouuu*, I hear Starlet say.

She likes Lorelei, or maybe just pretends too. Lorelei treats them all with mild disregard. I peek over my shoulder, see Starlet's arm draped round her Pakistani boy who's just taken a stool. Long red fingernails scratch his chest through his open shirt.

*Keep your eyes on the fucken coffee.*

Lorelei's servin up some breakfast piña coladas, cause this is Greece and it's not afternoon til they say it is. Starlet is screechin about an extra slice of pineapple, cause it's breakfast and she hasn't eaten yet. Lorelei's not havin it.

Give her extra pineapple, I say.

Lorelei won't be overruled.

Now they're shoutin. I'm just tryin to make my fucken coffee.

I shout and snatch up a slice of pineapple and jam it into the glass. But I've turned my back on the coffee. Rule number one, broken. Coffee's all over the show.

Fuck all o'yis, I shout.

I put a beer down in front of Kostas instead.

It's almost two anyway, I tell him.

Kostas has strict rules about his intake. But he's Greek, so he's flexible. He takes a glug, no protest.

Who's this, then? I say to Starlet.

This is Asif, she says.

And what does Asif do?

Starlet speaks for him. He makes lampshades, she says.

Oh yeah? A tradesman?

Apprentice, she says.

I grin. *Where does she find em? There must be a craft fair or marketplace where she picks all these guys up. All the same, every one.*

Lorelei's givin me the evil eye from about twelve feet away. Luckily I've taken to wearin the protection around my ankle — you know, the little bracelet with the blue eyes. I'm impervious to her foul magic. Lorelei is one of those frightenin blue-eyed Hellenes. Some kind of pure, terrifyin genes. Scares me, she does. That's why I've turned to the gods for help.

She storms past me givin me a shove with her shoulder. She'll be like this now til I take her upstairs and beat her a bit. Then we'll fuck and everything will be okay. It's nice.

How'd you meet? I say, turnin back to Asif.

Oh, Starlet says, Asif's brother came round to wire my flat. Asif was there helping out and we fell head over heels.

She scratches his unshaven chin with her nails and he blushes. A kinda sweet and pure guy, Asif.

Somethin's eatin at me and I go back over to Kostas.

I pour us each a glass of raki and lean across the bar.

134

*Yia mas*, I say.

We clink glasses and take a drink.

Everything alright at home? I ask him.

Sure, he says, all Greek and mysterious like.

Just that, your wife's gone and you're here alone, I say.

It is happen every year like this, he says.

I'm tryin to read him and I think he's tellin me straight. He's my guy on the street — I can't have him bent outta shape by some tiff or break-up.

*Ola kala?* I say.

*Ola kala*, he says.

*Everything is okay then.*


I go out back and downstairs into our storage. We took a little time settin up our facilities before we opened up, and I'm right proud of how it all turned out. It's proper hospital-like. All white and sterile and smellin of bleach and well-lit. We got six beds laid out all nice, with a full set of equipment for each. We got ventilators. We got drips and ventriculostomy tubes and intravenous catheters, and everything else you need for pumpin someone full of ridiculous levels of MDMA. I'm not sure what it all does. We got a man for that.

There are six bodies laid out in various states of comatose. *Comatosy?* Living carcasses, all drip-fed a constant supply of ecstatic pharmaceuticals that will drastically alter their body chemistry to the point that it can be used as a mind-altering drug itself.

Next to the 'sleep room' we got a cold room. This is where the choppin gets done. Culhannan's in there, sawin through a right arm. He looks up as I walk in.

Right there? he says.

Aye. You alright?

Hunky-dory, he says.

*Hunky-dory.*

We on schedule?

We will be when I get through this lot.

He nods over his shoulder at the two carcasses hangin behind him on the wall. One on the table and two on the wall.

They've to be out by tonight, I tell him.

Sure don't I know it well, he says, all calm like.

He took easily to the job, Culhannan. I don't know how Hugo found him, but he showed up here in Athens our first week of openin and a few days later he was sawin off legs and heads like he was born for it. One more lunatic for our little cabal of freaks. Culhannan's been through medical school so he has a fair knowledge of anatomy. He's a dentist by trade, and ran his own practice in Dublin til he was struck off for fiddlin with patients under heavy sedation. Was doin it for years, gassin up cunts and stickin stuff inside them and takin pictures. Earned the name 'Sex Dentist'. Then the fucker skipped bail and showed up in Athens and we gave him a job. And why not? Not like we can hire normal cunts.

I'm gonna have Lenny pull up round back at six, I tell him.

Right so, he says, all chirpy.

Whistles as he works, he does.

Right so, I say.

I head into the office and open the safe and pull out papers and a bunch of IDs. I scan the lot and put it all on an encrypted drive and close it up tight. Fucken Hugo. I wouldn't bother with it but he insists on it. I'm gonna have to start doin this soon as they come through the door, so's I don't have this stuff sittin round too long. Even locked in the safe, I'm skittish with it. I toss it all in a plastic bag and tie it. Then I make a couple of calls to our restaurants, make sure they know they got a delivery comin in later. All kosher.

I go back upstairs and call Lenny over and give him the plastic bag.

Go out back and burn this, I tell him.

OK boss, he says. *Basss. Oh-K Basss.*

Canadian twat, he goes to sit back down.

Now, I tell him.

He fucks off out back.

Sweeney's lurkin in the corner with his sweaty cat. Strokin it. Honestly, I'm fucken tired of him treatin this place like a shelter. Time for a no-pet rule in here.

Leave that filthy beast at home next time, I tell him.

Sukie's no filthy beast, he says. He hugs her.

*Sukie*. I shake my head. I look over at Lorelei but she's ignorin me completely. Perhaps it's time for a little afternoon delight. I know what to do. I go over to the jukebox and throw in fifty cents. I know just the song to get her hot.

Filthy harmonica plays. I walk in behind the bar and come up beside her.

*She's the demon child...*

She slaps me across the face with her small, hard hand.

*Sweet Lorelei. I know all your cues. I'll take you upstairs and make everything alright again. Ready for some primal screamin?*

Filthy harmonica is the thing.

*...Crawl a million miles*
*To see your dirty smile*
*She's the demon child...*

# 17

# Argentinian Beef

About six that evenin, Lenny pulls the van round back. I'm goin out on the delivery with him to natter with a few clients. Lorelei's holdin the bar with all the freaks.

We load the van with our finest five-day cured steak and head out into Athens. Crawlin, cloying Athens.

We got two restaurants sellin our product in the city: one right here in Psiri, one in Piraeus. Here in Psiri it's the Byzantine. The Byzantine is run by Michalis. We head over, where Michalis is settin tables for the evenin turn.

Michalis, I say, stop sendin me orders by text. We talked about this.

Michalis is fat and Greek. He's also kinda old school. I sat for two hours one afternoon and explained how to use encrypted messaging but he's still sendin me fucken texts.

Michalis tells me to stop breakin his balls.

Michalis, you text me askin me to send you kilos of this and kilos of that, you'll have the fucken law on me quicker than you can say *soudsoukakia*.

Michalis laughs, thinks I'm hilarious.

I'm fucken serious Michalis, do like I showed ya to do.

Michalis says *Ne ne ne…*

Yes yes yes, Michalis, just do like I showed ya.

*Old Greek bastard.*

We drop off the meat and head down to Piraeus.

Down in Piraeus, it's a place called Swim. Classy place, got a pool on the roof and a view out over the sea. Place is run by a proper Greek lothario, real sleazy prick called Adonis. Adonis is a piece of work. Like a bronzed and greasy Aids Joyce, but with an oily sex appeal. I've eaten here a coupla nights and it's obscene watchin him work. Shirt open, hand-feedin meat to the ladies, suckin on his fingers. May as well be rubbin his balls on the food for all the subtlety he has. I think he's a rank bastard, but the people who eat there seem to like it. Plus he's well-connected, so I can't tell him to fuck off. I suspect he'll be of some use to us, so I hide any feelins I have against him.

*Kalos irthatei*, he says when we go in.

Lenny carts our product off to the kitchen.

Adonis, I say, you're cleanin up. We can't keep up with you. The meat's just flyin outta this place.

They can't get enough of my meat, he says.

*Sure, Adonis, sure. We know you love throwin your meat around. We've seen you work.*

This is it for two days. No more til Friday, I tell him.

We have the Germans comin Friday. We'll need a delivery Friday afternoon, he says.

The German bankers. Ever since the takeover of Greece, the German bankers are callin the shots. They're the ones with the clout. They eat what they like, and they like to eat human flesh.

You'll have eighty kilos, I tell him. You need anything speciality?

If the IMF people show we'll need a couple of hearts, he says.

One of those IMF pigs loves to feast on human heart. He goes through two or three a month, the sick fuck. At ten grand a piece we don't care. Hearts alone pay for our weekly overheads. Medically, you can get up to a million for a heart in some countries, but when you take the heart of a fat fuck

140

or a drug addict then the medical value is non-existent. Still, people will pay to eat it. We could probably charge three times that and they'd still go for it.

We got a couple, I say. You'll have em Friday. Want some kidney or liver too?

Why not, Adonis says.

See you Friday, I say.

You don't have a drink? he says.

Nah, Adonis. I got work to do, I say.

See you man.

*See you Friday, you greasy cocksmith.*

\*

**Location:**
*Screamin Pope, Athens*
**Time:**
*20.20, Wednesday*
**Present:**
*Lorelei: succubus, tease*
*Ducasse: transcendental whoremonger*
*Foxy Maffia: frightenin fucken shemale*
*Lenny Sack: useless cunt*
*Sweeney: another useless cunt*

Back in the bar, Lorelei is takin care of a table of four Argentinians. They're well-juiced and gettin a bit pawsy for my likin, so I'm gettin ready to go over and say somethin when Ducasse walks through the door. Eyes red and twitchy, he looks hunted. Like he hasn't slept for three days.

Hugo's lookin for ya, I say.

I can tell he's wired so I throw a glass and a bottle in front of him. He rips into it, no hesitation.

Where the fuck you been?

He explains he fell down the rabbit hole at Madame Zhu's, whatever that means.

What does that mean? I say.

So Madame Zhu's girls, he says, pumped him full of *salvia divinorum* and hooked him up to some sex machine, and while he's gettin rid by this machine the salvia causes a tear in the passage of time, so that he's just spent a full year gettin fisted by a big black rubber hand. Swears to me a whole year has passed.

Hugo lost you three days ago, I say.

A year, he swears. Spent the first week in a kind of spasmodic ecstasy, the next three weeks in excruciating pain, slept for a full week, then had three months of intense meditation after which he attained a kind of enlightenment. Proper enlightenment, he stresses. The last eight months were passed in a stupor of suicidal boredom. The dildo is still hammerin away, mind, all this time, every second of his gone year, he says. Says his hole feels like a drainpipe.

I'm laughin at the prick but he's deadly serious. Tells me he spoke with Christ during his transcendental phase.

While you had the fist up your hole? I say.

He's gettin prickly, thinks I'm laughin at him.

Sri Sai Baba, I say, bowing down over the bar.

Go fuck yourself, he says.

Glad to see enlightenment paid off, I say.

Prick.

Ducasse is back. I call Hugo and tell him.

Tell him I need him back here, Hugo says.

He'll need a day or two.

Just send him up here.

Right so.

Ducasse is watchin Lorelei run around the bar.

Keep your hands off, you degenerate, I tell him.

Anywhere I can get an hour's sleep? he asks.

I throw him a set of keys. Up above, I say.

Cheers. See you in an hour.

Been through an ordeal, he has, I've no doubt about it.

As he's walkin out, in walks Foxy Maffia, one of our

shemale regulars. Where one goes they all go, and we get em all.

Foxy Maffia is a big black shemale of uncertain origin. We're not sure if she's black-Asian, or some queer blend of Latina, or some other freak mixture, and in fact we don't really give a fuck. Most call her Black Foxy when she's not around, and Foxy when she is. We like her but she scares us. She killed a man, and we know this cause Kostas helped her get rid of the body. She tends to attract small men with a chip on their shoulder. Small men who have control issues, small men with fragile egos. Lookin at her, you'd have no trouble picturin her beatin a man to death. She's big and mean. Muscular. Hands like vises. But mostly she's sweet with me. She sits down at the bar.

Heya sweetheart, she says.

Hey Foxy. Usual?

Sure, baby.

*Sweetheart. Baby*. All the usual talk, which I dig.

Whatcha doin?

Night off, she says.

We're in trouble, then, I say.

Nah, baby, I'm keepin it quiet tonight.

Good for you, honey.

I don't believe a word of it. She'll be goin batshit with the rest of em by ten. I throw down a coaster and place a gimlet in front of her.

You heard about Luna? she says.

No, I tell her.

Luna's a friend of hers. They share a flat.

Locked up, she tells me.

For soliciting?

Possession, she says.

Of what?

Two grammes.

Fuck.

Greek police are cunts for drugs charges. Three to five

years on possession.

She got a lawyer?

What do you think?

I knew the answer before I asked the question. Luna's Mexican, in the country illegally, livin hand to mouth. Maybe they'll deport her. Could be a good thing.

Across the bar, the four Argentinians are gettin rowdy. I nod over. You know any of em? I say to Foxy.

She looks over her shoulder, shakes her head.

One of the Argentinians has his hands on Lorelei, gropin at her. She comes back over with the glasses.

Hey look, I say, you stay in here behind the bar. Anything needs lifted from the table, I'll do it.

It's fine, she says, all Athenian and ballsy like.

One of em at the table is a big cunt. Ducasse has gone upstairs. Anything kicks off it's just me and a couple of ladyboys. Lenny's at the bar, but he's a big streak of Canadian piss. Sweeney, forget about it. He'll fucken run. Still, Foxy might have my back if any shit starts.

Someone's put on some mambo and everyone's a bit frisky. Half the shit in this place starts over the music. We'd nearly be better gettin rid of the fucken jukebox. Maybe I should just control the show from a laptop here behind the bar. Throw on a couple of playlists, end of story.

But I quite like readin customer's moods through their choice of tunes. It writes the story of the afternoon, or evenin, ya know? Everyone's pain, wide open. Weepin through the speakers.

I head over to the Argentinians' table to clear away some plates. They've eaten, but not our meat. We don't serve the good stuff to the blow-ins. We keep the freezer stocked with regular burgers and so on for the walk-ins. Our stuff is for clientele. The ones who know.

Where's the lil puta? one of the Argies says.

I look the cunt in the eye. *Keep still*, I tell myself. *Walk away*.

Finish your drinks, I say, indicatin the glasses on the table.

That's your last.

I go out to the kitchen and dump the plates. Lorelei's hangin out with Foxy, comparin nails all innocent like, ass in tight shorts and pierced nipples showin through the veneer of her blouse, blissfully ignorin the fire she's just lit at the table of Latinos, if you can call Argentinians Latinos. I squeeze her ass as I pass, realisin my mistake almost immediately. They're all watchin.

Hey Lenny, I say, you see that fire extinguisher behind you?

Yeah…

Those four cunts are about to kick off. If I go for one of em you gotta take that thing and spray the fuck outta the others. You got it?

He nods.

You sure? I say. Cause he's sittin there lookin at me all wide-eyed and dumb and Canadian-like.

I got it, he says.

But I write off Lenny.

One of the Argies is up swingin his hips, the way only a Latino guy can.

I look over at Foxy, she's lookin at me and I can see this is happenin. It's already happened in my head and now it's happenin, like I'm writin the trajectory of the thing.

The Latino is slouchin towards the bar.

Sure, I coulda said somethin different and it probably wouldn't be goin down like it is.

He's up against the bar and he's shoutin at Lorelei. Hey *bay-bee*, come dance with me, he says.

Probably could've avoided the whole thing if I had any kind of awareness.

He reaches over the bar and grips Lorelei's wrist.

No undoin it now. I swing a fist at the guy. I don't have a big fist but I have a little trainin and enough power. Nevertheless, I've been drinkin all day and I miss his temple which I was goin for. I catch him square in the neck, but there's enough clout to stun him. Over his head I see the others move. I've lifted one of those big ceramic ashtrays off the bar and I'm holdin it in my hand. I don't move until I see the cunt six feet from me and I fling it at his head. But the big cunt behind him is over me, and right before he floors me with that thick arm I hear a slap, an almighty slap, like *thwaaaaap!* A sound like a grenade in a foxhole. Foxy has cracked the guy and he hits the floor. Two are down and two are movin over the floor, and I look over at Lenny and he's fiddlin with the safety pull on the extinguisher, daft Canadian prick. The big one is conscious on the floor but is unable to get up, and he's wrapped his arms around my legs and I can't move. I feel a fist hit the back of my head, now I'm goin down too. I grip the first prick as I fall and he comes down with me. Then Lenny, bare fuckwit, has the safety off and we're gettin lashed, all of us: me, Foxy, the Argies, Lorelei, all gettin covered in clouds of thick, snowy anti-inflammable.

You fucken eejit, I scream.

Mambo pounds dully in my ears.

Then I hear a thrilled scream and a dull thud. I look up, and Ducasse is above me swingin a black club — could be a sex toy or a police truncheon, I've no idea, but it's game over either way. I hear skulls crack.

# 18

# Hearts

This wasn't how I pictured my Wednesday goin.

Now we've got four tourists tied to chairs in the back room in various states of consciousness. One of em is out cold, and I'm not sure if he's already dead or just in a deep and bruised sleep. Ducasse has pumped them full of barbiturates, so they're pretty docile. Lifeless. Problem is, what the fuck do we do with em now?

Ducasse is for killin em.

Look man, I tell Ducasse, we can still dump em out on the street and they'll wake up with a sore head and a broken skull and fuck off to the islands for some R'n'R. Chalk it up to a rough night.

You wanna take that chance? he says.

We've all got in a scuffle before, I say. You wake up, you try n'forget it and you go about mendin your bruised ego. End of story. You don't go to the cops and file a complaint, I tell him.

That mighta worked before I filled em with Seconal.

Then why the fuck did you pump em full of meds?

I was thinkin on my feet, he tells me.

This is the kind of thinkin I should've come to expect from people with longstanding and dedicated drug habits.

I'm callin Kostas, I say.

There's no need.

Fuck there isn't.

I call Kostas. Wanna come down here help us with somethin? I say.

Twenty minutes later he's in the room with us. Me, him and Ducasse. I explain the situation. Ducasse explains the situation in a different way. Kostas lights a cigarette, all quiet like.

*Gamoto*, he says.

*Fuck it* is right.

Kostas explains we got two choices: we can take the four pricks and throw em in the back of the van, and drive em down to Patras and dump em on a street corner. They wake up, freak the fuck out, make their way to the embassy in Athens and get the fuck outta the county. That comes with its own risks. You gotta make sure they remember *nothin*, or else someone's gonna come lookin. There's only so much Kostas can do. Or, he says, you kill em all.

Me and Ducasse are lookin at each other. He's murdered before, I know it, but it's not my bag. I'm no killer.

Give us a minute Kostas, will ya? Ducasse says.

*Ne re file*, he says. He goes out.

Look, I know what you're gonna say, Ducasse tells me, but I'm not gettin in a van and drivin to Corinth with four drugged Argentinians in the back.

What's the problem? We drive all over Athens every day with drugged fuckers in the van, I say.

Why make the work for yourself? Look, you've got four good meaty cunts here — that big one alone's gotta be a hundred-forty kilos. Why you makin a thing outta this? Just take em out to the shop, hook em up to the drip, then in three days turn them into steak.

These are not some strays from the back streets, these are tourists. These guys are gonna be missed. Cunts are gonna come lookin, I say.

Fine, he says. Tomorrow mornin I'll go down the port and buy four tickets in their names to Rhodes. I'll even use their
148

own credit cards. When cunts come lookin, they're gonna go lookin in Rhodes. For all anyone knows, they fucked off to Turkey after. Whadda we care?

He's got a point, too. He makes it seem easy. And speakin of weight, I'm doin the sums in my head and from what I can see of em there's about four hundred kilos of prime Argentinian beef right here — allowin for loss, that works out at about a hundred grand, thirty per cent of which is mine directly. I'm learnin quickly that it's often wise to let the numbers do the talkin, and this may well be one of those times.

Fine, I say. Let's get em out back and hook em up.

Good man. Probably best we don't share this with Hugo, he says.

*I figured.*

We take em out back. All our beds are occupied, so Ducasse lays out some pallets and we lay the Argies down and Ducasse goes to work with the pentobarbital. When we've got em all in a coma, Culhannan takes out the pineals then we start em on the MDMA drip. In forty-eight hours we'll kill em with a superdose, cure em, then feed em to our clientele. All my time here, I don't recall servin up an Argie before. That protein-rich diet — I'm curious to see how they taste. They are famous the world over for their beef. There's some kinda poetry in that, I'd say.

*Fucken Wednesday.*

Friday.

Friday's deliveries are prepared by Culhannan, hearts n'all, and delivered by Lenny. Saturday night is Feast night like in every other Screamin Pope across Europe, so I tell Culhannan we gotta prepare some cuts — ribs n'the like. But first we gotta spike the four Argies. Forty-eight hours on the drip, then they're ready to be topped. We do it like this: the drips are filled with about 5000mg of MDMA, which is way more than you need to kill a man, but don't forget we're creatin our own product in the process so it's very important the body

149

is flooded with all the right chemicals at this stage. Over the course of a single hour, the body is drip fed this stupefying shot of heaven right into the vein. Often cunts wake up on the bed all disco like, goin boogaloo. Sometimes we gotta administer the kicker early, the kicker bein a heavy dose of Lidocaine to stop the heart dead. If the cunt hasn't woken up, this goes into the arm about an hour after we start the MDMA drip, but if they go disco this needs to happen right off. You can't be tryin to oversee a delicate medical procedure to six bodies you got in a heightened state of pharmaceutical conditioning if one is poppin off and gettin his seizure on, causin a ruckus — you gotta put a stop to that shit. Lotta money on the table here. You take your eyes off the ball for a second and your meat is irreparably degraded. It's a delicate process, the last hour. So Culhannan is preppin the tubes and the drip bags while I double check they're all secured, ya know, that the straps are tight and they're not gonna go boppin mid-procedure.

They're all set. The four Argies are still vegetating on pallets at the back of the room, and now we got four Greeks and two Senegalese sisters on the beds. The two sisters were a fluke, but the Greeks are plentiful. Not cause we're in Greece, which helps, but the financial crisis gutted the country. Cunts up and down the land are on the precipice of fallin into unsustainable drug habits, so we've had no problem keepin our fridges full here in Athens.

Our biggest headache has been the archaic drug legislation. So far, we been drivin the MDMA down from the Dam. Aids Joyce puts a shipment together, mostly liquid. You can ship a half million milligrams of liquid ecstasy in five or six bottles of water, nobody knows a fucken thing. The problem is the pills. Pills are hard to hide, and we need pills, ya know, for our own recreational use. We're stuffin the upholstery of the car with it right now but that's a gamble. Trick is as old as it gets, and it wouldn't stand up to serious inspection. We've been okay so far but we need to change up strategy. Aids Joyce is gonna fly down in a few weeks so we can set up our own operation here in the city. Until then we're shippin it. We got a crazy cunt called Bo Schizzer drives down in a single run. Twenty-six hours from the Dam to Athens loaded on speed and Red Bull and probably Molly too, though for me it's never been a good drug for drivin. He pulls in, drops off his load, sleeps for twelve hours straight then drives right back.

The other problem with the drug laws is our houses are always bein raided. To that end, I've come up with a genius fucken plan that I'm gonna run by Hugo.

They all tight? Culhannan says.

All strapped, I tell him.

He's down close to the arm of one of the Senegalese girls, makin like he's checkin the needle, but I'm pretty sure he's sniffin her. Fuck knows what he's been up to with these two girls the last few days on his own.

I'm gonna flick the switch, he says.

He means he's gonna start the drip.

Go ahead, I tell him.

Interestin, watchin a body in a medically-induced coma get pumped full of MDMA. I mean, they're already full of MDMA, but now they're gettin dosed proper. First you see a high degree of rapid eye movement. Then the body will start a kinda sensual tremble, and maybe some groanin, and cunts like Culhannan are probably lovin this. It's highly sexual. Then the body gets to sweatin, and when the body temperature rises it's usually at this point that cunts will wake up outta the coma if they're gonna and we've gotta put out the lights. But those last moments, I believe, are happy. Gentle at first, with a kind of sensual ecstasy, then rising to an indescribable euphoria... then the all-consuming and unforgiving darkness. Lights out. *Time to go, Papi, but it was a helluva ride...*

And then they're nothin but meat for the cleaver.

Back in the food chain, all protein and gristle. Fat, calcium, plasma and water. What's a human more than this?

Nothin.

My phone rings. It's Lenny. He says we got a problem here.
Where? I say.

Down at Swim, he says.

Fuck it. I'm on my way, Lenny, I tell him.

I drive down. It's before openin so nobody's in there yet.
Lenny's standin with Adonis at the back, havin it out over the
trays of product.

You gonna leave those sittin out here? It's thirty degrees
out, I say.

Look man, says Adonis, I ask you for three hearts, and I
only got two here. I got a big party comin tonight and I need
three.

Naw man, Adonis, you asked me for two.

I say three, man.

Now, I was drunk Wednesday but I wasn't high. I remember
well.

What you said, Adonis, was a couple o'hearts. A couple is
*two*, not three.

Naw man, he says. A couple, like, three.

Fuck it, Adonis — say you got two people been datin for a
few months, or, they been married a while, what do you call
em?

A couple?

Exactly, man. Not three, or four. It's a couple. *Two*. Now, had
you said *several*, we could probably quibble over semantics…

A couple, several, he's shoutin, wavin his arms about now
in that Greek way designed to blind you with theatrics. I need
a heart, he says.

Adonis, man, you're just gonna have to get creative with
the cuts. I lift the cover on the tray. Look, there's about six
hundred grams of heart there, you just gotta play around a
bit. Next time you need three hearts, you tell me you need
three hearts. Not a couple. Or two. *Three*.

*Gamoto re malaka*, he says.

Cunt is gettin testy.

There's another thing, he says.

*Of course there is.*

One of my customers get sick, man, she go to hospital last night. What is this, man? You not checking your product?

Hold on now, Adonis, how the fuck do you know she got sick from the meat? Did she even eat our meat? Maybe she had seafood.

No man, she had your steak, he explains. Wife of the French Ambassador, too, *re*, not just any woman.

Fuck it, Adonis, I don't know what to tell you, but we have very strict quality control on our product. We check everything. How the fuck do we know one of your cooks isn't jerkin off in the steak sauce?

*How do we know you're not jerkin off into the sauce, you greasy pervert?*

*Ela re malaka*, I got the best people work here, and no one is fucking with my sauce.

Okay Adonis, I say, you got a sample of the steak she ate?

Adonis goes into the kitchen and comes back with a carton. I take it.

I'll have this tested first thing tomorrow, I tell him.

I can't have people gettin sick in my restaurant, he says.

I'm on it, man. I'm on it. And maybe get this into the fridge, I tell him.

Three trays of meat still sittin out on a table. This is how food gets tainted.

*Ne re*, he says.

*Fucken prick.*

Come on Lenny, let's get back, I say.

We head back.

*

*Location:*
*Screamin Pope, Athens*
*Time:*
*20.30, Friday*
*Present:*
*Foxy Maffia: shemale sex-worker in search of career change*
*Culhannan: Sex Dentist, failed romantic*
*Lenny Sack: streak-of-piss Canadian*
*Sweeney: self-abuser and patron saint of lost animals*
*Lorelei: moody nymphet*

Now I'm kinda wound up and I take to the raki. I feel it comin on, a silent, livid drunkenness. I can't stay here.

Hey Foxy, I say, you got a minute?

We sit down at a table.

Wanna job?

Doin what? she says.

Here. Bar work, I tell her.

She laughs. Honey, bar work don't pay enough.

A hundred a night, I say, then tips. A good night you walk away with three hundred. And you don't even have to suck any cocks.

She's smilin. Three hundred a night is good fucken money in this city post-collapse.

She thinks about it. Okay, she says.

I smile. Foxy on the bar. I like it. She's got a big hand and an efficient way of dealin with assholes. She'll be bouncer, too. Nobody'll start any shit with her here.

Go n'have another drink, Foxy, then pitch in with Lorelei.

Job done. Night off for me.

Mornin to night dealin with pricks, that's what you get when you strike out on your own. Everyone's a prick when it comes down to it. Now that I think about it, I was happy drivin around the Dam in my little white van filled with carcasses. Nobody fucked with me. Nobody broke my balls. A few grand in my pocket every month. I gotta ask myself, is it worth it, the stress? I'm makin coin, but fuck, dealin with cunts from mornin to night is takin its toll.

I take to a corner with my raki and survey the bar.

Some black tune plays, but I know it's me — it's me that's black. Everything else is dark when you are. I sink into my black mood as I survey the cunts at the bar. Culhannan is tryin to chat up some girl, and I watch with rising ire the seduction technique of a seasoned sex fiend. Women get a sense of these things and I'm sure she kens he's a wrong'un. She's tilted back in her chair, like tryin to keep her distance. Maybe it's the rapey vibe, maybe it's the aroma of meat, and not like Hugo — Hugo's odours have a seductive barbecue charm about em, but Culhannan just smells metallic and bloody. Not a winning perfume. Not sure it matters. Cunts like Culhannan got all kinds of tricks up their sleeves. Rohypnol, if all else fails. He'll find a way.

Lenny's over sittin with Sweeney in the corner again. Two rare ones. My blood boils lookin at both of em.

My blood boils up in me and I squeeze my glass like a stress ball. I swallow the firewater and hiss through my teeth at its warm anger.

Then I see Sweeney's cat at his legs. And another in his hands. A kitten. Now he's takin the piss. I get up and walk over. Look, I start to say, and I see it's not one but two kittens he's holdin in his arms. Look, you queer fiend, this isn't an animal shelter we're runnin, leave your cats at home next time you come in. We serve food here.

Sweeney's ballin somethin about strays, and kittens in bins, and *blah blah*.

I don't give a fuck, I tell him, knowin full well if he opens his mouth again I'm gonna smash it in.

But *blah blah*, he says, and he's opened his mouth and now I grip him by the lapel of his jacket and pull him off his stool. The kittens scarper. I throw him to the floor and smash him in the face and feel very fucken good about it too. So I do it again. Pretty soon I've lost it and his face is quickly turnin to pulp under the hot smack of my fist.

It's Foxy that pulls me off. I knew I did the right thing hirin her. Lorelei's come up beside Foxy and she's hittin me now, but she's only wee and I don't feel it, nor do I pay her any attention.

Let's go take a breath, Foxy says.

I got it Foxy, leave me be. I got it.

I drain the raki on my table with all them cunts lookin at me. Sweeney's still bleedin on the floor when I walk out the door.

Air.

Not the cool air of Amsterdam. Hot, thick, sweaty air. A humming air. Not an air to clear your mind. Not an air to make anything better.

I walk. All over. Just walk and walk. Psiri. Omonia. Kerameikos. Metaxourgheio. Exarcheia. Likavittos. Kolonaki. I walk in the hot, dark night of Athens, climbin deeper down into myself as I do, feeling the night close around me like a hot wet cowl.

I walk deeper into the hard, hot city, finding myself on lost city streets, the people of Athens passing soullessly, lookin at nothin.

On a bleak and anonymous concrete avenue, I stop outside one building, the door black, the windows lit softly in a burgundy light. It's the only colour that can comfort me on this night. Don't ask me how I know it, but I've found Madame Zhu's. I just fucken know it.

I knock on the door, and it's answered.

# 19

# Madame Zhu's, Again

I sink into a plush burgundy sofa with thick cushions. Some scent permeates the air, Asian in its muskiness, sickening its sweet perfume.

She tells me to sit and wait, so I'm waitin.

I feel like I've come back to some ancient home. The wanderer returned, all prodigal like.

Holy music from the walls.

Damask and bamboo. She knows, Madame Zhu.

*She knows what we need, does Madame Zhu…*

A little incantation forms in my head, and soon I'm reciting some mystical mantra, concerned only with burgundy perfume and Madame Zhu. Burgundy perfume? Colours and smells colliding already, and I haven't even imbibed any of her sweet poisons yet. *I'm comin, Madame Zhu…*

A woman descends the stairs, one of her many women, and to my disappointment it's not one of the Ethiopian sisters from before. She's black this girl, right enough, blacker than I've ever seen a woman, but not round and soft like the sisters. She's thin, clad in a very stiff kimono, and the effect is almost comical so clichéd it seems, but she's not laughin and so I don't either. She's serious. *I'm in for some serious business, I see. Madame Zhu's is not a place you get what you want. Madame Zhu's is a place you get what you came for. That's why you're here.*

She holds out her hand and I stand up and take it.

*Lead me.*

I follow her upstairs.

She takes me into the bathing room and leaves me. I know what to do. I strip, I climb in. A hot bath.

*Madame Zhu knows what you need.*

I drift off for a bit, and when I wake there's a girl in the bath, no more than a child, and she's cleaning me gently. The child has the eyes of sorrow, the eyes of sorrow, and I cannot look at her and I close my eyes and weep gently. I have so many things to tell you, child of sorrow, but I do not know how. Instead I will weep and die inside. I die inside and then I sleep some more.

I sleep some more and when I wake I think Hugo is next to me in the bath, but I know it can't be, so I sleep some more.

I feel the water grow cold and I climb out.

As I do the kimono girl returns, dries me, takes me by the hand and leads me down a darkened corridor. I can't see. She is my eyes and I follow her. We enter a room, dark but for the burgundy perfume, and I am laid on a great bed, soft from sorrow.

The bed of sorrows.

*Madame Zhu knows what you need.* Damask and bamboo, Madame Zhu…

A boy in a loincloth comes and lies next to me on the bed, speaking in a tongue I don't understand. He takes a pipe, lights it, and invites me to inhale. I do. I inhale from the pipe, the dark pipe on the bed of sorrows, and the smoke fill my lungs. That smoke, filled with damask and bamboo, and burgundy perfume, and sorrow and sorrowful children, and deep eyes of sorrow; and musk and ire and bloody fists, and the flat smell of paper money and the hardness of freshly-starched kimonos, and of Madame Zhu; and of small unwashed kittens that rot in trash bins, and of the metallic burgundy of plasma cells, and the sweat of Greek lotharios and the pumping of arteries; and semen and barbecue and unspent passions, all these, and everything else, I inhaled. I sucked it deep into my gut and I began to dissolve from the core out. I dissolved in the bed of sorrows, and the boy was gone, for you can only be alone on the bed of sorrows.

*Damask and bamboo…*

I saw it, then, the emptiness of mantras, and I laughed out loud. I saw the emptiness of religion and I laughed louder. I saw the emptiness in morality and patience and goodness, and I wept softly.

*She knows what we need, Madame Zhu…*

Some bitter poison climbed up in me, from my gut to my throat, clawed its way up my trachea and it shot out of me in a great ejaculation of vomit. With it I felt the bile, the anger and the sorrow rise up: bitter, metallic and bloody it spilled out of me, and I felt cleansed. I, the prodigal.

I had no more tears and no more bile, and no more sorrow, so I slept some more. Maybe I slept for an hour or a day, or possibly a week, I cannot say. The bed of sorrows held me and I slept in its cloying embrace, for is there a finer bed than sorrow?

No, there is not. That is why we go with living.

After a week in the bed I rolled onto the floor, and the child with the eyes of sorrow took my hand and led me out of the room and down a long hall, and into a room where I sat on a great and comfortable chair. I watched a man, who was Death, play chess against another man who was Sorrow. The game continued for one thousand years and Sorrow was the victor, and I understood he would always be the victor, for Death was hollow and Sorrow was gargantuan, fed on the dead souls of a billion.

The game over, I watched the feast of seven unholy men and seven raging women; they ate the meat of the living, plucked from the bodies of mothers and children. Meat was their food and tears their wine, and sorrow was the music that the orchestra played, the walls all damask and bamboo, the smell a burgundy perfume.

The perfume of the tears made me giddy, and the fourteen heard me giggle and invited me to their feast, but I could not eat for I was sated on sorrow.

Instead I retreated to a corner where a small boy was torturing a puppy. In his eyes was the purest joy.

As he went about his work he sang a sweet song, which may have been the words of the Bible but could have been the Decameron, I do not know. The beauty of his song caused the puppy's demise.

I left the boy with his dead puppy and found a window box, in it a man and a woman making love, a love drenched in the song of sorrows. They looked in each other's eyes and I held both their hands, and I felt the power of their union, but knew too that their progeny would be stillborn. I left them to their joy, for it would not last.

I found an old man under a tree by a bend in a stream, holding the bleeding heart of his dead wife in his lap. He had a single tooth in his head and he laughed a grating laughter which made the hairs on my neck stand on end. He dropped the heart into the stream and it was carried off into the eternal sadness, sadness which is tainted with the screeching laughter of crows. The old man took a pipe from his shawl, lit it and handed it to me, and how could I refuse, for how many thousands of years had it been since I'd had something to smoke? I smoked. The old man nodded and took his pipe, and handed me a knife, the very knife which I'd seen Hugo use to cut his flesh for the jade woman. I buried it in my robe.

At the foot of a mountain I found the gnarled bust of a Roman general with the name Lascivious, whose real name was Nero or perhaps Caligula. A small boy, not much bigger than a baby, was pissing on the head. From far off I heard the old man laugh. I felt I should piss on the head too, so I did, and me and the boy we pissed together and laughed, laughter tinged with the tears of besmirched virgins.

*Virgins*. Where are all the virgins? I said out loud to the stream, the stream where sailed the hearts of old women towards the great ocean of mockery.

And I was granted eighty virgins then and there, like a holy soldier of Allah. *Ask and ye shall receive…*

Eighty virgins were given to me, but I dismissed them, for they were dressed in robes of meat, and I no longer had the stomach for meat. Give me smoke and silk, and virgins of burgundy perfume…

*Burgundy perfume.*

In a room of yellow silk I lay down on a bed with a one-legged whore. She spoke to me like a mother so we didn't make the beast with two backs. Instead we looked into each other's eyes, and there I saw grief.

I am sorry I bore you, she said.

I forgive you, I told her.

I climbed a mountain where I found the cave of Plato. It was empty but for a table with a solitary glass of wine. I drank, for how many thousands of years had it been since I'd had a glass of wine?

It was bitter and full of canker.

I went down the mountain to find the old man by the stream, but he was gone, so I followed the stream that had carried his dead wife's bleeding heart towards the open ocean. It led me to a beach where two crones were beating each other with sticks for the right to the hearts. Each stood on a pile of hearts that reached the sky, and I left them to their petty quarrels for I found them droll and barbaric. I pushed a small raft out into the sea and soon was on the bitter green ocean, and there was no wind and I found myself adrift in nothingness. I thought to be free on the ocean, and here I was stuck in the wide Sargasso Sea. I was blown towards land by the acrid breath of the spurned virgins, and to my despair I found myself back in the bed of sorrows.

No, I cried, this is not my lot!

But I knew that it was.

I lay down with the sweet boy in the loincloth and now he administered myrrh and sandalwood to my body, and I understood I was being prepared for burial.

Must we? I asked the boy. I wept.

He did not reply, but lovingly applied the funerary oils to my body. He gave me a pipe to smoke, and I smoked, then I sank into a meditative silence for around one thousand years.

When I awoke, I was raised up on the shoulders of virgins and carried to the great arid plains of the Towers of Silence. I lay still and unmoving, carried across those plains by the whispers of virgins, whispers that spoke of blood and sand and the dust of bones. The whispers carried me on the soft winds, across the plains and up the Tower, where I was laid on the stone with the sky above me and the earth below. Eighty virgins kissed me on the forehead, then took my knife and cut my skin so that the metallic burgundy scent of my blood rose up into the sky. The virgins disappeared with a soft whisper, a whisper that said,

*'You came like water, and like wind you go…'*

I wept, the water of my tears melding with the blood from my veins, and a river poured down the spiral stairs of the tower and into the red earth. As the river ran so the great vultures appeared, circling above my head, brought to by the scent of fresh carrion.

Is this all I am? I cried. Carrion? Meat?

And I knew the truth of it and laughed bitterly as the first lumps of flesh were torn from my body. I was carried piece by piece skyward on the wind, and I saw my dissolution in the eyes of the vultures. Their eyes were resentful. The last of my body flew towards the heavens, and I heard it, the last cry of the virgins whose job was done and for whom there was no more sorrow, and they said,

*'Go like the wind…'*

I arose from my bed of stone and I descended to the red earth and I followed the wind, across the great plains of silence to Persepolis, where I felt the urge to dig up the great kings of the earth, but I could not, for I no longer had hands or fingers to claw the red soil.

I sailed on with the wind through the great cities of the earth, through Bukhara and Samarkand, on through Osh and Kashgar and across the Hindu Kush and the Himalayas to Mansarovar in the shadow of Meru, where all things dissipate in the cold desert wind, even souls and sorrow. I let it go there, my soul... a dust devil spun and was gone, with it my soul. I saw it disappear in the dusty air.

*Like wind...*

*Ego.*

That is all that's left of me now. I wander the earth, bodyless and soulless.

I've seen every corner and crevice, every wrinkle and fold, every run and rivulet of the earth's steaming husk. Nothing is left for me to discover. I've traipsed all over this foul, scabbed corpse, and know it's origin as well as its destiny. I know where it's going, where it's all headed. I've heard it in the susurrus of the stream and in the whisper of the wind, in the trees and in the pained baying of the oceans. It's a whimper, a death rattle, a cry for mercy, and it says, cries,

*Let me be.*

I hear her now, and know what she wants. We have taken all we can and are too much for her. Perhaps it is time, then.

*Let me be*, she cries.

Perhaps it is time.

# 20

# Sated

*Word is, there's a woman from back of Macau*
*ordained on Meru in the waters of the lake,*
*came forth like a daughter of the sun*
*and killed her way across the land*
*with a knife of green in her delicate hand,*
*feeding on sons and the woe of mothers.*
*Sated, she started on the daughters*
*til there were no more to spare*
*and she built a garden of bamboo and damask*
*and her bed was the dirge of the last ones,*
*the ones who saw that they were the last and no more would*
*follow*
*because there was no more need for flesh.*
*All were filled because she was sated,*
*and all we needed was burgundy perfume*
*which was her scent;*
*damask and bamboo and burgundy perfume*
*was all we needed now.*
*She gave it to us.*
*Her name was Madame Zhu.*

# Part Three

# 21

# Cunts Wanna Eat Each Other

Adonis called me up, urgent like, asked me to go down see him, so I went down.

We're sittin over a glass of raki and I'm waitin for him to get to the point, but I can see he's sizin me up for somethin. I'm waitin, while he yaks on about Greek pussy.

Yeah yeah, Adonis. Yeah.

I guess he sees me losin interest so he japs and jibbers a bit before he finally gets around to it.

So, he explains, he's got this client, see, even tells me who he is: IMF's head man here in Athens. A German. He comes here for the grub, loves a bit of human flesh. All these troika cunts knock about with each other, have dinner, socialise together, but now this IMF cat's taken a dislike to the head man of the European Central Bank here in the city, a Frenchie. They're both big fans of the Meat, Adonis tells me all proud like, and gives me a little pat on the leg, like *Kudos to you*. But now one's turned on the other. He doesn't know what's happened, maybe the Frenchie fucked the German's wife, who knows, he doesn't really care. This is where it gets sinister: the IMF cunt wants to *eat* the ECB cunt. Have him carved up like. Roast flesh. Roast French flesh. Made-to-order cannibalism. And he's asked Adonis to make it happen. Now Adonis is lookin at me, like, *Whaddaya say?*

Nothin surprises me anymore.

I sip on the raki. A cool breeze blows in off the port and I feel fine.

Sick *malakas*, eh? Adonis says.

I shrug. These thugs have sated themselves on the blood of the Greeks, now they've turned on each other. I like it. There's some kind of poetry to it, and, ya know what? Let's fucken do it.

It'll cost, Adonis, I tell him.

He offered a hundred grand, he says.

Nah, Adonis. Nah. Tell him a quarter of a million.

Adonis's eyes narrow. And me? he says.

You get ten per cent, for puttin it together.

He protests.

Ten per cent, I say.

He blows and flaps his hands all Greek-like, but I can see the deal is done.

We'll need time to prepare. Get me all the information you can on this cunt, I tell Adonis. Where he lives, works, where he has breakfast, lunch and dinner, who he's fucking, how he gets around… all of it.

*Egine*, Adonis says.

Done.

And this whole show just got a little bit sicker.

*

*Location:*
*Screamin Pope, Amsterdam*
*Time:*
*12.40, Monday*
*Present:*
*Hugo: barman, butcher, glutton*
*Ducasse: reformed rapist, artiste*
*Sweeney: bruised wanker, nurser of grudges*
*Danglin' Jimmy: unrepentant alko*


I drive through the night and get to the Dam the next mornin. I head straight to the bar, it's just gone lunch, and Hugo is at the table behind a great tray of Meat, a tray laden with ribs, strip steak and fuck-knows-what else. There's somethin that looks like intestine but I don't know what it is and I'm not gonna ask. But the size of the cunt… Hugo has eaten himself to almost twice his previous size, all swollen, like some gargantuan, beefy meat governor. I look at Ducasse who's sittin at the bar. Ducasse looks back and shrugs, like he doesn't know what's happenin. Some kind of transformation is underway from what I can see. What that entails, I can't quite figure. Hugo doesn't get up from the table, but that's okay, since it doesn't look like he'd be quite capable. Sweeney is sat behind him at the bar, nursin a beer, a kitten, and probably a hefty grudge. He's givin me the evil eye. *Fuck him*.

There he is, Hugo says when I walk in. Our man down south.

Now now, I say, don't be gettin up.

You hungry? he says, and gestures at the tray, and I lift some steak from the tray, cause yeah, I'm a little hungry.

So tell me about Athens, he says.

Tip-top, I tell him.

That it? That's all I'm gonna get?

Well, it's hot and it's sticky, and the city's a shitshow, but business is good. Great, in fact.

You're some pup, Hugo says.

He's fillin his face as we speak.

What about you? I say, sizin him up. You've put on a few kilos since I last saw ya.

Well, he says, Ducasse has taken a lot of the weight off my shoulders, and we got a new girl on the bar.

And as he says it, Starlet walks outta the kitchen and looks at me over Hugo's shoulder. She grins. I grin. Her hand isn't as big as Foxy Maffia's but I'm sure she takes no shit. Good girl.

So what, I say — you retirin?

He shrugs. I still gotta be here, keep the cogs turnin, but I've stepped back.

He tears at a rib with his teeth then sucks on the bone.

Why not, I say, and Starlet comes over with a Black Russian and puts it on the table.

New profession? I ask.

No more suckin cocks, she says.

Not even the ones you like?

Only one, she says. At a time.

Ha!

*Good girl, Starlet.*

So, says Hugo, you had somethin you wanted to talk about?

Yeah, I say, you wanna go out back?

Here's fine, he says.

Fine. So here's my idea, I tell him. And I give him the rundown. What I wanna do is this:

Kostas has no clout over the drug squad in Athens, so our houses are gettin cracked week in week out. We got no continuity in our lines of supply, cause soon as we got one house up and runnin the pigs get a whiff of it then they're shuttin it down. We're tryin to start up houses off the bat here and there, and it's makin us sloppy. Here's how we get around it: we buy a building in Psiri and set up a bogus health clinic, paint it up all clean like, kit it out with just enough gear to make it look professional, and put a few staff in white coats in as a finishing touch. Then we advertise drug trials, you know, standard double-blind experimental pharmaceuticals, offering handsome payment for participation. We get them in the door. So we got them comin in every day for their dose, building up those MDMA levels in the system, and they're gonna fucken love that and gettin paid for it too. After a week or two or three, we put them under, and in three days it's into the fridge with em. Job done.

Hugo's lookin at me. I can see he's impressed.

What about selection? he says.

We advertise at illegal raves, dive bars, street corners... the only ones we're gonna bring in are the headbangers. First day we bring em in, we test em, check the blood. If there's anything wrong we give em a couple of hits of E and tell em to fuck off. Their job's done. The clean ones we keep, and cultivate. We can even put in a cold room, move in all the butchery, put the whole operation under one roof. A one-stop shop.

Hugo's impressed. He's fucken impressed.

Do it, he says. I'll send Ducasse down with ya for a month to help ya get set up.

Alright then.

Anything else? he says.

Nah. *Nothin he needs to know.*

Go n'tell Ducasse to pack a bag, he says.

Right-o, Hugo.

I go up and sit at the bar between Ducasse and Danglin' Jimmy. Ducasse has an art pad in front of him. He's drawin a picture of Christ.

What's got into you? I say.

He doesn't reply. He's scratchin away with his pencil.

What's gotten into him, Jimmy?

He's gone all mystic on us, says Jimmy, just sits here drawin pictures of our Lawd Jaysus all day. Had some kinda mystical experience, went to his head.

Did he now?

Aww yessir, Jimmy says.

Buy you a drink, Jimmy?

Yessir.

A whiskey for Jimmy, Starlet, I say, and it feels strange, askin Starlet for a drink. *I used to be in there.*

How's the little lady? Jimmy says.

*Lorelei?*

How do you know Lorelei, Jimmy?

Sho don' I be in the bar ev'ry Sunday night, he says.

Naw, Jimmy…

Yes Jimmy, he says. Sunday's my night off.

You get around Jimmy, I tell him.

Sure I do.

The little lady's fine, I tell him.

She's a firecracker.

Yes she is.

That lil lady put the fear o'God inta me, and me a grown-ass man.

Somethin about her, Jimmy.

Sure is.

And that's our philosophical take on Lorelei. *Sure is.* Ducasse is still scratchin away at his portrait.

Me and you's goin to Athens, I say.

He looks up from his pad. Oh yeah?

Yeah, I say. We're gonna build a hospital.

Jimmy laughs out loud.

Yeah, I tell him, a hospital for junkies and pill-heads. With real doctors.

You fucken cracked, says Jimmy.

Yes we are, Jimmy. Hugo says to pack a bag, I tell Ducasse.

When we goin?

I'll finish my drink, sleep for an hour, then we'll hit the road, I say.

Ducasse is sniffin at me. You been to Madame Zhu's?

I nod.

I can smell it off ya, he says.

We hump it back to Athens in the car, me and Ducasse, with a load of MDMA — while we're at it, ya know? — and it's Sri

Sai Baba all the way to Dresden, at which point he pulls out his CD of Gregorian chants. There's only so much holiness you can take in a reformed rapist, particularly when you're aware he had his epiphany while strapped to a sex machine, so at Brno I tell him to take the wheel and I take two Valium and pass out.

I wake up in the Tempi Tunnel and *Ave Maria* is playing, and I think, this is it, I've passed over and I'm headin towards the dyin light, except there is no light, dyin or otherwise... but we barrel on through that tunnel and it goes on and on, me in the arms of the harp and darkness, blissfully forgetful of the fact that I'm sittin in a car with a holy rapist and enough MDMA to bring about the apocalypse. It's the tunnel, it has me, and it's never-ending.

I pass out again and wake up to the cloying dirge of Athens, and realise that heaven was nothin but a diazepam dream and that I'm back in the city that smells of suicide and semen.

We're here, says Ducasse.

*I know it.*


There's a lot to do. I need to get busy, but first I go see my little nymph. It's six in the mornin and she's wrapped up in the sheets with the fan goin above her head, and as I climb into beside her I see the hair blow gently across her cheek. She only looks happy when she sleeps, which makes me sad, kinda. But who'm I kiddin? What we got isn't really about happiness. She looks at me over her shoulder from her half-sleep and I kiss her and bite her lip. I slide my hand between her legs and she's wet, her *oh-so-sweet-Lorelei-born-of-the-sunsilver-Aegean* pussy is wet and warm, and so I slide in and we fuck. No beatings, no blood, no swearin; just sweet, tired love, and I think it's a first.

We fall asleep on the wet sheets, and I wake up alone, six hours later. Lorelei will've gone to open the bar. Me, I got shit to do. So I get showered and dressed, and Ducasse is waitin for me in the street, like he's now got access to my thoughts.

How long you been here? I say.

Just arrived.

How the fuck did you know what time I'd be up?

After twenty-four hours in a car together people get synced up, he says.

Perhaps he's right, but it's fucken creepy.

Fine, I say, let's get on this.

We got a realtor in Athens who helped us find the bar. He's up on Perikleous. We pay him a visit. Theodoros Mavromichalis. We call him Black Micky. He's a crook, but that's why we like him. We tell Micky what we need, he shows us a series of buildings that might suit our needs, we say, okay Mick, we wanna see this, this and this.

For you I get the keys, he says.

And then we're off down the back-arse of Psiri and Kerameikos lookin at dirty old buildings.

There's one, and we both agree on it. It's out behind the Athens market, an ex-dental surgery at that, and we walk in, me and Ducasse. We look at each other and without sayin anything we've agreed. Perhaps we are fucken synced after all.

The place is the ticket. It's already got a reception out front, with a long, retro-lookin counter, like somethin from the seventies, but I dig it. There's a dead starburst clock on the wall behind it. All this place needs is a lick of paint and few cunts in white coats and it'll be tickety-boo.

We look at the rest of the place. Won't take much fixin up at all. Lick o'paint here and there, a few prints on the walls, and a nice disinfectant-y smell to give that reassuring sterile vibe. I walk into one room with the old swingin dentist's light still there. Place is still kitted out with all the old machines. Some of em we can dust off and leave lyin around, make us look all medical and kosher like. The only thing we need to order is beds, and perhaps a load of sofas too. And lots of plants. We should go for a modern kinda ambience, maybe get some beanbags as well.

Beanbags, Ducasse, I say — whaddaya think about beanbags?

Fuck are you on about?

Get a load o'beanbags in, so the pricks can lie about in beanbags while they're dosed.

This isn't some kiddie day care we're runnin. We're gettin cunts in here so we can put them on the butcher's table, he says.

I know. But why not make their last days on this earth a little more comfortable? I'd be fine with movin on if I'd had a few days chillin in a beanbag whacked on MDMA. I'd be okay with that, I say.

You're too sentimental.

Well, I'm gettin beanbags.

Your place, he says.

*Fucken A.* Beanbags and potted plants, and we'll pump some Sigur Ros through the building… their last days on this earth'll be plastic and sterile, but a bit heavenly too.

So, my friends, says Black Micky, and he says 'friends' in a way you know the cunt is out to get whatever he can from ya.

So Micky, we like it and we wanna make an offer, I tell him.

One hundred and eighty? Micky says.

Nah, fuck that Micky. Make an offer of one-forty.

Are you crazy? he says.

Probably, but this is depression Athens and no way we're payin full fucken whack for the place.

Make the offer, Micky, see what comes back, I tell him.

So he does.


Two days later we've bought the place, hundred and fifty grand, and we're all set to get to work. I delegate to Ducasse and hand him the keys.

Here, you get started on the place, I tell him. I've got other shit to work on.

Like what? he says.

Just other shit. *And I do.*

Shout me if you need me, I say, and then I'm off down the port to see greasy Adonis.

We sit over a glass of raki. It's a rank day, hot like, one of those bastard oven days in Athens. Luckily Adonis is a classy cunt, so he's got those machines that blow cold droplets of water over your face, and I gotta say, that's what you need in a city like this, even if it is poncey as fuck.

Adonis has done his homework. He pushes a file, all gestapo-like, across the table. It's even got a red stamp on the front in German. I don't speak any German but for sure it says 'confidential'.

This is all very *spies-r-us*, Adonis, I say.

*Ti les?* he says.

Nothin, man. This is professional lookin. Very professional lookin, I tell him.

For the first time I'm gettin a sense of how real this is. We're gonna kill a man so some fat cunt can eat him.

I open the folder. Biography, schedules, pictures. Pictures of his home, his wife, his mistress, his cars. Very comprehensive. Security footage from inside his home, security codes for his home alarm system. Location of safe inside his home. Location of gun inside his home. *Cheeky bastard. What's he need a gun for?* There's also stuff on his staff, his doorman, his driver... it's all there.

*Right so. We're killin a man. Just to see what he tastes like.*

This is, uh, good work, Adonis, I tell him.

I sound like a prick. I don't know what to say. So I decide it'd be more professional all-round to just sit back and shut the fuck up. So I do. I sit back, arm over the back of the chair, and sip my raki and hiss through my teeth.

He'll pay fifty per cent up front, and the rest when he's on the plate, Adonis says.

I nod.

He says it should be clean.

I nod.

There'll be a diplomatic incident for sure, he says.

178

I nod. I like this, playin the bad cunt. *Hans Gruber. No. Anton Chigurh. Yeah. I kill cunts for money. That simple. Bone-chillin.*

He must disappear, Adonis says.

*We can do that. He's a fat fuck, but we'll make him disappear.*

We got just the right people for the job, I say.

Now I'm speakin in cliché.

Adonis holds up his glass. Let's drink to…

He stops mid-sentence, cause he's never done this before, and I've never done this before, and I've no idea what we should be drinkin too.

French cuisine? I say.

In poor taste, but Adonis laughs. Fuck, he roars.

To French cuisine, he says.

The clink of glasses dissipates quickly on the thick air.

We drink.

# 22

# Preparation

Ducasse works quickly. In a week he's had the place gutted, cleaned and painted. The reception has stayed pretty much the same, except for a lick of paint and a few requisite van Gogh prints, for what else says waiting room quite like van Gogh? The retro starburst wall clock is still there. Ducasse has fed it a coupla batteries and the thing still works, would ya believe.

Any music yet? I ask him.

Workin on it. There's a PA we're still tryin to get up and runnin, he says. Come out back til ya see the rest.

Three adjacent rooms have been set up with two beds apiece. Some of the old equipment has been dusted off and lies in the corner, doin nothin but lookin like it belongs there. Makes us look all medical. Stainless steel drawers for paperwork that will never be filed. Clean windows, open and bright. There's a little table between the two beds that Ducasse has placed a little bowl of Jelly Babies on. Now that's just fucken sick.

That your idea? I ask him.

He grins, nods.

Nice touch.

I gotta hand it to him, that's takin things to a new level.

Now come to ya see the rec room, he says.

Let's see it, I say.

We cross the hall. Ducasse has knocked out a dry wall, turnin two rooms into one, so we got this big, long chillout area, and whaddaya know, cunt's even thrown in a loada beanbags.

No you didn't, I say, all chuffed like.

Yeah I did, he says.

There's a TV on the wall hooked up to an X-Box. Beanbags litter the floor. Potted plants around the room, a nice scent in the air...

What's that smell? I say.

Juniper, or jasmine. I dunno, Ducasse says. We got some herbal thing burning down the end of the room there.

I like it.

Then, at the end of the room, he's installed a big one-way mirror. Right now we're lookin at our reflections in the glass.

What the fuck's that? I say.

A mirror. These cats think they're comin in here for drug trials. It's gotta seem like we're observing em. That's what that's for, he explains.

*Fuck me, he's a smart one. I'd never even considered it.*

There's a room behind there? I say.

Yep. With a fridge, a coffee machine, and a bowl of Es, he says.

A what?

A bowl of Es.

Ducasse, I say, you can't leave bowls of pills out round the gaff for any cunt walkin in.

It's not for any cunt, he says. It's for us. Me.

Whaddaya mean *you*?

Me, he says. I'll be takin a central role in the place. Administrator, like. Central command.

So what, you're gonna sit behind that big window poppin pills, watchin people pop pills?

Call it a human study, he says.

I get what he's about. He's gonna use this place as his own

182

personal playground. Get high and prey on patients to fuck. I wouldn't be surprised if I came back in a week to find his own personal sex dungeon installed. But frankly, I've got other stuff to worry about and it suits me to leave the runnin of it to him.

Nothin fucken weird, ya hear me?

Okay, he says.

I mean it. This place is for business, not pleasure. Keep your cock in your trousers.

He knows I know. Dirty bastard.

We're gonna need to double the capacity. Six a week comin through here just isn't gonna cut it, I tell him.

We're workin on the second floor as we speak, he says.

What can I say, but he's got it in hand. The place looks tip-top.

So, bout what, another week we can start bringin guests in? I say.

Should do it, he says.

Staff?

Got a couple of interviews later today, he says.

Where ya findin these cunts?

Got an ad in the paper, he says.

Ya fucken *what*?

Kiddin, he says. Black Foxy put me on to a couple of cats who're comin round to talk to us.

We can't be fillin this place with tattooed ladyboys, Ducasse. It's gotta be a professional lookin outfit. It can't be lookin like some cut-price Sokratou fuckhouse, I tell him.

Don't worry, he says. Foxy knows the score.

I'm not worried. But I'm worried.

Foxy single? he says.

You'd fuck a hole in the wall, wouldn't ya? I say.

Back to other business, then. We've followed this French cunt from a meeting at the Bank of Greece headquarters in Panepistimiou to the apartment of his mistress in the Plateia

Philikis Etaireas. He's got her set up in a nice little pad on the second floor overlooking the square, some little Italian hussy. Sees her Monday, Thursday and Sunday afternoons for a bit o'squeaky, and Tuesday and Friday evenins for more of the same. Nice little piece, she is: short, fat ass and tiny titties, and who would argue that isn't the perfect shape? Looks like high maintenance to me — she's got a suckin-lemon kinda face on her, but that pussy must be so so delicious. I followed her into the café below her building yesterday and she smelled like sweeties... like, ever passed a girl in a silk dress that smelled like sweeties? I swear, my prick went ballistic. I was ready to murder every cunt in the bar for a piece of her. A *mile-over-broken-glass* kinda piece, ya know?

Now I'm sittin here in the front seat wi'Lenny, thinkin about the slit between those brown Italian thighs which are open wide for some fat French fucker upstairs as we speak, and my prick is like granite and I wanna punch that Canadian whelp in the face.

I'm bored, he says.

This is the third afternoon we've tailed the Frenchie around Athens, in three different cars mind, cause this is the diplomatic district and fulla pigs, soldiers, and every other flavour of titled and striped asshole.

I pay you to drive, you dipshit, I tell him. Entertainment isn't part of the package.

So why're we following this guy? he whines.

Cause he's stealin from us, Lenny, I say. I say the first thing that comes into my head.

Oh yeah?

*Yeah, you daft Canadian wazzock.* If he wasn't such a safe ticket as a driver, I'd slap him silly and fire him.

Like, how much? he says.

Thousands, Lenny. Thousands. Plus he beats his Indonesian housemaid.

Oh yeah?

Yeah, I say.

184

Lenny laps it up.

What's more, I tell him, this guy's driver hit an old woman with his Mercedes last week. She died a day later in hospital.

No...

Yeah, Lenny. He's a cunt, and we're gonna fix him.

That shuts him right up.

I'm hungry, Lenny says.

*Jesus Christ. Like being stuck in the car with a nine-year-old.*

We go back to the bar and I give Lorelei a right good slap around. Fuck, my blood is boilin. I take off my belt and I beat her proper. I really go to work. As always, it finishes tenderly, me eatin out her pussy all soft like, gently kissin the lips of her cunt til rivers run outta her. Then I rub some lotion into the bloody welts on her thighs and we fall asleep, spooning, all sticky.

I get up and go down to the bar where Foxy's holdin the fort. Five o'clock and no cunt is in, cause nobody goes out when it's hittin forty degrees. August is round the corner. I'm not sure I'll be able to handle it.

I tell Foxy to close up, that we're goin out for a drink. She closes up and we go down the street to *Teras*, a terrace bar with no terrace, but that's okay cause they also got those machines that spray water over your face all *ocean-breezey-like*.

We nab a table right under the spray and order. Drinks come and we sit back, and she lights up a cigarette and I light one, and we smoke and we drink.

How you likin it at the bar, Foxy? I say.

She takes a drag of her cigarette, blows a long puff at the roof before answerin.

I'm happy, she says.

You still trickin?

I have a few regulars, she says.

*Why not.*

They good to you?

Yeah.

I'm glad to hear it, Foxy. Life's too short for cunts.

Yes it is. Speaking of, she says, what about your friend Ducasse? He was hittin on me last night at the bar.

He's a cunt, I say.

I thought so.

Yeah, a cunt. But a solid cunt, if ya know what I mean.

Yes.

But I'd probably stay away from him all the same.

I already decided to.

You're no fool, Foxy.

She says nothin.

Still, on the subject of cunts, I say, I know this woman who's asked me for help. Not a friend, but an acquaintance I suppose. Husband, some banker prick, is beatin her black and blue. She asked me if I could do anything. What would you do?

Foxy takes a puff of her cigarette and picks up her glass, and I'm not sure, but it seems her hand is tremblin. She takes a drink before looking at me.

Do you know? she says. I mean, do you know for sure?

I know what her face says, I tell her. Her face looks like a side of meat.

This gets her.

I'd fucken kill him, Foxy says.

I nod.

# 23

# Golden

I'm back with Adonis a few days later. I sit at a table out on the terrace and watch him work. It's thirty-eight degrees out and the fucker isn't sweatin. How does he not sweat? Confidence is his antiperspirant, I figure. Dumb, effortless, Mediterranean confidence, that's how. Still got that greasy vibe, though. He'll never lose his greasiness. I watch him jab his crotch at a woman on a table of four, her playin along. He's just stabbin his groin at her, all Adonis-like. *Go on, you grease-bagger, pull out your cock and lay it on the table. You know you want to.* I just know this cocksmith spends his Septembers on some beach in the Aegean in a pair of Speedos, strokin his bulge and smellin his own excellence. Fucken Adonis.

He sets these attention-desperate women up with lunch and come sits down at the table.

Adonis, you're a piece of work, I tell him.

What you say, man?

Nothin. How's it hangin?

He does that Greek thing where he raises his chin in the air, stretchin it out in a torturous motion while his mouth contorts at the corners. It can mean anything from *Fuck you*, to *I've no idea what the fuck you're on about*, to *Yeah man, everything is okay.* I presume the latter. Adonis is swingin.

So? he says. He's lookin out over the port, all casual. Like we're not discussin the killing of a man.

I nod, all slow and Greek and enigmatic.

The information is good, my friend? he says.

Yeah, your information is good, Adonis. It's all there. The guy's whole life. We been watchin.

So?

We can do it, I say.

When? Adonis says.

Man, we gotta get this right. We're plannin it all, plannin it down to the smallest detail. We got one chance. When we've got our ducks lined up, we'll do it.

Our German friend is pushin, Adonis says. He's flyin to Frankfurt in three weeks and wants it done before then.

Will he be here next Friday?

He is here every Friday.

Fuck it. We'll do it for then, I say. We'll be ready.

Not here, Adonis says.

Of course not here, you lunatic, I say. We figure on takin him from the girlfriend's house.

*His own place is out of the question. Surveillance inside and out and police either end of the street. Nah.*

Should be a walk in the park, I say.

In the park? Adonis says.

*I have to stop speakin in idiom.*

His girlfriend's house, Adonis. Smash and grab.

*Smash. Grab. Kidnap. Killin.* Is Adonis rattled? I swear that's a bead of sweat forming on the taut, smooth skin of his forehead. He lights another cigarette off his last. Below the table his arm moves. He's playin with his balls. A sure sign of nervousness.

I'm under the oceany-breezy water thingy. I feel fine.

Let me spell it out for you, Adonis, I say.

Maybe if I lay it all out, it'll ease his mind.

So Friday night our cat comes in and spends a few hours here as usual. This night, however, he's gonna be gettin a little extra with his steak. We're gonna give you somethin
188

to sprinkle on it, know what I mean? By the time he leaves here he's gonna be belly-itchin, and when he gets back to the girlfriend's he's gonna have some proper palpitations goin on. The girlfriend calls a doctor, and that's when we step in. We arrive at the door all friendly and medical like, just there to sort him out. We cart him off. Job done. You're out of the picture. He comes in here, he leaves. Same as every weekend. Nothin strange, nothin unusual. We do all the dirty work, I say.

Seems like you have it all figured out, he says.

Leave it to us. One more thing, Adonis.

Yeah?

I'll need the girlfriend's phone hacked.

I'll talk to our German friend.

Do that, I say.

And he does. Two days later, I've got it. A cloned phone. I can read her texts, her messages, hear her calls... I can even access her microphone and camera. Some shady cunt meets me at Swim at eleven on Wednesday mornin and shows me how to do all this shit. It's fucken thrillin but I try not to show it. Professional, like.

I don't know who this suit is, German intelligence or some private stooge, but he knows his stuff. In a half-hour I'm right up in this girl's private life. I'd like to be able to say I'm a better person, but I know I'll be abusin this. Sittin at the table with the guy, my cock is already hard thinkin about listenin in on this girl gettin fucked. I haven't forgotten her smell, not for a second.

I head over to see Ducasse to see how things are goin at the clinic.

We're fucken ready, he says.

He takes me in to meet the staff. A staff meetin. I'm introduced as 'the big boss', which makes me chuffed. *The big boss*. Which I am, in a way. We're all sittin round a table.

This is Vaso, Ducasse says. She'll be our receptionist.

We shake hands. Vaso is late twenties, dyed black hair and piercings. Got an ex-junkie look about her, but with a white coat and her best telephone manner, no one'll notice. Her big head of fuzzy hair is disarming.

These are our nurses, Vassilis and Alexandros, Ducasse says.

Two cats look like they can handle themselves.

Real nurses? I ask.

Vassilis worked in a juvenile detention facility and Alexandros is studying sociology at the Polytechnic.

*The fucken dream team.*

All speak English? I say.

They nod.

A big monster of a guy walks in through the door.

This, Ducasse says, is Fikrim.

Oh yeah? You Greek? I ask him.

Turk, he says.

I laugh. The thought of this big, monstrous Turk in Athens. *Brave boy.*

Fikrim's gonna be, you know, the general guy, Ducasse says. Fixin up things, helpin out, sortin out any shit when it happens. You know, the *guy.*

Good. I feel better with a big animal about the place. You stick a loada cunts in a building with an unlimited supply of pills anything can happen. We'll need a guy.

I feel good about this whole thing, I tell em. I think we're gonna have a good old time here, and I look forward to workin with you all. I'll not be around all that much initially, but Ducasse is gonna be here day to day. For the first month or two anyway, I say. Let me get you all more coffee.

Cause I'm just that kinda boss.


Me and Ducasse are walkin out the door. He's all excited. Never seen him like it before. Really takes to projects, he does.

So? he says.

I think it's class, I say.

When are we gettin people in?

We'll put out some flyers this weekend. I'll have Foxy track down the big parties, and we'll hit em up and put out the word, I tell him.

He's buzzin.

You get that other thing I asked you for? I say.

The wagon? It's downstairs — come on I'll show ya, he says.

Next time. I got somethin to do. Somethin important.

Right then.

I'll call ya later.

And I'm off. I hop in the car and head uptown. I leave that ballbag Lenny at the bar this time and drive over to the *plateia*. My prick has been hard against the inside of my leg from the minute I was handed that cloned phone.

It's nearly three o'clock. I check the folder for her whereabouts. She'll be comin back from the gym any minute. Then three-thirty she'll come down to the café. She'll sit for about a half-hour then head out for some shoppin.

So I wait, and soon she comes round the corner. She's in her gym gear, all athletic and sweaty. I watch her from the front seat of my car, rubbing my prick. She's too much. That thick ass and those tiny tits, her midriff exposed, tanned and toned. I imagine cummin all over that belly. I groan and stroke my prick. Then I look at her face and a great hatred wells up in me. The hatred makes my prick even harder. She disappears through the doors of her building.

*Excruciating.*

I stop touchin myself.

I wanna smell that perfume when I push myself over the edge.

So I wait. I sit in the car locked in some kinda tantric torture — my prick has never been so hard without the use of chemicals before, every atom of my body wants that release, that explosion, but I hold off. I deny myself. My heart is palpitating and my head spinnin. The edge of my vision has started to blur. There's a ringin in my ears. I feel I might have a seizure.

I turn the microphone of her phone on and hear her gettin into the shower. She's got the phone in the bathroom and is takin a shower. It's too fucken much. I check the camera but I only see the ceiling.

*Soaping her belly and her tits, and long fingernails scratching the back of her neck, before her hand slips down between those fat Italian thighs, those brown thighs, thighs that smell of juniper and oregano and cocoa butter, and of fat lecherous statesmen and precum, of black olive tapenade and summer grass, and of sweetie perfume and nail polish… fingers lingering just too long on fat labia, maybe she plays with it a little — and isn't that a soft groan I hear through the fallin water, water fallin on shoulders that fat, dirty men weep into, shoulders that peek through silken summer dresses and make fourteen-year-old boys tremble, shoulders that artists scream into the night over, screaming til their throats bleed… oh yes, certainly I hear a groan, as fingers play with labia and her ass brushes against cold tile, and a finger, the tip of a finger, slides into that warm nest where men may die happily…*

I freeze, on perhaps the edge of the most frenzied state of arousal I've ever experienced. I almost weep.

I hear the shower door, the water cease.

I turn off the phone, knowin that if I see her naked I will not be able to hold back. It's that scent I crave. When I unload, I wanna smell her.

And so I wait some more.

And wait.

Sweat runs into my eyes and I can't see or hear for the buzzin in my head. I am a sweaty pulse of black electricity, waitin to discharge into the empty void.

I wait until she appears through the doors, silken clad, shoulders exposed, brown shoulders to make boys cry. *And thigh, and calf, and fingers…*

She comes out and heads for the café.

I wait until she takes a seat and orders. She takes out her

phone, gets busy. Sweatin and on edge I get out and cross the street. My prick rubs my thigh and I fear I may lose it before I reach the café. But I get there, and as I step onto the pavement it hits me, the sweetie smell, the smell of candies in the mouths of children, and of sticky fingers and of misspent youth and of raspberry and sugar. I inhale it and my head spins, and I sit down at a table behind her. A waiter comes and I dismiss him, and I sit and inhale that heady scent, that scent of rhubarb and lime and strawberry, and I can't help it, I emit soft groans like a dog in heat, and soon I'll be howlin, so I take one last gulp of her odour, filling my nostrils and my head and my belly... it invades every atom, every cell, and *God-fucken-help-me* I can take it no more, so I stand up and retreat into the café toilets and touch my prick, my prick like a phallus carved from marble, a single touch, and I explode, inward, outward... I fucken lose it, I explode, and a great scream like a battle cry emanates from my lungs and my belly, and I quiver and dissolve.

I sit there for minutes, shaking, as my body reinvigorates.

Then I clean myself off and step outside, and maybe every cunt in the café is lookin at me but I don't notice, nor do I care, for I've just had a sensual epiphany. I know my purpose. Suddenly and unflinchingly, I know my purpose.

I walk past her into the street and inhale her scent as I go. Steppin out into the sun is like communion... it doesn't even feel warm, it's cool, like a slow drink of ice water. I stop there, in the middle of the street just absorbin it, that cool heat, and cars are blaring horns at me to get the fuck outta the way, but I don't care because I see it and feel it and know it.

Sure as fuck, I know it.

I can do anything in this world and it's all golden.

# 24

# Mr Pharmacist

Me, Foxy and Lenny hit up an illegal rave in the hills outside Athens Saturday night. We go out about midnight and the place is kickin off, a big sound system bouncin in the woody hills, loada Greek cunts gettin pilled up and lovey and delicious. We get in among em, Lenny's off his face himself so he gets carried away, me and Foxy are relatively straight so we settle in and talk to a few folk, explain what we're doin, spread the word like. We hand out flyers. All these pillheads are off their tits, so they'll forget everything in an hour, but if they wake up with a flyer in their pockets then our job is done. We talk to a bunch of pricks for an hour or two before we chill out and get into the spirit of things. We even pop a few ourselves, my first since comin to Athens.

*Oh baby, how I've missed you...*

So we dance into the small hours and we pop another pill, and we dance and hold hands and, fuck it, me and Foxy even kiss. Then we're rollin around behind a tree, and I tell her I love her and she tells me she loves me, and then we play with each other's cocks but we're both tits-high and nobody's gettin hard so we giggle and laugh and go dance some more.

Then we come down and we find Lenny, big dumb Canadian cunt, hanging upside down from a tree, and how do you explain that one? We cut him down and drive back to Athens and everything that happened is already forgotten and we fall into our respective beds as the sun rises in suicide city.

I wake up the next mornin and Lorelei's got a head on, like, *Where the fuck were you last night?*, even though I told her where we were but she's only pissed cause I was poppin pills and havin fun and she wasn't there, she was stuck in the bar with all the sweaty perverts.

*Sweet Lorelei. I'll beat you about later and everything will be nice again.*

She goes out to work and I take my cloned phone and switch it on, and fuck it if I don't turn on the camera and find myself lyin in bed with the hot little Italian bitch. Mornin face on her, and she's less abrupt without her makeup, and I find my hatred off her startin to thaw. But my cock is still hard and I squeeze it now, me lyin in bed lookin at the Italian, shoulders bared and tits peekin out of her night clothes, hair wild, bed hair, and, *shoot me please*, she starts to play with herself. So we jerk off together, her alone and me with her, lookin at her lips curl and hearing the soft groans, unintelligible words whispered in Italian, Italian words, *fuck me* and *eat me* and *I wanna suck it, Daddy* all whispered in angry Italian, and we writhe and moan and pull at ourselves until we spill out, spill over… spent and no longer angry.

I am being consumed by this girl, this girl that I don't like, that I hate, but who I want to fuck so badly and relentlessly and without restraint. I want her. I want her mouth and her brown skin smellin like raspberries, and the nape of her neck and her black nipples, and if I could, I'd take her heart and soul too. I'd take it, because I am possessed by her.

I've cum, but my cock is still hard and she won't let me go. I turn off the phone, cursin the Italian.

The enigma of *Cunt*.

I go through Sunday the same way, my cock achin for that sweet Italian slit. I jerk off four times thinkin about her; in the car, in the bar, at home and, believe me or don't believe me, in a back street in Psiri where I go to imagine her sucking me off in a dirty alley. A classy Italian piece in a dirty piss-stained alley. *Fuck. Girl has me gone.*

Monday mornin I wake up, go through it again in bed with her, with her image in the phone, with her groans in my ear as I pull the mickey off myself.

I can't go on like this. I'm turnin into Sweeney. I have a girlfriend, for fuck sake.

I get up to go and do somethin.

It's just gone ten-thirty so I head over to the clinic to see what action's happenin first thing.

*Fuck me.*

Over thirty Athenian pillheads have turned up, a couple of stray Spaniards and a Somalian, and none of us can work out what he's doin there, but he's a big strappin lad, so if he's clean, we'll take him.

Ducasse is with our nurses, he's got a pair of gloves on and he's gettin his hands dirty. We got our nurses takin blood samples, two at a time and the rest of the potentials in reception or chillin out in the rec room. Ducasse is pitchin in, though there's no way you'd find that lunatic puttin a needle in my arm. Fucken maniac.

Takes us two hours to get through thirty-three people, but I'm sure we'll get quicker as we iron out the creases in our operation. We get the blood and tell em to come back in forty-eight hours for the results. We all sit back and sigh a sigh of relief, before Ducasse and me get in the car and scoot over to the Central City Clinic where we got two analysts lined up to take on our samples day to day for forty euros per sample. We hand over thirty-two samples, which is thirteen hundred euros right there for a day's work — not a bad extra piece for a job that pays eight hundred a month. And that'll be comin every week. We can expect results back in twenty-four hours, all the big ones tested for: HIV, hep B and C — shit you wouldn't wanna be swallowin with your steak.

Our first day of operation and things are runnin pretty tight. I'm impressed.

We get back in the car.

Tell you what, Ducasse, I say, you've really nailed shit down. I mean, things are runnin nicely.

He smiles he does, all Sri Sai Baba quiet and mysterious like. Says nothin.

I mean it, I say. Fair play. Place is hoppin already. Wait til we tell Hugo.

And as I say his name, I realise I've hardly thought about him at all since we left Amsterdam, how long ago? I can't remember, since there's so much shit happenin in my life now that the days are all meltin into one, one big long day of Meat and Ecstasy, and now a rampant masturbation habit and killin a man so another man can eat him, and luring cunts into a fake clinic so we can dose em and serve em up to fat customers, and payin cunts off for this, that and every other fucken thing and somehow I'm stayin on top of it all and really, it's all golden.

We're killin it. I give myself silent applause as me and Ducasse drive back to the clinic.

*You're killin it, you are.*

*

*Location:*

Screamin Pope, Athens

*Time:*

15.30, Monday

*Present:*

Sweeney: cat-less creep

Lenny Sack: gobshite Canadian

Danglin' Jimmy: unemployed, dedicated alko

Foxy Maffia: big, solid and dependable shemale

Lorelei: pissed nymphet, soon-to-be ex

Kostas: lawman, afternoon tippler


I drop into the bar just to see how thing are goin, ya know, catch up on unfinished business and say hello to the clientele. I been a lotta time outside recently. Operations are expandin in various strange directions. But I'm on it.

   *Golden.*

Sweeney's in the corner, face almost healed and no cats or kittens, a good thing, because I mighta smashed his head off the wall. He side-eyes me glumly. Sack is with him, expatiatin over some guff or other. Jimmy's at the bar, and he turns round to see me come in.

Jimmy, I say. Fuck you doin here? I thought you only came in on Sundays?

Ev'ry day Sunday now, since I done quit my *jaab*, he say.

Jimmy done quit his *jaab*.

Now what you gonna do, Jimmy?

I'm gon'drink.

Wanna play piano here, Jimmy? We'll get you a piano.

Why in the name o'sweatin Jaysus would I wan'play piano in this godforsaken place?

   *Ha!*

I laugh, Foxy laughs, even Lorelei, stroppy little nymphet, laughs. He's right. Blues piano in here would drive us all to the rope or the blade.

Jimmy, I'm gonna help ease your suff'rin, I say.

So I go over to the jukebox and throw in a coin. The Fall booms.

*Mr Pharmacist…*

Jimmy, I'm gonna do somethin for ya in your hour of need, I say.

*… Please see me right today*
*In your sweet and loving way*
*Oh Mr Pharmacist, don't desist*
*Help me out with some vitamin C…*

I go out back and grab a handful of pills and pass em out, yes, even Sweeney, and I'm extra generous wi'Jimmy and we all bang a pill, me, Lorelei, Foxy, everyone in the bar, and it's startin to feel like the good old days again.

*Hey Mr Pharmacist!*

Oh yeah, I done quit my *jaab*, Jimmy says and we all fall around in a fit of gigglin.

Danglin' Jimmy, I say, and I raise my glass, here's to new beginnings. Whatever they may be.

Oh yeah, Jimmy says.

Jimmy looks happy.

Maybe I quit my job too, Lorelei says.

Yeah girl, says Foxy.

*Try to be a sound boss and this is what you get.*

I give Lorelei a good slap on the ass. She squeals, all playful like.

Bossman say no, Jimmy says.

Bossman is a monster, Foxy says, and now the women are turnin on me.

Excuse me, I say, and I extract myself from behind the bar and I go sit next to Jimmy.

What else you got back there? Jimmy says, all hush like.

What ya mean, Jimmy?

Like, you got any Ket or PCP?

*… Mr Pharmacist won't you please*
*Send me on a rollin kick…*

Nah, Jimmy, we do pills, man. None o'that horse tranquiliser shite. What you want that insane stuff for anyway?

Man, you never done Ket? *Woo-wee!* Man, you ain't been to the fair til you rode the merry-go-round.

*… I got some of that dab I need…*

Not for me, Jimmy.

I'll go out later and find us some Ket, and we'll go vibe on Athens til we pass out on a park bench or get arrested, Jimmy says.

Ducasse is your man, Jimmy. He'll be all over that action. Me, I'm not one for drama.

Whole life is drama, Jimmy says. Whole life is a play and we's on the stage, just playin and rippin and roarin.

I applaud your youthful vigour, Jimmy.

And I do. For a man hittin fifty, he's got more stamina than I'll ever have.

*Woo-wee!* Jimmy says.

Kostas comes outta the bathroom, surprisin all of us.

Where you been? I say. I look at Foxy. She shrugs. How long you been in there, Kostas?

I just went in, man, he says.

Nah Kostas, I been sittin here twenty minutes, you gotta be in there at least that long — you fall asleep?

*Ase, re*, he says. Leave me alone.

Here Kostas, you missed all the action, I say. I pass him a couple of pills. Get these down your neck.

He gives me that Greek chin-wag, but all slow and deliberate, and this time it means, *Don't mind if I fucken do.*

He necks a pill, and soon he's with the rest of us.

*Hey Mr Pharmacist!*

He da pharmacist, Jimmy says.

I suppose I am. Maybe I'll put that on a business card:

> *Mr Pharmacist*
> *Bossman, Screamin Pope*
> *Dispensary of Meat and Ecstasy*
> *Established in a state of time and mind*
> *entirely his own making*
> *Open all hours*

Bit wordy on it, for a business card. Could cut it down some:

> *Mr Pharmacist*
> *Dispenser of Ecstasy*
> *Available*

*Yeah. Get on that right away, you prodigy. Businessman of the year.*

Where'd you go? Jimmy says. He's snappin his fingers in my face.

Been dreamin up some stuff, Jimmy. You know me, always workin.

Come back down to earth, spaceboy, he says.

Right-o, Jimmy. You know what? I say, and I come up with a plan. A marvellous plan.

I think this party calls for some absinthe, I say.

# 25

# Down a Hole in Athens

Now we're in it.

Me, Ducasse and Jimmy wanderin around Athens in a great hole, a K-hole, and maybe a PCP-hole, and definitely an absinthe-hole cause that's what started this mess, and I know we've all got pocketfuls of Es cause we're passin em out like Smarties. Lenny was with us, but we think he's been arrested but nobody's quite sure. Athens has sucked us into the hole and everything we do spills in, lost to experience and recollection, never to be recovered. There's no climbin out either, none of us is showin the least inclination to, cause we keep poppin and snortin and drinkin — in the toilet of every corner bar, the cistern or the sink lined with white powder and sniffed, or a pill popped surreptitiously or, fuck it, plain as day just walkin down the street.

*Tcha!* Neckin pills and we're still kickin.

Omonia, Exarchia, Metaxourghio, Psiri, Monastiraki, Thissio, Plaka... it goes on and on, and I'm not sure if we're even eatin or just thrivin on booze and pharmaceuticals, all over a city which is not the least bit drug-friendly. But we're made of stern stuff.

Jimmy takes us to some crack den where we pay to see two women fuck each other, not in a nice way, but in a *broken-glass-and-smells-of-skid-row* kinda way, and I'm not diggin it so I got a better idea.

Let's take Jimmy to Madame Zhu's, I say.

Nah, you fucken clown, Ducasse says. Madame Zhu's is in the Dam.

Ducasse, I say, I was in it last week, or two weeks ago, or some time ago, I don't remember, but I was in it here in Athens.

You're off your head, he says.

*Yes I am, but I remember very clearly.*

I'll take you there, I tell him.

Forget it, you're dreamin it, he says.

I'll take you there now.

So I retrace my steps best I can across the city, the dark night across the city, left here, right there, past the Botanical Gardens, we all pop another pill, turn here, down a dark street, should be just about…

*But no. It's not where I left it.*

It should be right here, I say.

Told ya, you're off your head, Ducasse says.

Nah, Ducasse man, I tell him. It was right here.

But there's no burgundy, or perfume, or burgundy perfume anywhere or nowhere. It's gone, dissipated in the hot Athens night.

I know another place, Jimmy says.

No, me and Ducasse say, no more of your funky wrecked-pussy joints.

Let's go to Amsterdam, I say.

What? Jimmy says.

Let's go to Amsterdam and go to Madame Zhu's.

You fucken crazy, Jimmy says, and we all get to laughin, rollin around on the street, cause it's the funniest fucken thing we've heard all night.

We crawl down the street on our hands and knees, the three of us, one after the other, cause we've all simultaneously and inexplicably lost the use of our legs. Ducasse is spoutin about Countess Markievicz cause suddenly he's an authority on

Irish history, Jimmy isn't listenin he's just makin cat noises, and me, I'm tryin to make it down the street without puttin my hands in the broken glass that's all over the ground, all stickin up like on top of a wall you're not supposed to climb over.

Where we goin? I say, and when we hit the corner of the street, I look up and I see the café on the corner where we had those Black Russians, the ecstatic Black Russians in the café with too many chairs.

Ducasse, I say, that's the place!

What place? Ducasse, on his hands and knees, looks up.

Remember, where I had the Black Russian that drove me crazy?

I don't remember, he says.

Remember, I say, the place with too many chairs, wall-to-wall tables and chairs, and the fucken glorious Black Russians?

I think I'm drizzlin, Ducasse says, but he means dribblin.

Remember, you'd just been to a black hooker and came out with blood on your shirt?

Amsterdam, again with the fucken Amsterdam. We're in Athens, you lunatic, he shouts.

That's it, I tell him, that's the place.

Black Russian, spits Jimmy, who's stopped makin cat noises and now has a thirst on him.

We claw our way to our feet with the aid of a car and we stumble across the road to the café. We wobble up the stairs inside.

You see? I say.

Just like I told em, there's too many chairs — we're stuck in a maze of chairs, tryin to get to a table, panicked, like three zebra surrounded by wild dogs. Me and Ducasse have experience with this kinda thing but Jimmy's lashin out, they're closin in round him. Three staff watch us, terrified.

It's okay, I say, we're regulars — we're in here all the time. We're just here for the Black Russians.

Now we're screamin about Russians, and these people

are afraid. I've made it to the table, but Jimmy's on his knees clingin to a chair, *Help!* he's screamin. Ducasse pulls him to his feet, places him in a chair and does some weird massage thing on him and he chills the fuck out.

I'm still shoutin about Russians, black ones, in all languages but Greek, then I pull the Greek outta my ass and the guy says, *Yeah, Mavro Rosiki...* maybe they're thinkin if they give us what we want we'll get the fuck out.

So they rustle us up three Black Russians, and Christ, they're *glorious.*

Didn't I tell ya? I say to Ducasse, and we sit imbibing the black bliss of Russia.

This is really it, Ducasse says.

I know, I say.

This is the place, he says.

*It is.*

Remember this place, Jimmy, I say. Someday this place will save your life.

And Jimmy's all blissed out too, his phobia of too many chairs now soothed.

Now we just gotta find Madame Zhu's, Ducasse says.

I'm gonna tell you a poem, Jimmy, I say.

You go on now, Jimmy says, all blissed like.

I tell him:

*There's a woman from old Macau* (I sing it like Mac-*ooo*)
*risen from Meru in the waters of the lake,*
*came forth, a daughter of the sun,*
*killed her way across the land*
*with a knife of green in her delicate hand.*
*Built a garden of damask and bamboo*
 *For us, the children of the golden breeze*
*Damask and bamboo and burgundy perfume*
*to send us across the golden ocean.*
*She carried us over the ocean of whispers —*
*Her name was Madame Zhu.*

I sit back and grin. Now I'm no poet, I say, but I think that's pretty fucken sweet.

That's the most beautiful thing I ever heard, Jimmy says.

Thank you, Jimmy.

Fucken elegiac, Ducasse says.

I sup from my blissful chalice of poetry.

Ducasse takes out his phone and looks at it, noddin sagely. You know, we're workin men, he says.

I'm not listenin to him. *Leave us to our abyss*.

We have responsibilities, he says.

*Nah, now's not the time Ducasse, man*. I reach in my pocket for the coke but it's not there, and fair enough we've probably snorted it all.

I'm goin home, he says. *Just like that*.

Nah man, sit down, have one more, I tell him.

Fuck the pair of you, he says. And he stands up. We've been — Ducasse looks studiously at his phone — three days on a bender, he says.

Can't be. Tell him Jimmy, I say.

Ain't no three days, Jimmy says, spaced out like.

Three days, Ducasse says. And he turns his phone for me to see, like seein it makes any fucken sense to me whatsoever.

Wait a minute — what day is it? I say.

Thursday, Ducasse says.

No, no no no…

Whaddup? Jimmy says.

I gotta kidnap a cunt tomorrow, I tell him.

Wassat?

I gotta do a kidnap tomorrow, I say, like that's the way to say it.

Fuck are you on about? Ducasse says, and I realise too late he's not in on it, because if he's in on it then Hugo's in on it and that brings a whole different bag of shite to the table. But I go with it.

Tomorrow I'm gonna kidnap the head of the IMF so we can cook up the cunt and eat him, I say. *Hidin in plain sight, innit?*

Ha!

Jimmy's laughin and Ducasse is laughin, rollin about laughin among the chairs and the tables, cause that is some funny shit. I mean, that's the funniest fucken thing they've ever heard.

# 26

# Hot, the Athens Night

We're all set. I hit up Adonis in the afternoon and palm the stuff, the stuff that'll put the Frenchie on his back later. Now it's up to us. Me. Me, who's head is hot and brittle as blown glass. I mean, death was on me this mornin, and I've come around some with the raki but I'm only holdin it together. Just. One of those Armageddon mornins, all bile and paranoia and end of the world. I also woke up to an empty bed. Lorelei had cleaned out her stuff and moved out. I went down to the bar to discover she's moved in with Foxy. It's a token protest. Who can put up with a guy disappearin down the hole for three days without a word to say about it? No, not even a gone little nymphet like Lorelei. Let her have her tantrum.

So I leave the bar to the women, they've been runnin the show without me anyway while I went off on one. I head over to the clinic. Our people there have their shit together — they've let the partyheads have their fun, three days hoofin it on pills and loungin in beanbags and *what-have-you*, and now we've got our first six carcasses laid out on beds, coma invoked and on the MDMA drip, body flooded with all those good chemicals that make our meat so good. Six big slabs o'prime cuts, about four hundred kilos in all, over a hundred grand's worth at current market price. We got the next six lined up to come in week after, and the next week after that, and so on. We're rollin. We've moved Culhannan outta the bar and into the basement here. He's settin up his operation as we speak. Tailor-made shop to his own requirements. The whole thing's a roarin success. I'd like to get Hugo down here to have a look at it. He'd be fucken chuffed.

I go out back where Ducasse has somethin parked up for me — an ambulance, retired from service and purchased at auction. It's pretty knackered. Yellow and orange, still stickered up with all the Greek stuff and the logo, the rod of Asclepius with the snake coiled around the rod. Our wagon. Here to save Athens. It'll do what's needed.

Lenny and Foxy show up at the clinic. We went through it on Monday, but I go through it all again and we hash out the details. I've bought us all some uniforms, not quite exact but anyone in a raging panic'll never know the difference. We get changed and stand around grinnin at each other. Foxy is comical — a big black shemale in medical scrubs is not somethin you see every day.

Right, I say, this needs to go like clockwork, so I want you to get familiar with the gurney in the back. Once we're in there, it's gotta look like you know what you're doin. Go n'have a go at settin it up.

So they do, they put up the gurney and take it down, put it up and take it down. They got the hang of it.

Know how to drive an ambulance, Lenny? I say, but I don't need to ask. Lenny's a prick but he can drive anything.

I grin. So are we ready?

Oh yes, they're ready. They've been prepped. We're on it, we are.


Eight o'clock, I phone Adonis. Frenchie's in the restaurant with a loada cunts he works with.

How long's he been in? I ask him.

He's been here over an hour, just finished his main course, Adonis tells me.

Time to move. I drive over to the square in the motor,

Lenny and Foxy follow in the ambulance. We go nice and easy across town. Lenny and Foxy park up on Kanari, just off the *plateia*. I'm sittin on the square, got my eyes on the place. I turn on the phone to check on our little Italian piece. Audio on, I can hear some music playin in the apartment, all happy like. So I turn on the camera and she's lookin right into the phone. Wearin some kinda green silk top. I can see the top of her tits, olive-skinned, and that sweetie smell comes back to me… she's made-up and looks stunnin but still got that bitter look on her face and I feel the hatred rise up but my cock is hard too, and *no no no*… I turn off the video. I can't. That's it, no more masturbation for me, cause I do not want to turn into a wanker, a furious wanker like Sweeney, gaunt and slippery and empty inside.

Instead I listen. The music plays and I listen.

Foxy calls me. What's up?

Hold on, I say, I'll get back to ya.

It's pushin ten and Adonis hasn't rang. So I ring him.

Where we at Adonis?

They've paid the bill and are enjoyin some complimentary raki, Adonis tells me.

Well Adonis, I tell him, maybe you stop plyin him wi'drink and let him leave.

*Ela re*, he says, we take care of our customers.

Well, Adonis, we're about to kill the cunt so we can eat him, so it doesn't really matter, does it? He ain't gonna be a customer after tonight.

Don't say it like that, man, Adonis says.

*Let's not beat around the bush now. This is what's happenin.*

Hey, hold on, Adonis says. Looks like somethin's goin on, he tells me. He's gettin up to run to the bathroom.

Good good. That's what I like to hear, Adonis, I say. Maybe you should gently push him to order a taxi.

Okay, man.

Good man, Adonis. Call me when he's movin.

I call Foxy, tell her to be ready.

211

About fifteen minutes, I reckon, I say.

I feel fucken good. The death hangover is still on me, it's in my bones and my skin and at the back of my skull, but I feel alive. Adrenalin, I guess. We're about to kidnap a guy, and I feel pretty fucken good about it. I don't really need to, but it's pretty easy to justify killin a fat, predatory banker. A leech, suckin on the blood of innocents: workin people, single mothers, unemployed, the unhoused, those without medical insurance who suffer endlessly… and then to use your ill-gotten gains to eat and fuck all you like, that's pretty fucken despicable. I'll kill this cunt easy, and I won't lose any sleep over it. None.

Adonis calls back. He's in a taxi. Lookin pretty ill, he says.

Well good, Adonis, that was the idea.

I call Foxy. Five minutes.

*Why stop here?* Why not kill the lot of em, all the bankers and bureaucrats and lawyers, all the cunts that have eaten Greece from the inside out, obese on the fat of the land and the sweat of the people and washed down with the wine of sorrow, sittin in their ivory towers and pickin the remains from their teeth with silver toothpicks and scratchin their perfumed bellies? Who could raise any serious moral objection to it? None, I'm sure. Let's eat em and be done with it, and build the world new, aflesh.

The Italian's phone rings. He's almost there. Okay my love, she says, all sweetness. My prick is hard again.

*My love.*

I phone Foxy. He's around the corner.

Soon the taxi pulls onto the square and comes to a stop outside the building. I see him get out, fat bastard, and he clutches the doorway as he goes in. He pauses. He's in some discomfort already. Job is half done.

He goes upstairs and I'm listenin on her phone and I hear him come in, and there's some muffled conversation, sounds kinda anxious like.

Foxy phones me. Want us to move down?

Just wait, I tell her.

Some huffin and puffin on the other end of the Italian's phone.

*Just put in the call.*

It takes fifteen minutes, but she does eventually.

She knows Greek too, cause I hear her speak to the operator.

*Chriazomai ena yiatro.* I need a doctor.

*We're here for you, sweetheart.*

Right away.

*Yes yes — we're here to help, doll.*

How long?

*Oh, we're right outside baby.*

I call Foxy. Move, I say.

Evangelismos Hospital is right around the corner, so I'd say we got about ten minutes to get in and out.

Foxy pulls up outside the building. I'm waitin for em. They grab the gurney and we're inside. Lift up to the second floor. Apartment 12.

We knock and she answers, hot and flustered, all silk and olive-skinned.

*I'm here for you, my love.*

We get in and the fat cunt's on the sofa. We drop the gurney and roll the bastard on to it. Groanin and moanin, sick with the flesh and blood of the people. *You're sick, and you're a sick fuck. What would your little Italian piece think if she knew you ate human flesh?* Maybe I'll tell her.

Fat bastard is groanin, sayin somethin in French. *I don't speak it, you gluttonous fuck.*

Italian touches my arm, looks lost, worried, and I'm hard. I mean, my prick is like marble. I look in her eyes, tell her everything will be okay.

*My love, I'll take care of everything for you…*

He's on the gurney and we're out the door. I'm lookin at my watch. Four minutes since we pulled up at the front door of the building. We're fucken good at this.

Italian follows us out the door. I take her arm and squeeze

it softly. I look into her eyes again.

Best you stay here, I say.

I want to come, she says.

*I want you to come too.*

I touch her shoulder and I almost weep. I'm a fourteen-year-old boy, touching the shoulders of sorrow, but my prick is hard and I have the thoughts of a man, a man for whom everything is allowed and for whom everything is golden.

Stay, I say.

And we take the fat fuck downstairs. I turn to look at her in the door. Green silk and shoulders and olive-skinned and the smell of sweeties and, *my-oh-my*, what must be between those thighs…

We throw the fat bastard into the ambulance.

Get outta here, I tell Foxy. I'll follow you back.

Right, she says, and Lenny starts the wagon and I hear the wail of that beautiful horn, the music of disaster, *Oh, it's a beautiful sound.* I stand in the street and watch em disappear round the corner, in the hot Athens night smellin of semen and suicide. I inhale it. It's golden.

*I'm here for you, my love.*

I go back upstairs.

# 27

# Get Outta Town

Who's this? Ducasse says the next day.

We're standing over the fat carcass of Frenchie, IMF guy, hooked up to the machines and bein pumped full of MDMA. Ducasse is runnin the clinic for the moment, so he notices the extra body.

This fat fuck, I say, got all touchy-feely with Lorelei in the bar last night, started a whole ruckus and got knocked the fuck out. Bled all over the floor, too.

Ducasse wasn't in the bar last night, so I can bullshit him.

So why'd you bring him here? he says.

Cause he was knocked the fuck out, unconscious like. So I brought him here. Not gonna take him to the hospital.

Still, he says, bit risky.

You did the same thing in Amsterdam, I tell him, or did ya forget? That chick I picked up one night? Came downstairs the next day to find her on the table.

Easy, he says. Bit testy, aren't ya?

Just back off with your double standards, I say.

He holds up his hands, like, *Say no more.*

Frenchie's lyin in his underpants. Guy wears y-fronts. Culhannan has him stripped. The Sex Dentist likes to come up and massage the carcasses. Says it's good for the meat, ya know, like Kobe beef n'all that, but really the guy's just a bit of a sicko. But we've only got one butcher so we let him do as he pleases. *You wanna rub up on a comatose guy? Knock yourself out.* To each their own. We're no angels.

It doesn't hit the news either. Two days later and still nothin. Head of the IMF in Greece disappeared from his mistress's home, you'd think that'd catch a headline or two. But no. Two things goin on here, I reckon. One, they're keepin the mistress quiet, and two, the bigger problem, the head guy of a major international organisation has vanished. *Poof!* Gone like the wind. Trust me, he'll never be heard of again. He's pig food. The pigs'll make sure there's nothin left of him.

I keep my head down. No more trippin round Athens in an absinthe hole, or a K-hole, or any kinda hole. I stay low, do my work. Now at the bar, now at the clinic. Kostas keeps me updated.

There's a French team on the way, he says.

Oh yeah?

Special detective unit. Maybe a few anti-terrorism guys too.

Sounds serious.

You best stay indoors, he says.

Apparently there's a grainy photo of me, at least we think it is, leavin the scene in the car that's now burnt out in the Athens' hills. Kostas says it doesn't give away much, but the bloodhounds'll be out soon enough.

Look man, Kostas says, about the girl—

Told ya, man, I know nothing about that, I tell him.

And that's the last he says about it.

Still nothin in the papers.

All schtum.

Fuck knows it should be. I've paid off enough cunts.

Lorelei's back. Foxy talked her into comin back with me. Maybe Foxy just wants her space back. But I'm glad. With all the time I'm spendin indoors, it's nice to have her around again. Masturbation is not for me, at least not as a long-term prospect. We're back into our old routine — I beat her about, we make up. Back to bloody and sticky sheets. Just like before.

I'm tryin, but stayin low isn't easy. I felt somethin that night. Somethin changed in me. Ever since, there's been a buzz in my head, a hum, an itchin at the inside of my skull. I'm restless, antsy. I wanna get back out there, do somethin else. *That's* the new drug. Mayhem. Deviance. How can I put it? You might call it *horror*. I know what it really is, its true value: life, death, kidnap, murder, love, cannibalism… it's all the same thing. I've inhaled it all, and it's all *golden*. I wanna suck some more of the pipe of mayhem. It's in my veins like barbed wire. These fat cunts that can't get enough of human flesh, well, I'm gonna feed on em. That's my tonic. I know it now.

Kostas comes to see me.

Look man, he says, these French guys are really diggin. Maybe you should get outta town for a bit.

What you talkin about man? I'm stayin low, just like we discussed.

But these guys are on the scent. They're hungry, and I can't stop em. I can't even slow em down.

Okay Kostas, I'm gonna get out for a bit, just one thing I gotta do first.

So I hang about, just for a few more days. Why? Cause I wanna eat some of our guy. I wanna taste a banker, one who feeds on the people. I just know it's gonna be some of the richest, sweetest Meat I've ever tasted. So I'm stayin til Friday.

We butcher him Monday. Culhannan hits him with the overdose right after the last massage. I'm standin watchin as Culhannan is rubbin him all Kobe-like, those rolls of flesh, mostly fat, but down below is the good meat. Culhannan's gettin right down in there with his fingers, you can see the effort in his face, the way his mouth twitches, the way his neck muscles stretch, Culhannan's right down in there at the meat, the juicy IMF meat, the people's meat beneath the fat of the land. He pokes around in there like a shiatsu wizard, a shiatsu sex wizard: the belly, thighs, shoulders, the neck… shiatsu sex wizardry for our primest cut ever. And he loves every fucken minute of it. *Olive oil, did you say?* Olive oil, massaged right into his folds. This guy is gonna taste fucking delicious.

And right after the massage, *bam*, we dose him, phenobarbital and 5000mg of MDMA, the final dose.

Then we carve him up.

I watch Culhannan at work, the only time I do. He enjoys this too. He's no Hugo, granted, but he gets the job done. He goes to work with the cleaver, bone saw where he needs it. Hugo didn't need a bone saw. He'd go right through with the cleaver, bone n'all, didn't matter how big the carcass was. Hugo had arms like the thighs of body builders, all sweat and muscle.

The Frenchie carved up, we hang him. Five days. One hundred hours to be precise. He'll be eaten Friday.

So I wait.


Friday comes, and Lenny does the delivery down to Adonis's.

Along with the regular delivery, Lenny carries an IMF heart and two kilos of prime IMF cut. It's delivered into the hands of Adonis.

I go down there that night. Foolish, yes. But I gotta, I gotta taste him. I could stay at the bar, we could barbecue him up ourselves, but I'm also here for the spectacle. I need to watch.

You shouldn't be here, Adonis says.

He's had the law round, and he's spooked.

Don't worry, man, I say. I'm gonna sit down the back, all hush like and just watch.

He doesn't like it but he can't really say no.

*Egine.*

The German's at a table with the other cats, the fat cats, the ones who feast on sorrow and misery and the flesh of the people, all together, all sneers and howls and sinister remarks.

Blood-suckers. Eaters of meat in a world of gruel and thin soup. A sinister malaise hangs over their table as they sup and pick and get ready for the main course. Greasy, snide men, men who lick their mouths and finger their bellies and pull on their crotches. These are the men behind the scenes, decidin what happens, who lives, who dies. And now they're fucken eatin each other.

And I'm here to watch. So that I can enjoy an immersive experience, I'm gonna eat some of this French fuck too. While I watch.

I'll be havin the steak, Adonis, I tell him. You know, prime cut.

He knows.

I'll be havin it medium, cause that's the way I like it. Not too bloody. Just a bit pinky inside, like the flesh of fat bankers, I say.

And because I really know how to enjoy our meat, Screamin Pope meat, I pop a pill. By the time the plate hits the table, I'll be comin up, hittin those highs, so that the meat'll push me right over the edge. I almost wanna get up and distribute ecstasy to the bankers, but fuck em.

Meaty aromas fill the air. I sip exquisitely on a Barolo and wait.

My whole being is one big rich sigh.

The food comes.

I'm on steak, the German's on heart. I sip and wait for him to begin. I feel like I should say somethin before we begin, some kinda thanks, or whaddaya call it — *grace.*

Let us give grace, Lord, before we begin:
*To this we are about to receive, O Lord,*
*the flesh of fat fucks,*
*the Meat of the meat of the people,*
*fed on the tears of sold women and their suicided husbands and*
*gaunt hungry children,*
*made sweet by sorrow and juicy by greed,*
*massaged by perverts and matured to perfection...*

*for this, O Lord, we do praise thee,*
*for if it is thee from whom we do receive, then*
*it is thee we eat, thou flesh, thou blood;*
*Thee, O Lord, Meatiest of Meats.*
*Praise be.*

Or somethin like that I said as I came up on ecstasy.

And as I watch the fat German pick up with his fork a slice of his associate's heart, I spear with my fork a cut of his flesh. And we eat. Together. *In Communion.*

I watch him, eyes rollin up into his head as he eats the sweetest cut that ever fell from a fork, and me, the Meat of the meat of the people melting in my mouth.

I cannot describe it, so I will not try. All I will say is this: He who has fed on the people is divine.


Kostas is on my back again the next day. Look, he says, you gotta split for a bit. Head to the islands. Drink some cocktails, finger a few waitresses.

Okay Kostas, I say. You make bein on the run sound so much fun.

I call Ducasse. Get me a ticket outta here. I'm gonna head down to the islands for a month, I tell him.

Sure, man. He doesn't even ask why. Maybe he knows.

The next mornin my bags are packed and Lorelei's at the door pleadin with me not to go.

I got to babe, I say.

I'm comin with you, she says.

I need you here lookin after the bar, I tell her.

What if you meet someone?

You're my girl. There's no one else.

I love you.

I love you too, I say. I kinda mean it.

*Sweet Lorelei.*

Ducasse takes me to the port, hands me a ticket. *Mykonos.*

What'd you get me a ticket to the queer island for? I say.

Hey, go spend a week see if you like it, he says. We got a

beachfront apartment waiting for you. You don't like it, fuck off to Santorini.

Prick, I say.

Hey, just think about it — an island fulla queers. There's women there, but no-one's fuckin em. You'll be Daddy Cool, there to bring order to things again. Am I right?

You okay lookin after business? I say.

I got it, he says. I might even come down for the weekend, once things are runnin straight.

*Fuck. The two of us in Mykonos down the absinthe hole. That's a story waitin to be written.*

Stay in touch, he says, and I get outta the car with my bag, my single bag, with two shirts, a couple hundred thousand euros, and probably the same value in MDMA.

*What?*

I plan to do it proper.

# 28

# Mykonos

Hot, white sun, the silver Aegean and a cool blue breeze.

*Why-oh-why* have I been stuck in suicide Athens? This is where it is. This is the future. This is where I can make it happen...

Here I'm a god. The sun shines through me and the water does not touch me. I am golden. When I stand out on that beach it's like I've shed my flesh, cast off my body... I go with the wind, bathed in light. I feel every atom of my body pulsate: they quiver, vibrate, shimmer. People sense it. Emirs from Qatar buy me thousand-dollar bottles of champagne, Russian oligarchs invite me on their yachts and offer me their wives, the tanned and golden queer elite lie at my feet in the shade of umbrellas, their toes red and blistered in sand like burning coal. I am showered with adoration.

*This place...*

Within days I've concocted a plan.

We open up here, on Mykonos. Fuck Athens. Fuck Amsterdam, too. Fuck Frankfurt, Marseilles and Paris. Fuck Dublin and Dubai. Fuck Rome. This place right here. This is where we do it.

We'll need a slice o'the beach, but there's always a price. Everyone can be bought, and if they can't, we'll just eat em. We'll start with one beach, Psarou, then we can spread out, take a slice of Paradise and Super Paradise.

Just one of these clubs on Psarou is takin fifty million a year on champagne alone. Fifty million in Moët & Chandon — think of what we could do if we were sellin Meat here? These are the cunts that eat it, that like it, right here, all gathered together in one place, all on one fucken beach. It's a ready-made Screamin Pope! We just gotta bring the Meat. We wouldn't even have to hide it. We'd start off low-key, then, as business spread and the money was comin in — and it would come in: we could be chargin five, ten thousand a kilo here — we could buy up the island. Buy the council, buy the government, buy all the top heads, then just make our own fucken laws. Write it all anew. Make human flesh legal. Who could say no? Mykonos would be the place they would flock to for human meat. We'd still have the queers, cause they're minted, but the others would come in, more than before, the princes, the fat cats, the oligarchs and the heads of state, all here to satisfy their craving for Meat, the meat of the people, the blood of the masses. Fuck, take it as far as it goes, take it to its logical conclusion: in the end, you feed em each other, like I've watched happen already, the ECB cunt eating the IMF cunt, Germany eating France... we'd run it for a year or two, maybe five, then wind it up with em all feastin on each other, one great final orgiastic frenzy of blood and sweet meats, the fat fuckers of the world eatin each other out of existence. And after, *Utopia*. We'd be out of business, but fuck it, we'd be richer than God. But where would we retire to?

I climb off the sun lounger and down into the sand, into the hot, burning sand. It's okay, I don't feel it now, instead it's like aloe on my skin. My body is now just an inconvenience that I can treat with mild disdain.

One of my queer acolytes follows me down onto the sand.

Shall I put some lotion on you? he says.

Sure, I say. Please yourself.

Here let me help, says another.

Soon four of them are massaging me, rubbing oil into my

flesh in a soft and mildly irritating manner. *Where is a Sex Dentist when you need one?*

Harder, I say.

And their fingers poke through the layers of fat, the layers of fat that have been forming slowly ever since I became a consumer of human flesh. But I care not how I look. It means nothin.

Fingers on my back, my thighs, my shoulders… they are certainly no shiatsu sex wizards, but they try, god bless em, they try.

Harder, I say.

They pick and prod, claw and dig. Through the fat, through the flesh, right to the bone. They are digging. I meditate. I imagine myself as IMF Frenchie in his final moments… *I feel the Sex Dentist's fingers reach depths that no man can imagine, til his nails are scraping at my very marrow. I conceive of my death, moments away, when I will be pumped with a lethal dose of MDMA and phenobarbital, and I rise up on a crashing wave of ecstasy and aether into an all-consuming blackness.* The end. Or so I thought. But it isn't.

*I feel my limbs cleaved, one from the other, and I feel no pain yet I am conscious, not from any centre of my body but in all my atoms together and simultaneously. I am pulled apart, ripped, torn, and still I feel no pain.*

*I am hung, then, from the walls in the cold room, and there I hang for five days while my molecules degrade. My cells begin to rupture and my enzymes get hungry. They begin to feast, eating away at the cells of my body. But this, this is why I will taste so good in the end. My skin sags, begins to drop from the flesh, the layers of fat that hold it all together dissolving. Fluids seep from within forming blisters on the skin; everything, meat above all, becoming soft and supple as the molecules pull further and further apart.*

*I am mature. Ready for the plate. Eat me, before putrefaction kicks in.*

*I feel myself on the grill, flesh sizzling, but do not burn me please, for I am rich and succulent. Sear my flesh but remove me from the flame before I char.*

*There. Perfect.*

*I slide down the gullets of fat, rich men, me, the flesh and blood of the people. I am taken like a wafer of Christ into their bellies, giving life.*

*Pray, ye, who would take of my body.*

*And so it begins again, the great circle of life...*

Enough now, I tell my queer apostles. Leave me be.

I melt in the late-August afternoon sun, the smell of burning flesh teasing my nostrils.


That night, I'm on a boat with Ilyich Kharkovsky, oligarch, and his wife, Ekaterina. A whole host of other cunts with us too. Abelard Jacobin, some French tenor, with a whole host of queer groupies. You're nobody in this town unless you got your queer acolytes. I got mine, so I'm somebody. Abelard Jacobin, incidentally, looks fucken tasty. Big fat cunt like IMF Frenchie, but softer, cause he's an *artiste* like. Probably very sweet and juicy. Abelard Jacobin could make any prime menu. He's not the only one either. Now, as far as eatin human flesh goes, I've mostly eaten men cause, ya know, most of the carcasses we pull in are male. But some women just look fucken appetising. Foodwise, like. This one on the boat, proper arch-cunt, name of Ulyana Vovk, prime minister or president or somethin of Ukraine, has the look about her. Proper delicious, I'm thinkin. Somethin about her. She's a huge bitch, big, satiated on the people, but has an air about her too. *I'm rich.* Not wealthy, even though she's of course fucken minted, but *rich*: her meat is heavy, flavoursome, full of essential nutrients... zinc, magnesium, potassium, mineral-heavy, oily, like you need just a few cuts and your satiated. You can smell it off her. When you've eaten human meat, you begin to *smell* it, that odour, that tinge on the hairs of your nostrils. Metallic and bloody goodness.

*We'll have you here on Mykonos, our guest... we'll wine and dine you, fatten you, then we'll eat you. You will be the lushest.*

I catalogue her away in the great menu that is growin in my mind. World's finest cuts. Menu of the gods. She's on it. She's *aperitivo*.

Who else we got? George Blinnit. Old money America. Magnate of some description, and to be fair, I'm pleased to see the effort at American-Russian relations by his inclusion at the party, but then this kinda money transcends all politics and nationality. Fat cat in every respect. Not sure I'd have him on my menu though, he's lost his aristocratic edge. Too much time spent in a country with no class.

Sasha Katz. Fat Jew. Rich on the fat of Africa. Stolen diamonds. Could be edible. I'd eat him just for being a cunt.

Xavier Sosa. Argentinian, and we know those Argentinians taste fucken good. Probably made his money in cattle. Millions of acres of deforestation, land grabs, destruction of the native population. Fuck it, let's have him as *antipasto*.

Jorgen Ortenz. Dunno where he comes from, but he sells weapons. Probably tastes like machine oil.

Hatice Şahin. Turk form Istanbul, they say she made her money runnin refugees from Syria and Libya into Europe. Another arch-cunt. Not sure I'd eat a Turk, though.

The boat is full of em, cunts and arch-cunts, bastards and blaggards. Don't see anyone that would serve as *primo*, though. Still, he'll be here on Mykonos somewhere — I'll find him. Or her, for that matter. There's no room for bias anymore.

I spike the punch.

I mosey up beside the waiter, or whatever he is, maybe they got a special title on big boats like this, and say, Hey there, buddy, you mind freshenin up this Black Russian? He says, Yes sir, right away sir — nice kid — and I shuffle up next to the champagne punch and tip a vial of powder in there, I dunno, maybe 10,000mg. Who's countin? Besides, there's thirty to forty cunts on this boat, many of em huge, so I gotta be loose with the dose. Now I'm gonna sit back and watch it unfold. I bid my apostles to sup of the debauched punch — I wanna see them smashed, wrecked, and maybe I'll get them to do sick shit to each other later if this party gets dull.

I'm stood listenin to Ortenz tell some story about a trip to Mogadishu, you can tell it's an old story, told many times and well-practised, full of trigger words like black hawks and niggers and M-16s, and I'm thinkin, *When was the last time anyone was impressed by this?*

Hey Jorgen, you tried the punch?

Hatice Şahin asks me if I've been to Istanbul, I say no, Hatice, but you've got such a beautiful name, *Ha-ti-jay,* and I say it all slow and filthy like so's I can feel her pussy get wet just at the sound of it. May I? I take her by the arm and lead her to the punch bowl.

Sasha, your hand is empty, let me get you a glass.

Sasha tells me he doesn't drink. *You fucken miserable Israelite,* I think.

So I go over to the table of *antipasti,* actual Italian *antipasti,* and canapé, and *Yes, I bet the fucker eats caviar,* so I load up the caviar with some powder and say to my new friend the waiter, Hey buddy, I think that big fella over there is a touch on the hungry side. Why don't you bring him a bit o'this and a bit o'that?

Yes, sir.

Nice boy. I would never eat one of these nice boys.

And how do I get that Ukrainian arch-cunt high? She's alcoholic for sure, she'll do it all by herself.

Nobody is gettin away tonight. You're all comin with me on the good ship Ecstasy. I'll sink the fucker if I have to.

*All aboard.*


And very soon we're sailin into the warm night of dopamine, blown by the south winds of serotonin onto the gentle sea of euphoria. My, is she gentle. We are rocked gently on the sea of euphoria, all of us, cunts, blaggards and death-merchants, and fuck if my nice little boy the waiter is not stoned too — *You've been at the punch you cheeky little pup, haven't you, when no one was looking?* — all of us rocked gently on the good ship Ecstasy.

The moon. There's a moon. There's a moon and a soft breeze, stars too, water lapping against the side of the boat, *hear the sound*, and the tinkle of crystal glasses and the smell of the sea and of perfume, burgundy perfume over the salt of the sea. Yes, it is all golden.

Ekaterina has her hand on my shoulder, she's whispering into my ear, lips right up against my lobe, tickling the ultra-fine hairs there, and Ilyich is gettin a kick out of it.

Come, join us inside, he says.

He leads me into their bedroom and Ekaterina sits on the bed, her long sapphire-blue dress with the slit up to her waist, gown falls from her legs exposing the thighs of White Russia, legs long as frustrated dreams and thighs of milk, and I kneel, what else can I do, but I kneel before her. Ilyich watches. Ekaterina opens her love-long legs and now I see the inside, the inside of thighs the colour of long Russian winter, a winter spent dreaming of white thighs like these, like the ones opening in front of me. White silk panties flash... a slit, a glint in the blue sapphire, the muscles of the insides of her leg liftin the silk a touch from her cunt, and I can smell it, the perfumed pussy of White Russia... it's scent tickles my nose like her lips tickled the hairs of my ear only moments ago. This is it, perhaps the finest pussy that exists on a woman anywhere: *Pray, on your knees and eat. Eat, and drink from the chalice...*

Eat her, Ilyich says.

And every impulse, every aching groan in my body says *Eat...*

...and I will, but the pussy, the pussy of the glory of White Russia will have to wait.

Bring me a knife, Ilyich, I say.

He doesn't ask why. He does it.

He hands it to me and I say, No, Ilyich, a real knife, and he returns with a strop razor.

*Yes.*

Ekaterina is no longer moist, she is wet. The silk of her

panties darkens.

I take the razor and cut a slice of flesh from her thigh as she moans hard. I cut a long slice from the inside of her thigh as she bucks and moans, *Yes yes yes…*

Let us eat flesh instead. I look at Ilyich, who is biting the flesh of his hand between thumb and forefinger, drawing blood. He is deep in pleasure.

I take a bite of his wife's flesh and it tastes of the white snow of the steppes. I hold it out to Ilyich who takes it and eats the rest. He shakes, the throes of a man who has just awoken from a lifelong sleep. Blood drips down the thighs of Ekaterina, and I drink, and he drinks, until we are sated. She falls back in the bed, the mother of thousands, sated, knowing we are fed.

We all lie in each other's arms and drink champagne punch.


Like this it goes, night after night, on and on into the long night of Ecstasy on Mykonos.

Here we are.

I call Adonis. How you doin, man?

Yeah, he says, *Ola kala.*

Any more police? I say.

No, they stopped coming around, he says. I think we're okay.

Well, I'll wait it out a while yet, I tell him. What about the German?

He's back now, Adonis explains. Still eatin his acquaintance, piece by piece, week by week.

They keep cuts of him in the freezer and the German has a slice every week.

He'll be finished in a month, Adonis says.

Tell him we'll find him another, I say. I'm jokin, but not.

*Eisai trelos,* he says.

Yeah Adonis, maybe I'm fucken crazy by now, I say.

Then Ducasse shows up. Whole different shitshow about to happen.

Looks like you've taken to island life, he says.

Everything down here is fucken sweet, I say.

I take him to Psarou.

Yeah, I see what you mean, he says.

He's all over my apostles. What can we make em do? he asks.

They'll do whatever the fuck you like, I tell him. Boys, meet my friend Ducasse.

Two of my boys lie him down on the sand, peel of his clothes, pour champagne over him and suck it from his hairy limbs. Ducasse is lyin there grinnin like a kid with his fist in the candy box.

Don't just sit there, he says — order more champagne.

*Fucken Ducasse.*


Later, we're in a villa in the hills above the town, up on the hill where the breeze come off the sea like the breath of virgins. Me and Ducasse and the apostles are lyin round the pool, a barbecue lit behind us, and the heavy smell of coal whips and dissipates in the cool wind. We will eat. But later.

Who's the fattest fucker in here? I ask Ducasse.

He knows, he does, we're not just talkin weight. Whole lotta things to consider, like oiliness and flavour and suppleness and age.

Ducasse laid back sippin on champagne, livin now on champagne and MDMA, doesn't seem to have the need for food anymore, does Ducasse.

Gotta be him, he says.

I'm lookin at the guy he's pointin at.

Isn't that the president of France or somethin? I say.

With a waist like that, it's very possible, he says.

I think it is, ya know, it's the French president, or Prime Minister.

Eat him? he says.

I've already eaten one French cunt, and while he was delicious I'd rather expand my horizons, I say.

Then he walks in the door, and we look at each other, like,

231

*Yes, that's the one.*

You believe it? Ducasse says.

If we could eat that guy this'd be the greatest night of my life, I say.

Then someone turns the music up and suddenly we can't hear ourselves talk anymore.

Ducasse looks at me, I nod. I hand the vials to one of the apostles and he knows what to do with it. By this stage, we've spiked the entire island. Every bowl on the table gets a vial of pure liquid MDMA, how many doses I can't say, but this party is about to enter new realms. I sit back and neck a pill, so does Ducasse, and the apostles eat em from my hands.

*Let me just take the reins for a minute here...*

I find the DJ on the other side of the pool and requisition the decks. Everyone is comin up on spiked punch and sangria and it's time to introduce a tune. So I freak everyone the fuck out with a little 'Moonlight Sonata', and everyone knows somethin's goin on cause they got that tickle in their bellies, that fearful quiver rising up from their gut, and they hear the strains of the piano and they realise, *Here we go...*

Then I throw on some Radiohead, and after droppin the darkness thick as I can, thick like blood and syrup, I play 'Belfast', and now they know it's a fucken party. I feel it come off them in waves, like the joy of a hundred thousand people in a wet field or a newborn baby that smells like milk... Pure joy.

Ducasse is thrashing in his chair by the pool, the apostles are quivering, and the whole party writhes like an animal in its final moments.

I push it out to sea once again, the good ship Ecstasy, gentle as a daddy with his baby child.

I set it adrift.

I go and get Ducasse.

Come on, I say, and he knows what we have to do.

We go get him. *Primo.* Main course.

Hey there, Prince, Ducasse says, puttin his arm round him.

232

He's a real prince too, not some self-appointed Saudi cunt, we're talkin old school Prussian here, Saxe-Coburg-Gotha, or whatever the fuck they like to be called.

Guy's already comin up and doesn't protest. Ducasse takes a vial from his pocket and pours it into his drink.

Go on, he says — it'll make you a king. Laughs at his little joke.

Prince isn't sure, I can see the hesitation in him, but Ducasse isn't takin no for an answer, and the prince can see it in his eyes. Ducasse nods as the prince lifts the glass to his mouth.

Come with us, Ducasse says, and we lead him into the kitchen. Outside, the strains of 'Belfast' pour ecstasy down over em like buckets of pure dopamine.

Now, you pour ten grand's worth of MDMA into a man, you see the effects pretty quickly. Prince starts sweatin, then convulsing, soon he's on the floor foamin at the mouth. He doesn't last long after that.

Long live the king, Ducasse says.

What do ya know of butchery? I say.

What do ya need to know? Ducasse says.

We lift him onto a huge mahogany table and retrieve the biggest knives we can find from the kitchen, and we go to work. We hack, we tear, we slice, we gouge… the kitchen's a fucken mess. We're slipping around in this guy's insides, and soon we've put together a tray of what we think are the prime cuts. We season it. We carry it outside and throw it on the barbecue.

They're all dribblin, foamin at the mouth as the hunger sets in. We cook up the meat nice and rare like, and they swarm all over the barbecue for a piece of it.

That's when I see her come in, the jade woman. Comes in, sits down at a table other side of the pool, minder either side of her. I know what she's here for.

I go over and fall on my knees in front of her, and she stands up and approaches. I've left a bloody trail in my wake, and now it's my turn.

She pulls a knife from the folds of her dress and passes it to me, handle first. I take it, cut my shirt open. She watches as I cut a slice from my flank; I feel nothing but the warm breath of virgins.

The flesh cut, I hold it up, and it transforms to an asp in my hand and slithers onto her palm. She holds it up above her mouth and lets it slide down her gullet.

She speaks to me, sayin nothin, across the wind.

I know what I must do.

# 29

# Combustion

I left Mykonos on a Sunday. I know because bells tolled from a church somewhere within that white, cobbled maze, as if there was any religion left in that town other than that of consumption.

I got on the boat to Athens and sailed north, watching the silver Aegean the entire length of the journey. By the time I got off the boat my eyes were two slits, honed by the white metallic burn of the water. I hadn't eaten since we devoured the prince, but it didn't matter since food was no longer a concern to me, I subsisted on ecstasy alone — not pharmaceuticals, but by the secretions of my own body. With full control over my adrenal system, I could now regulate levels of chemicals in my system, flooding and starving it as I saw fit.

My eyes burned by the sea, I saw the beauty of Athens for the first time. It shone, a city of white on the edge of a sea of silver. I saw the city through two slivers of eyes, eyes sharpened by seasilver. I saw it all, and it was all beautiful.

I made my way home.

It was the middle of the day and the apartment was empty. Lorelei's things were still there, but I had no need to see her now, for she was not a part of me anymore. None of them were: Lorelei, Foxy, Jimmy, Kostas, even Ducasse... none of them mattered, for now I saw through eyes of white.

I got to work, doing what I had to do.

I went out and bought soap, gasoline and a couple of cheap, resealable plastic containers. I found a hardware store and bought some calcium carbide. Then I went home and built a firebomb. I heated up the gasoline and melted in the soap and poured it into the larger container. Into the smaller I crushed up some calcium carbide and sealed it up. I placed them inside a backpack, not too big but large enough to hold them easily. I tried it on. It sat comfortably on my back. I placed it into the boot of the car and made sure it was nestled safely.

I went inside, showered and changed clothes. I took a light jacket and fashioned a new pocket on the inside, large enough to accommodate two knives. I took my knives, the razor given me by Kharkovsky and the knife from the jade woman and put them into my concealed pocket. I went out to the car.

I left Athens and drove north.

The trip was pleasant as the world was now white, seen through eyes of seasilver. Fields of green and blue sea, all was white.

In Belgrade I stopped for gas and stabbed a man in the chest because he was not white. Blackness was in his soul.

I picked up two hitchhikers in Budapest, cut their throats and left them by the side of the road. Their hearts were black.

I killed in Vienna, Nuremberg and Stuttgart, and the further north I travelled the blacker it became.

Then I arrived in Paris. In the evening I went to a cinema in the second arrondissement and bought a ticket. I sat down in the packed theatre and watched a half-hour of the movie, before gettin up and goin to the bathroom. In the bathroom I lit a rag and placed it in the top of the napalm bomb then added water to the calcium carbide. I returned to the salon, placed the bag on the floor and walked out. I sealed the door and killed the staff on the floor. I heard the screaming as I left the building.

Before I left Paris I visited the Hôtel de Beauvau in La Madeleine and politely requested entrance to the building. I could have killed them easily but I was testing the limits of my powers. They opened the gates for me since they could not resist, and I went inside and slit the throat of the Minister of the Interior.

I left Paris and drove through the night to Belgium.

In Brussels I chanced across the German foreign minister who liked eating his friends, so I stabbed him in the heart with the knife of the jade woman. Then I drove to Kleine-Brogel.

At Kleine-Brogel I found the home of the highest ranking NATO general from the airbase, and invaded his home and held his family at knife point. I held the razor to the throats of his wife and his two young daughters, before taking him to bed, where, for three days and nights, I whispered my sweet poisons into his ear until he was ready.

Then I left Belgium with one of his daughters and drove to Amsterdam. I arrived at the weekend. I parked the car on Nieuwmarkt with the child inside and went to the bar.

Hugo was there, alone. Alone, because he'd eaten all the clientele. His gargantuan frame consumed the bar, and he sat at a table with the remains of his dinner on the plate. He put down a great bone as I entered and sucked through his teeth.

Where've you been? he says.

Athens.

The white city, he says.

It's beautiful.

It is. You're doing great things, I hear.

I've turned things round down there, I tell him. But Mykonos is where it's at. That place is the new Mecca.

I've no doubt you can pull it off, he says.

I nod.

Sit down?

I will. Play you a tune? I ask him.

He opens his arms wide. I've been waitin, he says.

So I got to the jukebox and throw somethin on that I know he'll like.

He hears it come on and I see a tear in his eye.

You know me well, he says.

*Not carefree ever after,*

*Silence, no more laughter…*

I sit down.

So what now for you? he says.

I sigh. I'm tired, I tell him.

I'm feelin somewhat in need of a holiday myself. Been feelin it for some time now, he says.

He sucks a greasy thumb and wipes his mouth with a napkin. I take out the knife and lay it on the table.

She sent you? he asks.

I nod.

Some woman, he says.

Let's have one for the road, Hugo, I say. And I get up and go to the bar and pour us a couple of absinthe.

*Crawling through the empty rooms…*

We sit down and we have a drink.

Good times, he says, and Christ, I have to agree with him.

Thank you, I say.

For what? he says.

*Now we come to the story's end…*

It was you, I say. You made me.

Aye, he says.

He's fingerin his belly.

Let's do it then, he says.

I stand and pick up the knife. Hugo, arms wide open like a father, is smilin, singin,

'Knowing me, knowing you'…

And I take the knife and slice open his belly and out pours a river of blood and absinthe, and swimming in it the corpses of a hundred babies, whole and undigested.

He's smiling as his eyes glaze over.

I slit his throat.

*It's time for me and you,*

*This time we're through…*

The major did his work. But I knew he would, since my poisons were the sweetest poison. As I was walking back to the car a plane was flying over Kaliningrad Chkalovsk, the plane's nuclear arsenal raining down upon the naval base. The first shots had been fired.

I got back to the car and took the girl by the hand and we sat down on the square. I wouldn't kill her, as I'd promised, but it no longer mattered.

I asked her if she knew Madame Zhu and she shook her head.

I asked her if she knew Kailash, if she'd been there, and I saw a glimmer in her eye, some distant, faraway glimmer, deeper than knowing flesh.

I took the razor from my pocket and opened it, and told I was going to do something and that it wouldn't hurt, and I proceeded to cut a slice of flesh from her thigh and she didn't scream out but merely wept, so great a soporific was her sorrow, her sorrow.

The flesh turned to an asp in my hand. I held it up and it slid down my throat to my belly.

The child of sorrow was weeping as the first flashes lit up the continent, great flashes of white that honed the eyes to slits of seasilver.

And as I watched, we watched, the world and all its blackness was turned instantly white.

I fell into a golden sleep, my head rested on the shoulder of the child of sorrow.

# Part Four

# 30

# Desert Glass

A cold desert wind howled over the plateau. A black tent, solid, sturdy, was the only thing that upset the rolling contours of the plain all the way to the mountains beyond, where the great hump of Meru loomed, snow-capped its black flanks.

Not far from the tent, a dust devil, about the height of a man, whipped and tore across the rocky ground before disappearing as quickly as it had materialised. The wind died, the plain fell silent. No birds there. Just a black tent, a few wandering souls within.

Inside the yak-hair tent the old woman busied herself over a kettle. Squatting in front of the fire, she waited for the old cast-iron beast to spit a cloud of steam.

'What's this, Nani?'

The old woman looked over her shoulder. The little girl was sitting on the edge of her mat poking at her belly button.

'That's where the world comes from, child.'

'The world?' The child dug deeper but found nothing. 'I don't see it, Nani.'

The old woman clambered up onto her feet and came and sat in front of the child and slapped her hand away.

'Now listen child,' she said. And she told her a story, about how in the beginning there was only one big fat woman, fat like Nani, and how before she died a great sea of yak's milk poured out of her belly button, and out of this sea of yak's milk climbed a great turtle. Manjushri, the bodhisattva, saw the turtle and shot it with a golden arrow and it rolled over on its back. And Manjushri, because he was wise, took five cereals given him by Avalokitesvara, and planted them in the belly of the great turtle. And that's how the world was born, all from the belly button of a fat woman. Fat like Nani.

'Will I have a world from my belly button?' said the little girl.

'Let's hope not.'

The old woman heard the pot whistle. She struggled up and took a ceramic mug from a heavy wooden box. She put yak butter and salt in the cup before adding the black tea.

'Put your clothes on,' she told the child.

The girl stood up and wrapped herself in her *chuba*. The old woman placed a felt hat on the girl's head before handing her the cup of tea.

'Here — go give this to your grandfather.'

'Yes, Nani.'

The child took the cup in two hands. Not taking her eyes from the tea, she pushed her way through the thick doors out onto the plain. She turned and made her way out back of the tent. She knew where the old man would be, where he was and where he would always be. She found him sitting cross-legged by a bend in the stream.

'Nana!'

The old man turned round.

'Your tea,' said the little girl.

The old man took the tea in his hand and tousled the girl's red, flushed cheek.

The girl squatted next to her grandfather and listened to the patter of the stream, for she liked to hear the steam when she arose.

'*Willa wolla wibble wolla*,' said the little girl.

'What are you saying to the stream?' the old man said.

'I'm asking if it knows what a turtle is.'

'Of course it knows.'

'Do turtles live in streams, Nana?'

'Some do. But not this stream,' he said.

They listened to the *willa-wolla* of the stream together.

'Are you going to do some hunting for me today?' the old man said.

'Alright,' said the girl. 'But Nani told me I'm not to take any more sticks from you.'

The old man laughed a grating laughter.

'Alright, child,' he said. 'No more sticks.'

And the girl jumped up and ran off into the plain in search of dust devils.

The old man sipped at his tea and listened to the stream.

Later, when the afternoon was coming on them, the girl was still rooting around on the dusty ground with her digging tool. She dug with an old axe handle that had no head, and had not had a head for many, many years.

As she dug she hummed a nonsense ditty, born of the wind and the stream and of turtles and grandmothers:

*'On the willa-wolla stream, the turtle sings,*

*'Go away wind, will you never go away,*

*Blow blow blow away.*

*And the wind blew away, so now we sail,*

*Me and my turtle on the willa-wolla stream,*

*Going to the lake where the turtles dream...'*

Even far off in the tent the old woman heard the song and smiled a toothless smile.

The little girl, tired of her searching, struck the earth with her tool. And as if by some childish magic, a dust devil sprung up a stone's throw from her. She leapt up and ran at it. It disappeared as she chased it, but the child fell to the ground and started digging at the place it had dissipated in the air. After some moments she squealed in delight.

'Nana!'

She jumped up and ran to the stream.

She found her grandfather, unmoved, sat where he was and where he would always be.

'Look Nana!'

The child fell in front of him and held up her find for him to see.

'Oh, that's a nice one,' said the old man.

He reached out his hand but the girl snatched it away.

'What will you give me for it?'

The old man laughed a grating laughter. He reached into his *chuba* and pulled out a weathered copper coin, old, maybe Chinese, maybe Afghan. He held it up for the girl to see.

She grinned, took it from the old man and handed over her find.

The old man peered at it in his hand. A hard black marble, glassy like obsidian. Polished. He could hear it, too; the little girl with her ears of innocence could not, but he could.

He closed it in his fist.

'Take the cup back to your grandmother,' he said.

The girl slid the coin into her pocket, lifted the cup and ran off with the bubbling of the stream in her ears.

*Wolla-willa.*

The girl gone, the old man placed the marble on the ground and started to dig. About six inches down he struck a glass jar which he clawed from the earth. He shook the dust from it. As he shook it he heard the rattle of glass on glass. Inside, his collection of marbles, thousands, polished and black.

He opened the jar and the sound poured out into the air — the tormented screams of a thousand, born of the waters of sorrow and lost on the winds of ages. He picked up the girl's marble from the ground, hearing it, a solitary searing howl in the cold desert. He rolled it between his fingers before dropping it into the jar and sealing the lid.

He placed the jar in the ground once more, covering it with soil and tamping the earth.

He turned his ear to the gentle susurrus of the stream.

**End**

Many thanks to Dave Migman and Emma L.

Thanks to Bumbayo Font Fabrik for the font.

Latest news at
blacktarnpublishing.com

Available titles:
https://blacktarnpublishing.com/books/

Follow us on Twitter:
https://twitter.com/blacktarnbooks

## About the author

Ultan Banan started writing as a way of getting his head straight, discovering in the process that staying busy is the only way to stop oneself going insane. He devotes what time he can to writing, doing his best to avoid gainful employment by increasingly creative means. He lives on the move but dreams of a small cottage on a foul and inhospitable coast somewhere. Currently in Italy.

Lightning Source UK Ltd.
Milton Keynes UK
UKHW041832211221
395850UK00006B/31